Praise for the Posadas County Mysteries

Less Than a Moment

"The Posadas County that Havill has created is so tangible, you feel that if you walked down its streets, you would be greeted by old friends."

—*Bookreporter*

Lies Come Easy

Best of the West 2019–3rd Place in 20th- to 21st-Century Western Mystery Fiction by *True West Magazine*

"Havill has again written an engrossing mystery that focuses on the people of Posadas County and the intricate ways in which their personalities and lives intertwine."

—*Reviewing the Evidence*

"This compelling novel contrasts the loving family and community life shared by Reyes-Guzman and her retired mentor, Sheriff Bill Gastner, with the troubled lives led by victims and criminals in the county. Series devotees will eagerly welcome this latest installment."

—*Library Journal*

"Havill's irresistible twenty-third mystery set in tiny Posadas County, NM, combines a police procedural with a complex family saga. Havill's inviting world welcomes newcomers and keeps fans happily coming back for more."

—*Publishers Weekly*

"Master of mystery Steven F. Havill accomplishes that rare and remarkable feat of making each book in his compelling series even better than the one that came before it. With meticulous attention to detail and a warm storytelling style, Havill transforms ordinary people into extraordinary. Evildoers, no matter how twisted and complex, don't stand a chance against hard-working Estella Reyes-Guzman and her legendary mentor, Bill Gastner. If you haven't yet discovered these wonderful mysteries, you are in for a treat!"

—Anne Hillerman, *New York Times* bestselling author

Easy Errors

★ "Fans of the long-running series will be drawn to the backstory here, which fills in gaps in the stories of both Torrez and Gastner. They will also respond to the qualities that have made this series so appealing over the years: meticulous plotting, multidimensional characters, sharp dialogue, and a vivid sense of place. This is one of the very best entries in a consistently excellent series."

—*Booklist,* Starred Review

Come Dark

"The twenty-first Posadas mystery is a compelling mix of dusty small-town ambience, complex plotting, and an authorial voice imbued with compassionate humanity. Each of the Posadas novels plumbs the collective heartbeat of a community. Those beating hearts belong to characters who range from despicable to saintly, but together they make up one of the most vivid worlds in mystery fiction."

—*Booklist*

"Series regulars, including former undersheriff Bill Gastner, interact with a number of intriguing new characters, including Miles Waddell, the owner and sole funder of *NightZone*. Newcomers will enjoy this entry as much as longtime fans."

—*Publishers Weekly*

Blood Sweep

★ "The story line is satisfyingly complex, but the novel's great strength is its well-rendered setting, from the opening description of a silent, motionless antelope to the evocation of a dry riverbed. The concluding note of empathy for the many people trying to cross the border is moving without being heavy-handed."

—*Publishers Weekly,* Starred Review

NightZone

"The nineteenth Posadas County Mystery places the focus back on the retired Gastner after a few episodes in which the mysteries revolved around his successor. No matter the protagonist, Havill's work is believable and well plotted, and never, ever includes a character who isn't a viable human being. Another fine book in a terrific series."

—*Booklist*

★ "Gastner's capabilities are plausible for a septuagenarian, and Havill peoples the book with believable characters."

—*Publishers Weekly,* Starred Review

One Perfect Shot

"Gastner and Reyes complement each other well in an entertaining preview of a decades-long partnership. A welcome entry in an always satisfying series."

—*Booklist*

"Undersheriff Bill Gastner of Posadas County, NM, meets Estelle Reyes, the once-and-future undersheriff, in a welcome, well-wrought prequel... Gastner and Reyes charm from the get-go."

—*Kirkus Reviews*

Double Prey

"Havill is a master at using procedural details to expose the complexities of small-town relationships, but he also excels at drawing meaning from landscape. Like an archaeologist sifting history from the ground, Reyes-Guzman digs clues from the guano-splattered floor of the cave where the jaguar's skull was found. One of the stronger entries in an always-satisfying series."

—*Booklist*

The Fourth Time Is Murder

★ "The Posadas County Mystery series notches its sixteenth with all its signature virtues intact: good writing, an unerring sense of place, and a protagonist it's a pleasure to root for."

—*Kirkus Reviews,* Starred Review

"Havill is especially good at showing how connecting facts depends on recognizing relationships within a family or a neighborhood. Arid, harshly beautiful Posadas County turns out to be full of captivating stories."

—*Publishers Weekly*

Final Payment

"Havill takes the reader through an all-terrain investigation to an edge-of-your-seat finale."

—*Publishers Weekly*

Statute of Limitations

"The primary appeal of this series continues to be its evocation of daily life in a small New Mexico town."

—*Booklist*

Convenient Disposal

"As intelligent, carefully plotted, and insightful as its predecessors. The original star of the series, former undersheriff Bill Gastner, drifts in and out of the action these days, but Havill has successfully switched the focus to Reyes-Guzman and her struggle to balance a young family and an all-consuming career. An outstanding series on all levels."

—*Booklist*

"Literate, lively, and sharply observed as ever. Mystery fans who haven't yet made the trip to Posadas County, consider yourselves deprived."

—*Kirkus Reviews*

A Discount for Death

"Interpersonal issues, usually sequestered behind closed doors in insular Posadas County, take center stage in both cases as Reyes-Guzman follows a trail that leads from troubled lives on the edge of despair to her own thriving family. Mystery series too often lose their way when the author attempts to replace an appealing hero. Hats off to Havill for making the transition work smoothly."

—*Booklist*

"Undersheriff Estelle Reyes-Guzman gets her second star turn here, and longtime fans of Posadas County, New Mexico, won't mind a bit... A first-rate police procedural, small-town division. And Estelle's a charmer."

—*Kirkus Reviews*

Scavengers

"Throughout this low-key, character-driven series, Havill has managed as well as anyone in the genre to balance the particulars of cop procedure with the often unspoken emotions at the core of small-town life. The focus on Reyes-Guzman and her family brings a different dynamic to the series, but the human drama remains equally satisfying."

—*Booklist*

"Skilled investigation, happenstance, and cooperation mesh through every phase of the puzzle, ushering the reader along to one satisfying conclusion."

—*Publishers Weekly*

Red, Green, or Murder

"Havill shows us yet again how random bad decisions spur unnecessary tragedy. As always, a fine mix of village drama and carefully rendered police work."

—*Booklist*

"Another highly entertaining entry that shows those unruly New Mexicans doing what they do best. Long may they stay homicidal."

—*Kirkus Reviews*

"Havill's characters have a depth and a clarity that's refined with every new book in the series. It's a pleasure to see them operate not merely as lawmen or suspects or witnesses but as members of a community where flaws and quirks are understood and accepted."

—*Publishers Weekly*

Bag Limit

"The quiet pleasures of small-town life are again at the center of this appealing series as Gastner reaffirms his belief that even the encroaching evils of the modern world can be endured with the help of friends, family, and a properly prepared green-chile burrito."

—*Booklist*

Dead Weight

"Havill is every bit as good at evoking procedural detail as he is at capturing small-town ambience. This series continues to provide a vivid picture of change in rural America: small-town values under siege from within and without as a big-hearted sheriff tries to keep the peace one day at a time. Quiet yet powerful human drama resting comfortably within the procedural formula."

—*Booklist*

"Nice, easygoing, entirely literate prose, and if the approach is a bit too 'cozy' for some tastes, others will delight in dollops of local color and in Sheriff Bill, of course, who may well be the most endearing small-town lawman ever."

—*Kirkus Reviews*

Out of Season

★ "Gastner's calm, experienced leadership guides his staff, as well as FAA officials, through several prickly conflicts with a couple of fiercely independent ranchers. For readers, his considerate, methodical approach will prove a welcome change from the angry, violent paths trod by so many cops in other novels. Full of bright local color and suffused with a compassionate understanding of human motivation, this intelligent, understated mystery deserves a wide and appreciative readership."

—*Publishers Weekly*, Starred Review

Prolonged Exposure

"Another excellent small-town caper in which common sense, compassion, loyalty, and decency are law enforcement's primary tools against an increasingly brutal world. It's a good thing Gastner has had his heart mended because it may be the biggest in contemporary crime fiction."

—*Booklist*

"Fine storytelling married to a spicy Southwestern setting marks the latest Bill Gastner mystery... Gastner remains a solid center, using his knowledge and experience to good effect as the various cases of burglary, kidnapping, and murder play out."

—*Publishers Weekly*

Privileged to Kill

"The fifth Gastner mystery is a crystalline gem of dusty atmosphere, small-town personalities, and razor-sharp plotting. It also raises questions regarding the law—especially small-town law—and its attitudes toward the indigent, the homeless, and the privileged. Toss in Gastner, one of the most endearing mentors in crime fiction, for a mystery that is disarmingly simple on the surface but ultimately reveals surprising depth."

—*Booklist*

"Havill's fifth quietly continues a project virtually unique in detective fiction: anchoring his tales of crime and punishment as closely as possible in the rhythms of small-town friends, routines, and calamities."

—*Kirkus Reviews*

Before She Dies

★ "The fourth Gastner case is easily the best, no small feat in a series as strong as this one. Gastner is compassionate, intelligent, bulldog tough, and painfully aware of all his limitations, both physical and emotional. The same inward eye that provides insight into his own soul can quickly swivel outward to discern others' hidden traits. And if what you're hiding is motive, Gastner will ferret it out and do what needs to be done. An outstanding mystery."

—*Booklist*, Starred Review

Twice Buried

"Gastner is an incisive investigator whose two most valuable qualities are compassion and insomnia. Unlike other fictional detectives who approach murder as a personal affront, Gastner sees himself as the victims' advocate, striving to even the scales of justice for those no longer able to do it themselves. This is definitely a series to watch."

—*Booklist*

"Bill and his hardscrabble neighbors—especially Estelle, who seems destined for a return to Posadas next time—are as modestly appealing as ever, and in his third outing, he does his best detective work yet."

—*Kirkus Reviews*

"Havill sensitively explores the area's Mexican American culture in this increasingly estimable regional series."

—*Publishers Weekly*

Bitter Recoil

"This one's a winner all the way."

—*Washington Times*

"The authentic flavor of the New Mexico locale is so real you'll be tempted to check your shoes for fine red dust."

—*Mystery Scene Magazine*

Heartshot

★ "Gastner is a unique and endearing protagonist who certainly deserves plenty of encores."

—*Booklist,* Starred Review

"Septuagenarian undersheriff Bill Gastner of Posadas County, NM, is the skeptical, endearing narrator of this mystery debut by a writer of Westerns... If the villain's identity is not surprising, readers still will enjoy this caper and look forward to future appearances of curmudgeonly charmer Gastner."

—*Publishers Weekly*

Also by Steven F. Havill

The Posadas County Mysteries
Heartshot
Bitter Recoil
Twice Buried
Before She Dies
Privileged to Kill
Prolonged Exposure
Out of Season
Dead Weight
Bag Limit
Red, Green, or Murder
Scavengers
A Discount for Death
Convenient Disposal
Statute of Limitations
Final Payment
The Fourth Time Is Murder
Double Prey
One Perfect Shot
NightZone
Blood Sweep
Come Dark
Easy Errors
Lies Come Easy
Less Than a Moment

The Thomas Parks
Medical Adventure Series
Race for the Dying
Comes a Time for Burning

Westerns
The Killer
The Worst Enemy
Leadfire
Timber Blood

NO ACCIDENT

NO ACCIDENT

STEVEN F. HAVILL

A POSADAS COUNTY MYSTERY

Published by Poisoned Pen Press, an imprint of Sourcebooks
P.O. Box 4410, Naperville, Illinois 60567-4410
(630) 961-3900
sourcebooks.com

Library of Congress Cataloging-in-Publication Data

Names: Havill, Steven, author.
Title: No accident : a Posadas County mystery/ Steven F Havill.
Description: Naperville, Illinois : Poisoned Pen Press, [2022] | Series: Posadas County mysteries ; book 25
Identifiers: LCCN 2021024317 (print) | LCCN 2021024318 (ebook) | (trade paperback) | (epub)
Subjects: GSAFD: Mystery fiction. | Suspense fiction.
Classification: LCC PS3558.A785 N6 2022 (print) | LCC PS3558.A785 (ebook) | DDC 813/.54--dc23
LC record available at https://lccn.loc.gov/2021024317
LC ebook record available at https://lccn.loc.gov/2021024318

Printed and bound in the United States of America.
SB 10 9 8 7 6 5 4 3 2 1

For Kathleen

Chapter One

"Oh, Mama!" Squarely in the center of the Broken Spur Saloon, Johnny Rabke crouched, hands on his knees, panting, a sheet of blood curtaining down from just below his hairline. He blinked against the blood and grinned foolishly at Undersheriff Estelle Reyes-Guzman. Straightening a little, he pressed his right hand to his forehead and extended his left toward the undersheriff.

"Mama, take me, please!" His grin widened. Blood flowed between his fingers, down along his nose, and disappeared into his shaggy mustache. "You ain't going to zap me with that, are you?" He cocked his head so he could see the Taser in the undersheriff's hand. "I mean, *you,* darlin', can take me anytime, any place." He staggered upright, shifting his feet to maintain his balance. He extended both arms toward the undersheriff, wrists crossed, miming being handcuffed. The hand that had held his forehead together dripped blood, and the gash on his scalp gushed anew.

In one fluid motion, Estelle slipped the Taser back into its holster. As Rabke blinked back the blood, she slapped cuffs on his left wrist, spun him in place, and wrenched his right arm behind him.

"Sit," she commanded and booted a chair against the back of his knees.

Rabke's apparent opponent, a man whom Estelle did not recognize, was curled up tight against the bar's boot rail, right arm awkwardly embracing the legs of a barstool, the other obviously broken but his left hand managing to keep its grip on a hunting knife.

A family of four—mother and father, along with a daughter and son not yet in their teens—cowered at a table by the side window. An upended table and scattered chairs blocked their route to the front door. Victor Sanchez Junior, the owner of the Broken Spur Saloon, crouched behind the bar, staying close to his bartender, Maggie Archuleta—maybe expecting her to protect him.

"Aw, come on," Rabke whined, still oblivious to the blood coursing down his face. He tried to rise from the chair, awkward and in obvious pain.

"Sit still." Estelle shoved Rabke back, and before he could protest, secured a zip tie around his ankles. She knew the young ranch hand well, including his thick file at the Sheriff's Office to which most of the deputies had contributed at one time or another.

Even as she jerked the tie in place, she was looking beyond to the other combatant. The man's right arm still hugged the legs of the barstool. His head had drifted down to the floor, eyes half closed.

"Behave yourself so you don't fall on your face." She wadded a bunch of bar napkins together and pressed them against the wounded forehead. "Keep your head back." He did so, gaping at her, still grinning foolishly. She left Rabke and crossed to the other combatant. She knelt and touched the side of his neck.

Scruffy, burly, and fragrant with sweat, booze, and now with the addition of other bodily effluents, the young man was dressed in jeans and a T-shirt adorned with a logo for a popular brand of Russian vodka. He was barefoot, but Estelle saw the abandoned leather sandals under one of the tables. His pulse was erratic. The ugly bruise rising on his right temple—just about the size appropriate to a billiard ball—explained how he'd been sent to dreamland. She didn't move him, didn't untangle his arm from the stool.

Estelle reached to her collar mike. "PCS, three ten. Request ambulance to this location. One male unconscious with head injury, second male conscious with knife slice to the forehead."

"Ten four, three ten. They're rolling," Wheeler replied. "ETA about ten or so."

"Three ten, three oh four is six minutes out." Sergeant Pasquale didn't sound enthused. He'd been home, nursing a head stuffed with a sinus infection. He was something of an adrenaline junkie and had responded without hesitation to dispatch's call for backup for the undersheriff at the Spur. He was probably disappointed to miss the action.

"Ten four, three oh four. Take your time. Situation is resolved."

"Oh, Mama," Rabke whispered. "Look at me." He let it go at that.

"Just relax and the EMTs will be here in a couple minutes." She bent down and looked more closely at his head wound, now just oozing a steady curtain with no arterial pulsing. The front of his shirt was a red mess, and rivulets of blood had coursed down across his gigantic rodeo belt buckle. The five-inch slash arcing across his forehead was the sort of thing that might be inflicted by a utility knife or a skilled assailant with a hunting knife—deep to the bone, clean and bloody.

She gently rearranged the flap of scalp. "Keep your head back," she instructed.

"You got my hands locked behind me, Mama. I can't hold nothin'."

"Just sit still."

She stood up and looked across at Victor Junior, who had remained behind the protection of the bar. He rested both hands on the bar's polished surface as if he were waiting to be cuffed.

"I need a clean bar towel," Estelle said. Maggie moved swiftly and handed a folded towel across to Estelle. With a hand under Rabke's chin, she swept the soggy napkins aside and pressed the towel against his forehead, trying to keep the flap of scalp in place. He hissed through his teeth. "I bet," Estelle said gently. "Keep your head tilted back. Hang tough, cowboy. You've suffered worse."

She turned to the saloon owner. "How did this ruckus start?"

"I don't know," Victor said. "Really, I don't. I was in the kitchen."

She raised an eyebrow in Maggie Archuleta's direction. The young woman had stepped a pace or two away from her boss.

"This one," Maggie said, pointing a hooked finger down in the direction of the unconscious man hugging the barstool. "He was saying that bull riders are all pansies." She made a face. "He didn't use those exact words, but that's what he meant."

"Just that?"

"Well, they traded insults for a little while, but then this one," and she again pointed down at the unconscious man, "pulled out his knife. That's when Johnny went after him with the pool cue." The stout handle half of the pool cue lay on the floor, its slender tip broken off at the mid-shaft joint.

Estelle turned around and regarded the family. The man nodded agreement with Maggie's description of the action, while his wife and children looked terrified.

"*¿Comprende, Señor?*"

"That's exactly right," the man said in perfect but heavily accented English. "This one, he drew a knife and this one," and he nodded at Rabke, "defended himself with one of the billiard balls."

So which was it? Estelle thought. *A pool cue or a billiard ball?* Stepping around Johnny Rabke, Estelle knelt by the prostrate man below the bar rail. His pulse was unimproved, and his half-mast eyes showed no signs of conscious return. After a moment to slip on a pair of latex gloves, she worked the knife out of his limp grasp, stood up, and placed it on the bar.

"Three ten, EMT unit is three minutes out," dispatch radioed, and without hesitation, Deputy Pasquale's voice followed.

"Three oh four is ten ninety seven."

Rabke squirmed in place. "You gotta let me have my hands, Mama."

"That's going to happen, all right. Keep your head back, cowboy. So tell me... What started this mess?"

"Well, I don't know. Things just got kinda rowdy, you know?"

The saloon's door opened, and Sergeant Tom Pasquale managed to fill most of the doorway.

"That one needs to be transported ASAP." Estelle nodded at the victim by the bar. "That's his knife on top. Bag and tag it."

"He pulled that on me, and I socked him with the cue ball," Rabke murmured. He sounded proud of himself. Outside, a siren shrieked, and the kaleidoscope of colored lights flashed through the Spur's broken window. Pasquale lifted the towel and examined Rabke's forehead. The young man grinned at the sergeant. "Hey, uglier'n me."

"You just can't stay out of it, can you, Johnny?" Pasquale's voice was hoarse, his nose and eyes red. He felt the pulse on the side of Rabke's neck. He shrugged. "You might live."

The two EMTs appeared and at the same time, the father of the tourist family pushed his chair back and started to stand. "Officer, maybe we should go?" He sounded politely hopeful.

"Relax," Estelle said. "Be patient. I need to take a statement from you. Then you can go. For now, just sit tight."

He nodded uneasily and sat back down. Barry Evans, one of the EMTs, moved the unconscious victim just enough that he could listen with his stethoscope. Apparently, he didn't like what he heard and then didn't like the message sent by the BP cuff. He parted the man's hair and examined the head bash, then beckoned to Cassi Trujillo, his partner. Together they gently untangled the victim from the barstool, eased a cervical collar in place, moved his broken arm away from the footrail, and maneuvered him onto the gurney. In a moment, he was splinted, IV'd, sucking oxygen, and out the door.

Estelle took the opportunity to retrieve the man's wallet.

Pablo Ramirez's paperwork was the minimum, and the twenty-two dollars inside wouldn't take him far. His Mexican driver's license reported that he was twenty-four years old, most recently living in Janos, a few miles south of Estelle's childhood home in Tres Santos.

"Hey?" Johnny Rabke said.

Tom Pasquale held the door wide for the EMTs and the gurney. "I can take him in," he told the EMTs.

Barry Evans grimaced. "I don't *think* so, Sarge. We can take two easy enough. You don't need him bleedin' all over your unit. And if he shuts down halfway there, what're you going to do?"

"How come I gotta be handcuffed?" Rabke tried to sound reasonable. "I mean, *he's* the one who pulled the knife."

Pasquale watched as Evans deftly bandaged Rabke's head. "Good sharp knife. Not even going to have a scar, bro. We're going to transport you to emergency, and then they'll take it from there," Evans said.

"And before you shoot off your mouth," Pasquale added, "you have the right to remain silent. You think about that before you do something stupid."

"Oh, come on," Rabke bleated.

Pasquale quickly went through the rest of the Miranda litany. "Do you understand what I've just recited for you?"

"No, man, I don't. Why am I under arrest? I don't get that." He squirmed in the chair.

"You're under arrest because you attacked a man with a dangerous weapon, first the pool cue, then the eight ball in the corner pocket," Pasquale said, and turned his head to sneeze. The EMTs returned with a second gurney, and in a moment, Rabke was positioned and secured. Estelle found the alleged missile—actually the nine ball—where it had rolled over against the east wall, tangling in a thick nest of cobwebs near the jukebox. She toed it deftly into another evidence bag.

Estelle knelt beside the young combatant, now secured with cuffs in front and cozy under a blanket. "Sergeant Pasquale will take you for booking after they patch you up in emergency, Mr. Rabke. I'll talk with you then. In the meantime, you are being charged with aggravated assault and aggravated battery. If you know a good lawyer, I'd recommend spending your phone call to contact him or her."

Rabke's jaw dropped as he stared hard at Estelle. "Are you shittin' me? Mama, I thought you was going to be my friend."

"Tough love." Estelle patted his shoulder. A few moments later, as the ambulance screamed away, Estelle came back inside.

"You're all right? You sound and look terrible."

"I'll live, I think," Pasquale said.

Chapter Two

After propping the saloon's CLOSED sign in the remains of the front window and locking the door, Estelle swung a battered chair around and sat at the end of the Durans' table. The whole family—father, Hernán; mother, Josefina; son, Ricardo; and daughter, Josie—watched nervously as she introduced herself, set the small pocket recorder on the table in front of them, and then opened her notebook. Across the room, Maggie Archuleta busied herself with cleanup, and Victor vanished into the kitchen.

Hernán, a short, stocky man in blue jeans and a white Western-style shirt, had difficulty meeting Estelle's gaze. His brilliant blue eyes zigged this way and that, and he cleared his throat half a dozen times. She knew exactly why the family was nervous—caught in the middle of a ruckus, now under the scrutiny of foreign law enforcement, even if their hometown was only fifty miles south.

"Does the Toyota parked out front belong to you, *Señor*?"

He nodded vigorously, as if relieved to be asked a simple question. Estelle indicated the tape recorder, and Duran understood immediately. "Yes. The truck is ours. The Toyota."

"Where are you folks from?"

"Janos. It is a little town."

"I know it well, sir. Did Mr. Ramirez ride up here with you folks, Mr. Duran?"

He glanced first at his wife, then focused on the table's grimy surface. "Since Tres Santos. We stopped in that village, and at the new little store there, he approached us and requested a ride across the border. I agreed, of course. He is from Janos as well, and we know each other. In fact, I know him from when he did some work for my brother."

"He didn't ride with you from Janos, then. You met him in Tres Santos."

"Yes."

"And no trouble at the crossing?" For years a daylight-hours-only crossing, the border facility at Regál had recently upgraded to 24/7...not a decision greeted with cheers by the tiny village's residents.

"No." The monosyllabic responses surprised Estelle since nervous folks usually went the other way—blabbing nonstop as they tried to be overly cooperative.

"At the border, they did not question Mr. Ramirez?"

"No. They did not look in the camper."

"I see." She smiled wearily. "And you folks? Where are you all headed?"

"My wife, Josefina...she has a sister in Denver. We have not seen them in so long, you know."

"What time did you arrive here, at the saloon?"

"I suppose just before nine." He looked again at his wife, who nodded.

"Late night for the kiddos," Estelle said. Both Ricardo and Josie had been watching her closely, but when she looked squarely at them, they quickly looked away.

"Too late, I think," their father said. "There is the nice motel in Posadas right by the interstate. I think we will spend the night there. Denver, you know. It's a long drive."

"It is that. Let's go through a few things, and you can be on your way." She led them through the events of the evening, and it was clear from their recitation of events that Johnny Rabke had had the upper hand when the altercation actually started. That Pablo Ramirez had been sucking on a flat bottle of liquor for most of the trip was no secret. He'd been sucking on it in Tres Santos when the Durans picked him up, and the empty bottle had been abandoned in the back of the Toyota.

Keen little Josie had even noticed the brand—Red Ginger Brandy—when Pablo Ramirez had secured the bottle in his back pocket.

Reduced to shorthand, the replay of the bar fight sounded simple enough. Insults first, then a drawn knife, a hard swat with a heavy pool cue swung like a baseball bat by a major leaguer, and then, when Pablo Ramirez no longer appeared to be a threat with his wrist broken, a further and probably unnecessary assault with the heavy, lethal nine ball, flung hard sidearm at the injured Ramirez as he staggered to regain his balance.

They were halfway through the Durans' recitation when Estelle's phone vibrated. She recognized Captain Jackie Taber's number and stood up, walking away from the Durans' table.

"Hey, my friend," Taber said. "I'm here to give Sarge a hand with processing the Rabke kid after the hospital patches him up. I'll go over to emergency in a little bit. You doing okay?"

"I'm fine. How was your candidates' ruckus?"

"Oh, just spectacular." Jackie laughed. "This being unopposed helps."

"That's a good thing," Estelle said. Barring catastrophe, Jackie would be the next sheriff. For incumbent Sheriff Robert Torrez, a career of thirty years was enough, and with a competent successor waiting in the wings, he had decided the time was ripe for retirement.

Because of the candidates' forum at the high school, Estelle had volunteered to take Jackie's swing shift. A bar fight or two was par for a quiet Wednesday night. "Thomas will appreciate help with the paperwork. He feels awful. He shouldn't be on the road."

"Then I'll send him home. You're wrapping up some prelims?"

"Yes. A family from Janos was in the grandstands for the fight."

"Ah."

Estelle thought Taber sounded preoccupied.

"Here's the deal, though," Taber said. "Dr. Guzman is giving the other young man, Ramirez, little chance of survival. He's called for an airlift to Neuro in Albuquerque. Lots of subdural bleeding, a messy skull fracture, and bone chips driven into the brain. Scary stuff. Those billiard balls are heavy, and Rabke apparently has a mean pitching arm."

"So we want all the witnesses nailed down," Estelle said. "If Ramirez dies, then Rabke is sure to find himself in front of the grand jury. He'll probably end up there, no matter what."

"Exactly. So who do you have down there watchin' this circus? Who are our witnesses?"

"Junior Sanchez and Maggie, and a Mexican family—father, mom, two kids. They're on their way to Denver to visit relatives. In a bit of bad luck, they gave Ramirez a ride across. Picked him up in Tres Santos."

"He's illegal?"

"Sure."

"But this family saw the whole show?"

"Yes. From beginning to end. As did Junior and Maggie. Junior didn't do anything to stop it, but that's what I'd expect from him. Not like the old days when Victor Senior would take a cast-iron frying pan to stop the ruckus."

"You got a good statement from them? From the Mexican folks?"

"Not as good as it will have to be if Ramirez dies. Not if the grand jury pops with a murder or manslaughter charge against Rabke. The father says that they're going to stay at the Posadas Inn. I'm having them come to the Sheriff's Office for further processing. Ditto Junior and Maggie. The DA may want a video statement."

"Sounds good. Brent Sutherland just walked in, so he can take over for you while I deal with Rabke."

"Brent doesn't need to do that. I can..."

"Well, yes, he does." Jackie Taber interrupted and then drew in a deep breath. On the other end of the phone, it sounded a lot like a windup. "I just talked to your son. To Francisco."

"You did?" The question was automatic. "He's in New York."

"True. He wants to talk to you but didn't want to call your cell. He didn't want to interrupt you in the middle of something. Ditto with your husband. So he didn't call his father either. Being the sharp cookie that he is, Francisco called the S.O. to talk to dispatch. He asked for Bobby, then was passed on down the line to me."

"Jackie...what did he want?"

"He didn't say. Just to get a hold of you as soon as you went ten-eight."

"Okay, I'm on it. *Ay.* Let me get all these folks herded that way, and I'll see what's up."

"Yup. Maybe it's no biggie."

"Maybe." Midnight calls were never just to chat. Her son knew that there were times when his mother was not free just to drop and run, any more than Dr. Guzman was free to toss his scalpel onto the tray if a call came in the middle of surgery. Middle of the night or not, emergency or not, her talented sons, Francisco in New York, Carlos in Briones, California, knew better than to barge in via cell-phone calls. But the fact that Francisco had persisted and had called dispatch—where someone was always free to talk to him—started the flutter of butterflies in her stomach. He had called, so maybe the emergency didn't involve him. But his wife, Angie? Their son, William Thomas, now going on two years old and into everything?

Even in their safe apartment in New York, even at what would be nearly one a.m. Eastern, there were so many risks. New York City was an incomprehensible place to someone living in a tiny, remote New Mexico town. An unwanted collection of awful scenarios spun through her head.

But Francisco had said to wait until she went ten-eight—clear and available. So whatever it was, how bad could it be? And another rush of worries stirred her imagination.

Everything at the Broken Spur now seemed like an enormous nuisance. Even Captain Taber's hesitation to break the news to Estelle—choosing to work her way through the needs of the current bar brawl situation before telling Estelle of her son's phone call—even that chapped Estelle a little bit, even though she knew it was the right thing to do.

As soon as the saloon was locked and the six witnesses on their way to the Sheriff's Office, Estelle followed in the Charger, intentionally keeping her speed down to a dull roar—not to shepherd the witnesses, but so that she had time and opportunity to call Francisco in New York.

Her thumb was poised to scroll to the quick contact, but her phone beat her to it, vibrating its little self like a living thing. She recognized Sheriff Bob Torrez's cell number, its short-timer owner supposedly camped somewhere in Texas following a long day of feral-hog-hunting—his latest and most consuming recreation.

"Guzman."

"Where you at?" The sheriff's greeting was typical, vintage Torrez.

"On State 56, coming up on mile marker twenty-one, inbound. And good morning to you, too."

"What's goin' on?"

"We had a little tussle at the Broken Spur. One Mexican national down, one local cowboy arrested, a handful of witnesses headed for the office to make detailed statements."

"The Mexican in bad shape?"

"We think so. And a few things that don't click about the fight. I didn't actually witness the main event, so we're going to have to rely on witnesses...and you know how *that* usually goes."

"Huh. Who's the cowboy?"

"Johnny Rabke."

Torrez scoffed, well aware of Rabke's long list of accomplishments, along with his frequent mild tangles with the law.

"What are *you* up to in the middle of the night?" Estelle asked. "Chasing hogs in the dark?"

"No need to do that, many as there are around here. Look, when you're clear, give your son Francisco a call. Sooner rather than later."

"I was about to dial him. He called you?"

"Yep."

"Did he explain what he wanted?"

"Nope. He just wanted to make sure you got the message to contact him. Talk to you later, then." The sheriff cut the call, and for a moment, Estelle sat motionless, letting the cruise control pace her flight through the night. Tires thumped on the concrete joints of the bridge across the Rio Salinas, and she scrolled the phone to her son's closely guarded, unlisted number. The phone rang only twice before Francisco's quiet voice greeted her.

Chapter Three

In the background she could hear a little voice dabbling through an imaginary alphabet. A wave of relief tried to dull the edge of her nerves. Her grandson was one of those lucky youngsters who awoke always on the right side of the crib, happy and eager for whatever the day might bring...even if all the adult clocks claimed that it was still the middle of the night.

With the stroke of an electronic button or two, the phone link routed through the car's radio, and Estelle dropped the phone into her lap.

"Think of it this way, Ma. At least I didn't wake you."

"*Hijo,* you know how I love to hear the sound of your voice. But don't keep me in suspense any longer. What's up?"

"Where are you headed?"

"You mean right now? This instant? I'm on 56, headed toward town. I have a couple of bar fight participants headed to the hospital. I need to talk to a handful of witnesses. The usual stuff, *hijo*. What prompts this middle-of-the-night call?"

Francisco hesitated, and she could hear him whisper something, followed by more happy infant nonsense from William Thomas.

"Did you put 'em there? In the hospital, I mean. You beat the crap out of two drunks?"

Estelle laughed. "No, I didn't put them there. I'm just playing cleanup. How's Angie?"

"Angie is fine, and packing. Look, we'll be flying out in about an hour or less," he said. "That puts us in Posadas right around seven a.m. your time. Racing the sun."

Estelle felt a wave of intense relief, along with joyous anticipation. She knew that October had been a frenetic month for her son and daughter-in-law, with a tight schedule of concerts and recordings—made tighter by a torrent of interviews and appearances that their agent had insisted were necessary evils.

"That's wonderful news, *hijo*." But still no explanation for the middle-of-the-night call.

"Yeah, that's the good news." He hesitated. "The bad news is that both Carlos and Tasha are in Temerly Trauma Treatment Center in Briones." He fell silent, giving his mother time to absorb what he had just said. Estelle braked hard and swung the Charger off onto the shoulder of the highway, out of habit flipping on the array of emergency lights. She waited a few seconds for her pulse to stop hammering in her ears as she tried to put her thoughts in order. She had heard her son clearly...and Francisco would never invent such a thing.

"What happened? I'm listening, *hijo*."

"Carlos is still in surgery, and probably will be for at least another hour or two, maybe more." Francisco spoke slowly and distinctly. "Tasha is now listed in serious condition with multiple fractures but is out of danger."

"Did you talk with her folks?" Although she had met the Qarshes only twice, it seemed as if they had been the warmest of old friends for decades.

"I did. I offered them a ride out. They declined but said they'd make their way out as soon as they can."

Estelle realized she was trying to press the brake pedal through the floor. She jammed the gear selector into park and tried to relax and listen. "But what happened? Do you know?"

"As nearly as anyone can figure out, Carlos and Tasha were

riding their new tandem bike along a roadway somewhere in that area. I wrote down the map names, but they don't mean anything to me. Anyway, they were riding on this sort of park-like macadam road and were clipped from behind by a pickup truck."

"*Ay*. In the dark? They were riding in the dark?"

"Yes. Following the bike path, though, with good lights, reflectors, helmets, the whole works." He hesitated. "At this point, that's about all I know. I have the name of the investigating officer. He didn't want to take the time to tell me anything beyond the basics. I have his name and cell, though. If you want that, I can give it to you now or bring it with me when we come."

Her ballpoint pen somehow was in hand, but for a disjunctive moment, she couldn't figure out how to operate it. "I'll take it now," she said, straightening her pad on its aluminum clipboard.

"Sergeant Jake Kesserman, with the Briones PD. He's the guy who called me." He dictated the number and extension.

"*Carlos* gave the sergeant your number?"

"Apparently so. I do not know why Carlos wanted it that way, Ma. It would seem faster, more direct, if Kesserman had called the S.O. as the fastest way to reach you. But that's my brother for you."

"Whatever he did, it worked well. Bobby called me to say that you had contacted him as well."

Francisco laughed gently. "The man. I knew Big Bad Bobby was hunting, so that was worth a shot." Estelle heard voices in the background. "I would have called Dad's cell, but one of the nurses said that they're up to here with some business that the Sheriff's Department sent them."

He said something off-phone, then added, "And the cab is out front to take us to the airport, so I'm going to cut off here for a little bit. Serious as things are, though, it just made sense to grab the jet. It's in New York anyway, and I'm thinking that might be why Carlos gave me as a contact. Even if it's nothing much—if he's up and walking around? What the heck, it'll still be good to see him and Tasha. We can give him a hard time about his nighttime biking habits."

"And well deserved, probably," Estelle said. "*Ay.* Tasha is all right, you said?"

"Listed as serious. That's all I know. Carlos is in surgery. And that's all I know about him. My suggestion is that we wheels down in Posadas for about ten seconds, pick you and Dad up, and then head for Briones. Is that going to work for you guys? The two of you will find a way to schedule this so you can make it work? Tell me you'll make it work."

"You're feeling that it's necessary for all of us to descend on him? Is that what he said?"

"The suggestion wasn't his. It was the sergeant who said that. It's the sergeant's opinion that Carlos really took a serious whack. I haven't talked with anyone on the medical staff, but I assume that this Kesserman guy has."

"I can call him direct. Carlos, I mean."

"No, you can't, Ma. He's in surgery. And will be for a while, and then in ICU. Look, with us free for a couple days, with the jet here in New York and available, it just makes sense for a little reunion. And it's easy and convenient to pick you guys up on the way, if you and Dad can find a way to break free. Carlos will get a kick out of seeing you."

"*Ay.*"

"Yep, *ay.*"

"How did it happen, do you know?"

"No, I don't know, other than at night, and somehow involving a truck and the cops. That's the extent of what I know. But a little jet time answers all questions, face-to-face."

"You've made up your mind to fly out...how about this. You go ahead, and then give us a call and let us know what the situation actually is. Then we can fly commercial if need be."

"I don't think so, Ma. I don't think this is any time to be messing around trying to fly commercial. For one thing, there's no air service to Briones. You'd end up in SFO, or Alameda, or someplace like that, and still have to face the traffic out to Briones. Look, if this hadn't been serious, the cops wouldn't have bothered to call. Or you could call Tasha's cell, but if she's hurting, we don't want to bother her. So let's do this the easy way, all right? Let us provide the ride. Let Jackie or somebody handle the bar fights."

"Hijo..."

"Just do it, Ma. Look, I gotta go. So talk with Dad and arrange coverage, and I'll touch base with you again when we're in the air. If you really can't break away, we'll just give you a wing wobble when we pass overhead. But I really hope you'll go with us. Love you." He broke the connection.

For two minutes, Estelle sat quietly while the car idled and blinked. She tried to pin down one coherent thought, one *do this first* direction...so easy to do until things turned personal. With the unconscious, battered, and billiard-balled Pablo Ramirez headed for the hospital, with a pending emergency transfer for him to Albuquerque, Dr. Francis Guzman was having a busy night. Estelle hated the interruptions that cell phones inflicted, but at this moment she was proud of her older son's command approach, his decisive "do this first" mentality.

On top of that, at this moment she wanted the reassurance of her husband's gentle touch and the ocean of calm that always seemed to envelop him. With emergency lights still breaking the night, she pulled out onto the highway and headed directly toward Posadas General Hospital.

Willing her hands steady, she scrolled down to Captain Jackie Taber's contact. The captain answered on the first ring.

"Jackie, I just got off the phone with Francisco. It looks as if we're going to be headed to California here in a little bit."

"Carlos?" Without painful probing, Taber had been able to put the pieces together.

"Yes."

"What can I do?"

Estelle took a deep breath. "Nothing that I can think about

right now. In fact, I can't think straight about much of anything. I'm headed into the hospital to talk with Francis. If you'll follow through with this saloon mess, I'd appreciate it."

"Done. You do what you have to do."

"Thank you, Jackie." Was it that simple to just drop everything in one life and charge off into another? She tried to relax back into the seat, but her spine felt as if someone had welded all the vertebrae together into one inflexible rod.

Chapter Four

The Gulfstream 650 charged down the runway with a ferocious acceleration, the early morning sun chasing it. Estelle gripped her husband's hand until her knuckles turned white, concentrating on the tiny window view of the tawny New Mexico prairie until they had gained sufficient altitude to see over the San Cristóbals, deep into the shadow-striated heart of Mexico—where Pablo Ramirez's family would be trying to cope with their own change of fortune.

Refreshments came and went, and Estelle relaxed enough to guide her two-year-old grandson through the slurping of a plastic lidded cup of chocolate milk. Her own Earl Grey breakfast tea went untouched. Her husband, son, and daughter-in-law did their best to keep the conversation light, but Estelle didn't follow it, so loud was the cacophony of questions and scenarios running through her head.

Dr. Francis Guzman spent some time on his phone and once rose from his orthopedic leather seat to wander toward the rear of the aircraft as he conversed, hunched to avoid the low, curved ceiling.

He returned to his seat after a few moments and folded Estelle's right hand in his. "We're just going to have to be patient," he said. "They told me that Carlos is still in surgery, for the second time. Tasha is in recovery." He shrugged helplessly. "There's nothing I can do from here, and you know, there's probably nothing I can do out there either. The kids are in good hands."

"We can't just barge in." Estelle heard herself say that, and wished the world spun the other way. "They'll have their own way of doing things, both the cops and the hospital. Could you talk with the attending, though?"

Francis shook his head. "I talked with a surgical nurse. The nurse couldn't—or wouldn't—tell me much except that the internal injuries were 'significant.' Who knows about that. I've had about as much luck as you've had trying to reach the cops."

The third time she'd tried calling had not been the charm, nor the fourth, fifth, or sixth. The geological magic of the Grand Canyon was passing under the right wingtip when her cell phone vibrated, and she recognized the number. "Hold this guy?" she said, and urged the squirming little boy onto her husband's lap.

"Guzman." For a moment, the phone was silent.

"Undersheriff Guzman? Good. You've tried to call me a number of times, and I'm sorry I wasn't able to get back to you any sooner," a husky male voice said. "This is Sergeant Jake Kesserman with the Briones PD."

"I'm sure you've been busy, Sergeant. I've been anxious to hear from you."

"Well, yes." He snuffled something that might have been a weak chuckle.

"We're headed your way, Sergeant. We'll be landing at Jackson in an hour or so."

"Jackson? You're not coming commercial?"

"No. I'm told that Jackson Field is closer to Temerly Hospital, where they tell me that the kids are."

"Indeed it is. Jackson is home to one of the air ambulance services as well. Okay, look. I'm sure you have a whole basketful of questions. Is your husband flying with you?"

"Yes. And my son, Francisco, and his wife and son."

"Oh, wow. That's good. Look, we're making some progress at this end, but let me calm your nerves a little. The two of them—your son, Carlos, and his fiancée—were close to Temerly when the crash happened, so that's a plus."

"Who hit them?" The cop mantra prompted the questions, as if at this moment it mattered.

"We don't know that yet. It turns out that the truck that hit them was stolen. We've recovered that, but we've got a snarl. The vehicle is tied in with another vehicle theft incident somehow. It's been like workin' with a bunch of dominoes." He drew in a long breath. "Some things I need to talk with you about, but it'd be best to wait for you all to get here."

The flight attendant, who looked as if she might be someone's sprightly grandmother, appeared at Estelle's elbow. "About twenty minutes," she whispered, and Estelle nodded her thanks.

"I heard that," Kesserman said. "Christ, you must have rented a rocket. That puts you here just a little after eight, our time. Look, I'm going to have a driver meet you folks at the airport and take you where you need to go. Later, if you want to corral a rental car, that's fine too. So there's four of you? Plus the child?"

"Yes. Four adults and a two-year-old."

"Ah…a terrible two. That's right. I remember reading that somewhere. I'll see if I can dig up a child seat for him."

"Sergeant, I…we…appreciate your efforts. You can't imagine how much."

"No worries, Sheriff. Glad to do it, and I'm sorry it's under these circumstances. As it happens, my mother—she's ninety-one, bless her—she's one of your son's biggest fans. The pianist? Francisco, isn't it?" He laughed. "We've done a little background work." He sounded sympathetic, but what came out next was almost ominous as he lowered his voice to deliver the theatrical line: "We know who you are."

"My husband and I aren't coming out to look over your shoulder, Sergeant. I want you to know that. We're just worried, and so far, we're in the dark about what really happened."

"Yep. I hear ya. If you can, just try to relax. Your son and his fiancée are in the best of hands, and we're optimistic. We'll talk when you get here. See you in a little bit. Travel safe."

A few minutes later, the descent to Jackson Field was steep and fast, enough to make little William Thomas chortle with glee. Catching glimpses outside, Estelle saw verdant hills studded with occasional rock outcroppings, and patches of dense forest splotched here and there by the encroachment of the city. To the north and east, the view opened up to reveal vast vineyards that looked like extensive corduroy.

They skimmed altogether too close to expressway traffic before the pilot settled the Grumman on the runway numbers and kept the aircraft rolling briskly until they turned off on one of the taxiways near the FBO.

Beyond the airport office building, in front of a yawning hangar, she caught a brief glimpse of a black Suburban, parked with its grill strobes dancing. As they drew closer and then turned to park, she saw a uniformed police officer waiting by the Suburban's driver's door, hands folded in front of his belt buckle, shoulders square, the brim of his uniform cap a neat two fingers' width above the bridge of his nose.

As soon as the jet wheeled into its parking spot and the engines spooled down, he moved away from the Suburban toward them, left hand activating the radio mike on his lapel. He met them as they stepped to the tarmac.

"Welcome to sunny California," he said, extending his hand. "I'm Officer Troy Dinsman with Briones PD. Sheriff Guzman?"

"Undersheriff Estelle Reyes-Guzman," Estelle said. "This is my husband, Dr. Francis Guzman, and my son and daughter-in-law, Francisco and Angie Guzman."

"And the little one," Dinsman added with a warm smile for William Thomas, a smile that was tinged with just enough sympathy to hint that he knew the background of this meeting.

William Thomas, though only two years old, had seen plenty of cops, and he'd flown dozens of times. But this particular set of circumstances caught him with his mouth hanging open and his dark, bottomless eyes wide. Dinsman squatted, reached out, and poked the little boy in the gut. "Welcome to California, son."

The officer stood up. "My instructions are to provide whatever arrangements might be needed to make your visit..." He hesitated. "Well, a little less difficult for you than otherwise." Estelle's stomach clenched.

"If you wish to go first thing to the hospital, I'll be glad to take you there right now." He turned and pointed off to the northwest. "That squat, mostly glass building over beyond the interstate is Temerly Trauma Treatment Center. Triple-T, we call it. Maybe four minutes from here. If you wish to rent a car for your stay, there are at least three rental agencies here at the airport." He swung around and pointed off to southwest. "That brown building complex in the forest of eucalyptus is the Holiday Express. It's the closest decent hotel, easy in, easy out."

"Ma and Papa, may I make a suggestion?" Francisco said. "How about you let Officer Dinsman run you both over to the hospital, and Angie and I will get us wheels and rooms. As soon as we do that, we'll join you at the hospital."

"Good deal," Dinsman said briskly. "Sergeant Kesserman is at the hospital right now. I informed him and the captain of your arrival. I know that Captain Mitchell would like to talk to you. Get you squared away with what's going on."

"Let's do it," Francis said, taking Estelle by the elbow. She hesitated and looked at her son and daughter-in-law.

"You're sure?"

"Come on, Ma. Get a grip. If I can rent this buzz-bomb a couple dozen times a year, I guess we can manage a Toyota and a couple of rooms. We'll leave the luggage on the plane and pick it up when we have wheels."

She reached out and hugged him, one arm drawing Angie in close. "You two are incredible, you know that? Come right over, then, all right? As soon as you have things sorted out?"

"Of course."

She turned back to Dinsman and nodded. "Officer, we appreciate this."

He handed her a business card. "Put that number in your phone. If you run into a snag, give me a buzz. Like even if you just need a chauffeur who knows the city," and he nodded. "You have the sergeant's number as well?"

"I do."

"Then let's roll."

For a few moments, after dropping Francisco, Angie, and the toddler off at the terminal's car rental entrance, it seemed as if Officer Dinsman was heading who-knows-where, but eventually the maze of streets made sense as Temerly loomed closer. Even as they swung into the hospital access road and Dinsman headed straight for the looming portico of the emergency entrance, Estelle's pulse pounded. She wrapped her husband's hand in both of hers and shut her eyes. Dinsman parked directly in front of the NO PARKING ANY TIME sign.

"Through that door," Dinsman said, "then the interior door, and at every intersection, head left. Eventually, you'll meet up with one of the nursing stations." His hand swept toward the west. "It'll be easier when your son returns with the rental car if he parks over there in the open lot."

Just ahead of them, in an area marked "Official Vehicles Only," a pair of police cruisers were parked, one unmarked but obviously a police interceptor, the other in full regalia. "Sergeant Kesserman will probably find you before you find him." He smiled sympathetically. "Good luck with all this. And don't hesitate to call me if there's something I can do. I mean that. I know what it's like to flounder around in a strange city."

"Thank you, Officer," Francis said, and Estelle nodded. She was grateful for the seemingly limitless hospitality, for the unwavering VIP treatment, but right then she wanted nothing more than to exit the Suburban before her clenched gut revolted from the stress and apprehension. Still, she was able to detach herself from this moment enough to realize that it was no wonder victims of highway tragedies, family violence, or a host of other senseless crimes made such lousy witnesses. Turn the gut inside out with apprehension, and logical thinking knotted with it.

As she passed through the second set of automatic doors, the waft of hospital fragrance prompted another flinch. No matter what air purifier they used, no matter how much sweet disinfectant they dumped in the mop water, the heavy, cloying hospital miasma was the same everywhere.

"Oh, *por Díos,*" she exclaimed, as at least part of the mystery came stunningly clear. Two cops stood in the hallway, the taller one engaged with his cell phone, his back turned to the door. He was so thin that his shoulder blades poked at his light nylon jacket. His partner was not much taller than Estelle's five foot seven, but brawny and standing with hands on hips as if waiting for a crowd to try and rush the door. Captain's bars winked on his shoulders. What hair was not covered by his captain's cap was short and tightly curled, heavily accented with gray.

"Eddie?"

He grinned—an expression that she hadn't witnessed often. Eddie Mitchell had experienced a few years as a patrolman on the streets of Baltimore, and that, coupled with a nasty divorce, had hardened his attitude. Then he'd left the East and found a home in Posadas County, New Mexico, first as a deputy and then patrol sergeant. Now he seemed to find satisfaction, if not pleasure, in dealing with the "California Crazies," as Jackie Taber called them.

"You folks made good time." Mitchell reached out a hand and gripped Francis's. "Good to see you again, Doctor. I'm Eddie Mitchell, plus a few more pounds and a lot more gray hair than I carried around during my Posadas days. The guy with the phone stuck in his ear is Sergeant Jake Kesserman." He turned to Estelle, extended both hands to grip hers. "Let's find a quiet place and catch you up."

"Eddie, you're treating us like royalty," Estelle said, and pulled him into a hug. "Thank you *so* much. Is there a way that we can visit with my son right away?"

He frowned and guided them down the hallway, a hand on her elbow. "There are some issues, Estelle." He could have clubbed her with both fists and not made any greater impression.

"I...we...can address those one at a time," Estelle said, sounding more confident than she felt.

He nodded and glanced across at the sergeant, who trailed a step or two behind Francis. "Sarge, maybe you'd keep a watch for her son and daughter-in-law. Save them some time and frustration with navigating this place." He flashed a wide smile—something Estelle had *never* seen him do. "You'll recognize 'em."

"You bet." Kesserman replied. "Folks, I'll be checking in with you later."

After a moment or two, Estelle began to feel like a nervous spelunker—that she should have tied a ball of string to unwind behind her to mark her path. This hall, that hall, then an elevator, then more polished hallways, some with small groups of people gathered, some of those folks looking nervous, some hopeful, some with barely contained tears. As they walked, her husband's grip on her right elbow became more than just a casual comfort. This was *his* world. Yet so far, he hadn't found a single word to say. She tried to steady her breathing, tried to relax to let Captain Eddie Mitchell and her husband be her guides.

A man she guessed to be a physician, who had been behind one of the counters of the nurses' station near the vast suite labeled as the Intensive Care Unit, looked up as they approached. A white lab coat framed the colors of his paisley shirt. He laid the clipboard down, and with long, slender fingers adjusted the stethoscope that decorated his neck. With a nod at Mitchell, his gaze then shifted to take in the captain's companions. For several uncomfortable seconds, he regarded Estelle and her husband.

"This is Dr. Tobias Baines-Smith," Mitchell said, as if

prompting the young man to say something. The physician extended his hand slowly, as if the entire arm were on hydraulics. His careful demeanor sent a clear signal. The corners of Dr. Baines-Smith's eyes crinkled as he more cradled than shook Estelle's hand, at the same time reaching out to take Francis Guzman's with his left. "Blame my father for the name." His voice was a soft tenor with no recognizable accent. "Dad was British military, my mother was Nigerian. My father's last posting was as an attaché at Scott Air Force Base in Illinois. But..."

The physician's circumstances—in some ways so similar to Tasha Qarshe's, her younger son's fiancée, born of a Somali father and Irish mother—were such that Estelle's curiosity would normally have been intrigued. Now, she could not care less who was who. "Is it going to be possible to see our son, Carlos Guzman? And his fiancée, Tasha Qarshe."

"Of course you can. Has the captain given you any background at this point?"

His left eyebrow lifted in question as Estelle's unblinking gaze riveted him.

"At this point...no." Another small part of her psyche knew that hundreds of times she'd done this same thing, stalling a frantic relative before delivering the heartbreak. It was never easy. Knowing how the system worked didn't make it any easier.

"I understand," Baines-Smith said. "If you'll accompany me, please." He paused at the counter until the elderly nurse looked up. "I'll be in ICU-3. My phone will be off for a few moments." The nurse glanced at the large wall clock and nodded. Then her gaze shifted to Captain Mitchell. Her eyes narrowed, one eyebrow drifting upward.

"Let's not have a congregation in there," she said.

"Absolutely not." Mitchell managed to keep his tone deferential. Once again, he took Estelle by the elbow and lowered his voice. "There's a little family room just down the hall. I'll wait there. We'll need to talk in a bit."

"Thank you."

Dr. Baines-Smith led them through a maze of glass-walled partitions, each panel covered by immaculate white curtains. Estelle tried to ignore the electronic hum of myriad machines, the rhythmic hiss of ventilators, the clicks that marked cycles and pulses of something—an entire symphony of gadgetry that gave patients something to listen to when they could do nothing else.

The last sound that Estelle expected—an almost childish giggle—floated out from behind the privacy curtain of ICU-3. Dr. Baines-Smith stroked the curtain to one side and was greeted by a beaming nurse, a sturdy individual whose face bore an interesting history of deep scars that mapped his ebony skin down his neck to his left collarbone. His name tag announced Reese Patton, RN. He smiled at the visitors and leaned closer to Dr. Baines-Smith. "He's awake…just."

Patton pointed a finger first at Estelle, then at Francis. "Mom, Dad?" Without waiting for an answer, he added, "He won't be very responsive, but he's doing great, all things considered. Go easy on him. In about thirty seconds, I'll be back to kick you out." Patton's tone said he was kidding, but his piercing gaze said otherwise.

Estelle moved close to the bed and looked down into her son's face. Without additions, he could easily be Francisco's twin—dark complexion, black wavy hair, heavy eyebrows, and already in need of a shave. Three neat stitches smeared with clear petroleum jelly marked Carlos's left cheek in front of his ear, and behind the ear, a four-by-four-inch bandage was centered in a shaved patch, covering more souvenirs. A white sheet drawn up to his chin concealed everything else.

"*Por Díos,* they gather for the wake," Carlos whispered. He opened his right eye and sort of looked at her…or at the ceiling behind her head. It was hard to tell. "The gathering of the clan…this is not a good sign."

"Hijo…"

"I'm just fine, Ma. Don't let 'em tell you otherwise." He

heaved a breath and flinched. "I feel like I got run over by a truck is all." He shuddered through a deep breath. "Dang."

Dr. Baines-Smith grunted with what might have been amusement and handed a folder to Francis. "Doctor, he's had a rough time. We can expect that he'll be in and out for a day or two, even when he's out from under the anesthesia," the physician said. And sure enough, Carlos drifted off. "And the rest of this day is going to be a rough one for him. More surgery in just a little bit. And then he'll probably wish that he could be sedated far more than we'll allow." He puffed out his cheeks and sighed heavily. "But he's a tough young man."

He glanced across at Estelle, who had not taken her gaze from her son's face. "Tasha Qarshe has been moved out of ICU to a private room up on the second floor." He flashed a smile and waved to what might have been the north. "About a mile that way."

"Is she awake?"

"Not at the moment. Sedated into dreamland. She's scheduled for some orthopedic therapy on her right hip. That will happen tomorrow. At the moment, she's in considerable discomfort, mostly because of a championship collection of road rash. A hellacious bruise on her right hip and nasty fractures of three fingers on her left hand."

He gestured toward Reese Patton, who stood at the curtain, managing to look more like an MP than an RN. "Let's go talk some. Dr. Guzman, you might want to take that folder and chart with you. You're welcome to study it as long as you'd like. Carlos may be more responsive by this evening. And by then, you'll know more."

Patton turned and startled, eyes wide. "My God," he said in a theatrically loud stage whisper, then looked quickly back at Carlos's silent form before he extended his hand toward Francisco Guzman, who had appeared around the corner of the curtain. Patton clamped his hand on the young man's shoulder.

"You and your brother surely are out of the same mold, aren't you?" Patton said, his smile wide. "For a minute, there…I mean, we specialize in fast healing around this joint, but not *that* fast."

The words that floated up from the hospital bed were weak but distinct. "The guy who plays the requiem is here… Now I know I'm in trouble."

Chapter Five

"In a nutshell, this is what we have," Dr. Tobias Baines-Smith said. With everyone seated, he pointed at each in turn. "Just to make sure I have everyone straight, this is mom, dad, older brother, sister-in-law, the little guy who looks as if he'd rather be somewhere else...and our own Captain Mitchell. So. Let's start here."

He turned the computer monitor a bit so that it faced them all. "And, Doc, forgive me for sticking to the basics, but I want to make sure that everyone is following."

"Basics would be good," Estelle said.

"First of all, his left leg was badly shattered, taking the brunt of the initial impact. That's in part why Carlos spent so long in the preliminary surgeries. You can see the plates and rods in situ above and below the left knee. That whole mess is going to require some more work...some *extensive* work, before that leg—especially the knee joint—functions at least halfway normally.

"That won't happen here, though. Here at the trauma center, we get him stabilized, then find the right orthopedist to improve his condition in the long run." He moved the cursor. "Also, a compound fracture of the left lower fibula, just above the ankle joint." He moved the cursor to yet another panel. "And a cracked left femur." He touched the screen. "Right behind the ball, there. We—*he*—got lucky with that one."

He swiveled his chair a bit so he could face the group. "Let me tell you, this was a *hard* hit, folks. This wasn't just a case of the truck's wing mirror slapping them as it passed by and knocking them into the underbrush. This was a *hard* hit. The captain is going to talk to you folks after I'm finished. Anyway, your son's left leg absorbed most of the first impact, a hard blow that twisted the patient into the bike frame and smashed him to the pavement." He mimed the impact with both hands.

"In at least one way, he was fortunate. The pelvis was spared entirely. And that's good. And now, the cut on the head? Maybe part of the bike, maybe something else. It's nasty, but there's no sign of subdural hematoma—bleeding on the inside. So that's good. All of those are concerns, but are not the biggest concern."

"*Por Dios,*" Estelle murmured, and her husband's hand found hers.

"The second strike is troublesome, from both the captain's point of view and from mine. It appears to us that the driver of the truck smashed into the tandem bike, then braked hard to a full stop, and then backed up to effect a *second* impact. I'm told that's what the marks on the pavement show." He paused and offered a hand toward Mitchell. "Captain, I may be talking out of turn here, so correct me if I'm wrong."

"What you say is accurate," Mitchell said.

"Doctor, you're saying the driver deliberately backed up and ran over Carlos *again*?" Francisco asked incredulously. "I mean, he wasn't just stopping to see what he had done?"

"That's exactly what we think. The marks on the pavement tell the story, and the bruising is distinctive. Before your brother was able to free himself from the mangled bike, the pickup driver hit him again." He prompted the computer to bring up more images. "This mass you see here in his lower torso is internal hemorrhaging. Some significant damage there. Four fractured ribs. One of them tore into his spleen. We removed that successfully earlier this morning."

"The spleen or the rib?" Francisco asked.

"Well, actually, both the spleen and a piece of shattered rib. And as you can imagine, the bruising is severe, inside and out. There's some critical damage to the stomach, to the diaphragm. There's also evidence that his left kidney has been damaged and is bleeding. I'm expecting another surgical session, or even two, before we're out of the woods. That will happen a little later this morning."

"The fact that he's conscious at all is remarkable," Dr. Guzman said.

"Absolutely."

"And Tasha?" Estelle's voice was small, more of a croak. "And Tasha?" she repeated, stronger this time.

"The truck apparently came in from the side, like so." Captain Mitchell stabbed one hand into the other at an angle. "It missed her, and hit Carlos. When the bike crashed down, she sustained injuries consistent with a typical bike smashup. We don't think the truck actually touched her. Her left hand got caught up somehow in the bike's frame."

"Hence the fractures of the three fingers," Dr. Baines-Smith said. "Lots of bruising, as I said, especially around the right hip. Lots of road rash. Fortunately, the secondary strike by the truck missed her entirely. So, she's very, very lucky. I think it's best if we keep her here for a day or two under observation. Just to be sure.

"At this point there's not much else I can tell you. For your son, it's going to be touch and go for the next forty-eight hours. I won't kid you about that. But he's a strong young man. And it matters a *lot* that you folks were able to come here so fast." He rose and nudged the computer so that it pointed away from the door. "You may have questions for me at this point? I don't mean to charge off, but I have to."

"I don't even know what to ask." Estelle's voice was husky.

"I understand that. Now, when you're ready to visit with Tasha, I'll be happy to take you up to her room. Or you can ask Reese Patton, any time. He might be easier to catch. I'd really recommend that either Reese or I escort you up there. Her attending nurse is...well, she's interesting. And very protective." He turned and shook hands with Mitchell. "Captain, good to see you again."

As the door closed behind him, Estelle turned to Eddie Mitchell. "You've had a chance to speak with her, Eddie? With Tasha?"

"Yes, but I gotta tell you, Estelle, she doesn't remember very much. It was so fast, so violent, not much registered with her. We know," and he held up a hand to tick off his fingers, "one, it was a Chevrolet. She remembers seeing the logo on the tailgate. For an instant there, it was backing right toward her. Two, it was dark blue or black with chromed wheels." He shrugged.

"One occupant? Two?"

"She doesn't know. And sorry to say, at this point, there's a whole sea of things we don't know. Did your son and his fiancée know the assailants? We don't know. What prompted the attack? We don't know. We *do* know that it was an attack, not an accident. Hit hard, not just a glancing blow. Then stop, back up, and a second strike." He took a deep breath and held it for a moment. "The truck was significantly damaged after the primary collision, and that's helped us some."

"What does my son tell you?"

"Not much, Estelle. What he said to you a few moments ago was the most we've heard from him since the accident. Surprised the hell out of me that he's even that cogent, I gotta tell ya. The good news is that during these brief moments of consciousness, he's been completely coherent. That quip he made about Francisco playing the requiem is a good example. In and out, in and out. What he might be able to tell us? I don't know. You and I both know how unreliable witness testimony can be. And in this case, we have two witnesses romped and stomped, without warning. An unexpected attack—that's how I'd describe it. A beautiful, warm evening, and they're out for a pleasure ride. They never saw it coming."

She regarded Captain Mitchell as if waiting for more.

He held up both hands again. "By the time emergency help reached the scene, your son was unconscious, so we got no statement there. We're working the scene every which way, so we'll see what we come up with. There may have been some traffic in the area, but no one has come forward. There's the possibility of some security cameras in a couple locations, so we'll see. Later on, I'll run you out to the scene, if you'd like."

"Who found them?"

"A passing motorist. She didn't see the crash, but when she drove by, she says that Tasha was struggling on her hands and knees. It must have been just seconds after the crash." He took a deep breath. "You know, it's the most common thing for the bike rider—or riders, in this case—to be thrown way free. Carlos apparently was *not* thrown. He went down in a tangle with the bike, and they ended up near a stand of saplings that bordered the highway shoulder." He grimaced. "A really hard hit. As I said, I'll be happy to run you out there."

Estelle shook her head. "Until I'm convinced that both Carlos and Tasha are completely stable, this is where I intend to be."

"I understand that." He handed her a business card after jotting a number on the back. "That's the phone I'll answer twenty-four, seven—if you need anything. In the meantime, we're out there."

"Thank you, Eddie."

He stood up abruptly, then hesitated. "And if Carlos has anything to say to *you* about what happened," and he pointed at the card. "Twenty-four, seven." Sergeant Kesserman and Officer Dinsman are both with the Briones PD, and they're assigned to the hospital until we say otherwise. Primarily, we do that until we know what the hell is going on. We want to make sure there's no follow-up strike against either of the kids. As I said before, this wasn't just a slap with the wing mirror. We're way beyond that. With that in mind, one or the other of the cops will be here, all the time. But they'll stay out of your way." He extended his hand to Francis. "Doctor, not good to see you under these circumstances, but…it's good to see you."

Dr. Guzman offered only a silent nod, and Mitchell bent toward him. "A great medical team here, Doctor. In that sense, your son is fortunate. They're the best."

"I appreciate that," Francis whispered.

"And you two…" the captain said, offering Francisco and his wife a warm smile, taking Francisco's hand as the young man stood, and then reaching out to Angie's with the other hand, drawing them together. William Thomas leaned as far away from Mitchell as his mother's grip allowed.

"Here you are, top of the world. We're all proud of you two. While you're here, we're going to do our best to handle the press, but I gotta tell ya, you know about the paparazzi better'n I do. I'm guessing that they'll find you, for sure…if they managed to find a way past Kesserman's roadblock. If they *do* find you, if they ask any questions about the accident, I hope you'll just refer them to me or the sergeant. And don't hesitate to call hospital security if you see somebody with a camera headed your way down the hall."

"Yes, sir. Thank you."

When it appeared that Estelle was about to follow Mitchell out of the waiting room, her son spoke up. "Ma? Some logistics?"

She turned to her son with a "What are you talking about" look on her face. He reached out and urged her to a chair, at the same time beckoning Dr. Guzman to the couch beside her.

"Angie and squirt, here, are going back to the hotel for a little bit. He's going to need a nap or he'll get cranky and attack a nurse or something." Francisco held up a key fob. "This is to the white Toyota Camry parked down in slot six, just west of the front door. Slot six." He waited a second to make sure both

Estelle and Francis were focused. "That's your chariot to use for whatever. It's from the airport, so it's easy to return...whenever." He held out the keys and his father nodded, taking them.

"This is your room key," Francisco continued, passing the folder containing the heavy plastic card to Estelle. "Room 407 at the Express, just down the block. Your car's parked facing the hospital's main entrance. Just drive out, then one block left, and a quick right. It's an open reservation. I know that right now you don't want to leave the hospital, but there may come a time when a hot shower will feel pretty good."

"*Hijo*..." Estelle started to say, but her voice cracked.

"Not to fret, Ma," the young man said. "We're in room 409, right next door. Now, here's the deal. The jet is set to take us to New York later this afternoon for a dinner meeting that we can't skip, then we'll be back. We thought about a teleconference, but that's not going to work in this instance. Then we're clear on through the weekend, and we'll be back here as soon as we can." He held up a folded sheet of paper. "I jotted our probable schedule here for you. I have to be in Atlanta for a recording session on Monday, and then both Angie and I will be in Los Angeles with the movie people for some dubbing stuff on the following Wednesday. In between times," and he held up his phone, "we'll be either in New York or here, and you have my number as well. If we have to make changes in our plans, we will. But we have reason to be optimistic."

The sight of her son's phone reminded her that several times in the past uncountable minutes her own phone had come to life, and she had ignored it.

With one arm holding her husband close, she pulled Francisco into a tight hug. "You are amazing, you both," she murmured. "Sorry if I seem so scattered."

"No one is ever ready for something like this, Ma."

Chapter Six

Dr. Francis Guzman was sitting in a corner chair, reading the voluminous patient record for the fourth or fifth time that day, in addition to all the supplementary paperwork Dr. Baines-Smith had provided in a near-constant stream. Estelle stood beside the patient's bed, one hand resting feather light on Carlos's chest, counting the respirations, feeling the strong heartbeat through her fingertips. Her eyes were closed, her concentration total.

A flash of irritation interrupted her thoughts when her cell phone vibrated in her pants pocket. As if he could hear the vibration, Francis glanced up from his perusal of the medical files. "It might be Francisco," he whispered.

They had taken a few moments to visit their motel room, to wish Francisco and Angie—and little William Thomas—smooth traveling as the young family departed for engagements in New York. The phone would have to serve as the young couple's link with Carlos's condition. His periods of wakefulness were already more frequent and prolonged, and during the afternoon he seemed in less distress.

Estelle glanced at the phone's little screen. "*Ay.*" She stepped away from the bed, loath to break her contact with her son's body. She stood apart, left arm extended so she could rest her left hand on her son's right wrist while she manipulated the phone. "Guzman."

"Hey." The quiet, almost whisper sounded as if the sheriff of Posadas County, New Mexico, were in the next room. "So what's goin' on?"

"Watchful waiting, Bobby."

"You able to talk with him yet?"

"A little. He's in and out."

"Eddie says he's stable now."

Estelle was not surprised that Bob Torrez had made contact with Eddie Mitchell. The world could go on without her.

"Stable, but more surgery to come."

"Eddie said the one kidney is probably too damaged to save."

"So we're told. That decision comes today, I think. What day is this?"

She was only half kidding, but Torrez's answer was sober. "It's still Thursday. Five fifteen p.m."

"So." A long pause followed, and Estelle let it linger. She gently shifted her fingers so she could feel her son's pulse, and she watched the sweep of the second hand on the wall clock as she counted. Her count agreed with the monitor's display.

"I know you ain't got a schedule yet," Torrez said. "But Pablo Ramirez crapped out on us. He died just before noon today. I thought you'd want to know."

For a moment, Estelle drew a blank, then shifted mental gears to connect with another life, far away and far in the past. "Were you able to reach his family?"

"They've been notified."

How cold that is, Estelle thought. *Your son is dead. You'll never see him again, never talk to him again. Deal with it.* And now the tables were turned. Once again, she felt a surge of gratitude for how Dinsman, Kesserman, and Eddie Mitchell had handled the incident with her son and his fiancée. A brief, impersonal phone call was all that was called for "by the book." They had gone far beyond the book, and she knew she had Eddie Mitchell to thank for that.

"Schroeder is going for grand jury, lookin' for an indictment against Johnny Rabke," Torrez continued.

"I'm sorry to hear about that, on both counts," Estelle said. "Did Ramirez ever regain consciousness?"

"Nope. You know Schroeder's going to want your testimony for the grand jury."

"I suppose he will."

"Pasquale says that by the time he got to the Spur, the fight was over, so he didn't see it happen. But we got the Durans, we got Maggie Archuleta. I don't know if dumb butt came out of the kitchen in time to see what happened, but maybe he can tell us something. So you were the first cool head on the scene."

First on the scene, another world, another lifetime ago. "I need that cool head right now, Bobby. You've read Maggie's deposition? And the Durans'?"

"Yep. They all saw the same fight. They all agree that after being cut, Rabke clocked Ramirez with the billiard ball, *after* first breakin' his arm with the pool cue. That Ramirez was on his knees at the bar, out of the action, no longer a factor, when Rabke cut loose with the ball and popped him in the head."

Estelle closed her eyes, picturing the interior of the Broken Spur Saloon, remembering the exact spots where she had first seen the two combatants—Johnny Rabke bent and bleeding but still on his feet in the center of the room, Pablo Ramirez curled up, unconscious under the bar rail.

"What's Schroeder going for?" *And why does that matter?* she almost added.

"Manslaughter is my guess. Can't be nothin' beyond that. Even that's going to be a gamble, what with Ramirez makin' contact with the knife. 'Kick 'em when they're down' kinda goes with the territory in a bar fight."

Estelle didn't respond.

"I'm thinkin' Schroeder's going to need to know your schedule, here comin' up."

"If I knew, I'd give it to him, Bobby. But I don't know. I don't know how long I'll be here."

"No guesses?"

"No. Schroeder has my number. He can call me if he wants. But my answer will be the same."

"He'll want, that's for sure."

"I'll do what I can, Bobby. That's all I can say at this point."

"Yep. Somebody will pinch hit for ya, if it comes to that."

"I appreciate that. I asked Jackie to do that, so I'm confident."

"Yep." It sounded as if the sheriff wanted to add something else but changed his mind. "Do what you gotta do," he said. "Any change, call me."

She felt pressure on her hand, and realized that Carlos had turned his arm so that his hand held hers.

"You don't need to stay here," he whispered. She looked hard at him, searching his face, looking deep into his eyes.

"Are they keeping you comfortable, *hijo*?"

He managed a wry smile. "Drugs are great, aren't they?" He squeezed her hand. "But I think that for a while, this is as good as it's going to get, Ma." Francis joined her at the bedside, and Carlos squinched up his eyes in a grimacing smile. "Any good reading, Doctor?"

"Fascinating stuff, *hijo*."

"I was hoping to see Tasha today."

"She wheeled in, what, three times so far this afternoon?"

"I must have been asleep."

"She thinks you're trying to avoid her."

Carlos almost laughed. "She's okay, though?"

"She's okay," Estelle said. "Some broken fingers, bruises, road rash. They're going to release her sometime tonight or tomorrow morning, I think. Your dad is going to take her back to the apartment so she can pick up some things."

"Nobody needs to hang around here, Ma."

"That's true," Francis said. "We can leave you to the nurses."

"That one—the dude? General Patton? He's something else.

Cracks me up. Hurts to laugh, though. He's a little bit of a sadist." He shifted carefully and looked at his father. "So tomorrow's the day?"

Francis nodded. "OR is scheduled first thing in the morning."

"Another part of me."

"You won't miss it, *hijo.*"

"Will you be there?" The question was directed at Francis, but Estelle flinched—not so much at the thought of her son losing a damaged kidney, but more so because at that moment Carlos sounded more like a forlorn little kid than a twenty-four-year-old architectural engineer.

"I'll be breathing down their necks," Dr. Guzman said.

"Then that's okay." He settled back a bit, digging his head deeper into the pillow. His grip on Estelle's hand eased, and she realized that he'd fallen asleep.

"He's conked out again?" She turned at the sound of Captain Mitchell's voice.

"In and out." She did not relinquish her grip on her son's hand.

"That'll be the way of it for a while, they say." He regarded Carlos thoughtfully. "We found the truck, by the way. Kesserman mentioned that to you, I think."

"He probably did. I wasn't listening too much."

"In a way, that's one concern down. The truck was stolen, no surprise there. It was found over on the college campus, parked in a visitors' zone. One of their security folks found it."

"A sure thing?"

"That it's the right truck? Seems so." Mitchell shrugged. "They're workin' it up now. Wyoming plates, carries one of those big grill guards that ranchers like to use, lots of scrapes and dings. Some small strands of what looks like Spandex, some blood and tissue smears." He reached out and rested a hand gently on Estelle's shoulder. "A problem there, though."

"How so?"

"The Wyoming tag comes back to a 2020 white Subaru

Outback, owned by a salesman in Laramie. He was down here visiting his sister's family, and he claims his license plate was stolen a day or so ago. He reported it, as far as that goes."

"And the truck?"

"VIN shows it belongs to a construction worker here in Briones. Name's James Wayne. James Patrick Wayne. We talked to him a bit ago. He's working at a project near the college and says that he loaned the truck to his ex-brother-in-law for a week or so. No one is sure just when it was stolen."

He stopped talking when Nurse Patton entered the cubicle.

"Guys, time to hit the road. Carlos and I have some things to do." Patton placed the bundle of bedding and other paraphernalia near the patient's feet, then drew close to Carlos. He settled a hand on Carlos's forehead, and at the same time watched one of the monitors nearby as if monitor and forehead were linked.

"One to ten?" he asked, a question Carlos had obviously heard before.

"I think he's asleep," Estelle said.

"No, he's fakin'," Patton said. At the same time Carlos gave Estelle's hand a little squeeze that the nurse didn't miss. "See what I mean? So, where are we at, guy?"

"About a sixteen," Carlos mouthed, not even a full-fledged whisper.

Patton nodded, then looked at Estelle. "We're going to make some adjustments here, so best you folks and the captain wait outside."

Carlos tightened his grip. Estelle saw one eye open, and the shake of his head was the slightest twitch.

"Do you want me to stay?" she asked.

The twitch of the head came again. "No," he whispered. "You don't want to do that."

"No, ma'am. You don't," Patton added. "Doc will be in here in a minute, and we'll be replacing a tube or two. That's not something you need to have nightmares about."

She squeezed her son's hand. "I'm sure I've seen worse."

"I'm sure you have. You've probably rolled on a thousand accident and crime scenes that would make the average Joe toss his cookies. This is worse than that, in one important way. This is your son here. And you're going to react like a mom, not like a dispassionate cop." He offered a gentle smile. "You don't need that. And you know, we don't either."

"Go get a cup of tea or something," Carlos whispered.

"Give us an hour," Patton suggested.

Her consent was reluctant at best.

Chapter Seven

Rising almost gracefully out of the wheelchair, Tasha Qarshe slipped up behind Estelle and hugged her, her grip across Estelle's shoulders strong and lingering before she settled back in her chair.

"The good doctor?" she asked, referring to Dr. Francis Guzman.

"He's observing, consulting, kibitzing, trying his best to stay out of the way," Estelle said. "Please...join me."

Tasha maneuvered her wheelchair until its arm nudged against Estelle's chair. Even battered and bruised, Tasha was a beautiful girl. The aluminum finger splints on her left hand with their white bandaging, the gauze pad near her right elbow, an unbandaged scuff on the left side of her high forehead—all served as exclamation marks against the rich ebony of her otherwise flawless skin.

"The tea would be all right if their city water wasn't half chlorine," Estelle offered. "What can I get you?"

"I'm too twisted up to eat or drink much," Tasha said. "I talked with Francisco and Angie for a little bit before they left. They said that most likely they'd be flying back here toward the middle of the weekend. But if there's a problem, they can make it back Saturday morning."

"One day at a time," Estelle said. "That's how we have to take this. Are your folks going to be able to visit?"

"Tomorrow, they think."

"That's good news."

"Is it true that you used to work with Captain Mitchell?"

Estelle nodded. "He did a stint in Baltimore, then came to the Southwest. We were his first stop. He's a good cop, Tasha. Some folks thought he was a little hard-nosed for a small town." She shrugged. "He's mellowed some."

"A small world."

"It is that." She regarded the girl, enjoying the elegance of her profile. "We haven't had much of a chance to chat, Tasha. Your hip's doing okay?"

"It'll be fine. Just a deep bruise. At first they thought I had dislocated it, but no." She held up her left hand. "The hand is going to be something of a challenge. My advice of the day? Don't go sticking your fingers in bike sprockets."

Estelle grimaced. "I'd be interested to hear your recollection of what happened."

"I wish I did recollect. I know the front fender of the truck just missed me as it came in the first time. I remember that. But *bang*! Just that fast, with no warning. Over we went. We weren't going very fast, and I don't know if that's a good thing or not. The impact didn't toss us off. It just kind of slam-dunked us hard to the ground. I think. I don't actually remember the falling, but I sure remember the impact. So hard. And I remember that my left hand somehow was smashed into the crank and forward gear cluster. And then I remember the truck charging backward toward us." She opened her mouth and closed her eyes, as if the memory had frozen her speech. "I remember the word 'Chevrolet' on the tailgate."

"There are always so many questions," Estelle said.

"That's what Captain Mitchell said. What do you think?"

Estelle started to pick up her Styrofoam cup, then thought better of it. "It's not unusual that victims of violence don't remember the episode that hurt them. The most common words that we hear from the survivor of a terrible wreck are, 'What happened?' Everything cartwheels out of control so fast that the mind can't process it. And yet—there are incidents where survivors claim that the whole scenario went down in slow motion."

"I'm one of the former, I'm afraid," Tasha said. "Bang, slam, there's the pavement. And an instant later, the image of the truck roaring backward toward us."

"You had no time to see the driver?"

"No. Not even a vague shadow. Just the big, looming, dark form of the truck."

"And I'm left wondering. The truck was stolen, I'm told." She stared off into space, eyebrows knit. "He takes the truck, then decides to be clever and steals the license plate off another vehicle and puts it on the truck. Why he's trying to be so clever with the double dealing, we don't know. Then he uses that truck to attack you two. Then he dumps the truck and goes his merry way."

"How would he know?"

"About you and Carlos? That's a good question. That's *the* question. How would he know, in advance, that the two of you were biking out there? When? Where? And on a tandem, no less...not on separate bikes."

Tasha gazed at Estelle as if waiting for the answers.

The Posadas undersheriff added, "It's obvious to me, as it must be to you, that this isn't just an unfortunate highway accident. The driver of that stolen truck hit you on purpose, and then hit you again after your crash. He did not just stop and run to your aid. He didn't just stop, take a quick panicked look, and then drive off, like a typical hit-and-run." Estelle shook her head. "It's possible that the first hit was by accident, I suppose. But I find that unlikely, based on what happened next. I think he *meant* to hit you and Carlos. Twice. It wasn't a hit-and-run. It was an *attack*-and-run." Estelle hesitated. "Unless the only thought in his little pea brain was to try and neutralize any possible witnesses."

Tears glistened. "How could anyone..."

"Sweetheart," Estelle said quietly, "there is no limit to what awful things people are capable of doing. I know that. But what really confuses me are the logistics of it all. How did the attacker know? How could he plan such a thing? Those questions are going to be the key. I have to admit, though...I don't have the head for it just now. I am focused on you and Carlos, and nothing else matters."

Dr. Francis Guzman appeared in the doorway, face grave. "They're going to operate now." He walked across and rested a hand on each woman's shoulder. "Rather than waiting for morning."

"His kidney?" Estelle's words came out as not much more than a chirp.

Guzman nodded. "He'll lose his left kidney, yes." He looked down at Estelle with deep sympathy. "And Eddie said that if I found you, that he really needs to talk to you. And Tasha, to you as well. He's down at the nurses' station right now."

"I can't do that. Not now, *Oso.*" Estelle stood and leaned forward, resting her forehead against his shoulder. "Eddie doesn't need me involved in his investigation. This is *his* turf, not mine. He works for the Contra Costa Sheriff's Department. The others are with the Briones PD." She held up a hand and twined two fingers together. "They're cooperating on this, with the captain leading." She nodded vigorously. "And all I want is for my son to pull out of this." She bumped her head against him. "I want him back, *Oso.* I don't care about anything else just now."

"Let's go back to ICU, then," Francis whispered. "You won't have long, but a few minutes, maybe."

It was less than that. Estelle had time to rest one hand lightly on her son's forehead, the other just touching his chest when Nurse Reese Patton parted the curtain.

"About two minutes." Patton's face was sympathetic. "We

have a lot of prepping to do. He's already on drip sedative. Surgery will be ready for him in about..." and he examined his watch. "Yup. Just about two minutes." He held up both hands to fend off any discussion and backed out of the area.

Sedated as he was, Carlos had trouble focusing on the faces hovering over his bed. "Get rid of the broken parts," he whispered. "As long as they don't go takin' things I only got one of." He managed a tired smile.

Estelle ignored the phone vibrating in her pocket.

"Be tough, *hijo*," she said.

"Yeah, I'm tough." He looked from Estelle to Tasha. "I'll come back so two gorgeous women can wait on me hand and foot."

"Yeah, *that's* going to happen," Tasha scoffed good-naturedly.

Carlos raised his head a fraction and looked down. "I still got both feet? Yeah, I do. That's good."

"And about fifty pounds of hardware," Tasha observed.

"Ballast," Carlos whispered.

"Folks?" Patton had reappeared. "Transportation time. He'll be back in about...in about I don't know. As long as it takes." Behind him, Dr. Tobias Baines-Smith appeared, and Patton moved deferentially to one side. Carlos lifted a hand and found Estelle's.

"Go have a nice dinner or something," he whispered. His eyelids drooped. "And tell...and tell the captain..." His eyes closed, but then, as if he had massive lead weights attached to them, he fought his eyes almost open. "Tell...him I know..." The "know" tapered off as he slid into unconsciousness.

Dr. Baines-Smith took Estelle by the elbow. "He'll be fine, Mrs. Guzman. We'll get this all ironed out, get the internal bleeding stopped, and the healing can really begin." He flashed a reassuring smile that Estelle didn't find the least bit reassuring.

Chapter Eight

"He knows what?" Captain Eddie Mitchell looked skeptical. "If he's saying he knows who the driver of the truck was, just how does that work, especially when the truck was a stolen vehicle? It was dark, there were no streetlights in that particular section, so who's going to see detail? Carlos apparently never saw the strike coming, so he isn't going to turn his head and get a look—plus the truck's headlights would have precluded that."

He stopped and gave Estelle a moment to respond. When she didn't, he added, "Did the truck first drive by from the other direction, maybe? Window down to give Carlos a look at the driver? I suppose that's a possibility." He looked hard at Tasha Qarshe. "Is that what happened?"

She returned Mitchell's hard gaze without flinching. "I don't know. I was second seat on the tandem, and I wasn't paying attention to traffic in the far lane."

"So you don't know if the truck drove by in the oncoming lane or not. That maybe it drove by, then turned around."

"I don't know that."

"But let's face it , folks. This may not be what Carlos was trying to say. Maybe he was just saying, 'Tell him that I know he's looking at every angle.' Nothing more significant than that. 'Tell him I know that I'll be all right. Tell him...whatever.'"

He hooked one of the yellow plastic chairs out from the table, spun it around and sat, arms crossed on the chair back. "Let's see what we do know." He nodded at Estelle, who had remained silent through the questions. "You feel free to jump in if I forget something, all right?"

Jump in? She managed a silent nod, and Mitchell turned back to Tasha. "Did he have any arguments with anyone recently?"

"I've never known Carlos to argue with anyone. Not in all the time I've known him."

Mitchell shrugged helplessly. "He never spoke of issues from work? Problems with colleagues?"

"Never."

The captain rapped his heavy onyx ring on the back of the chair. "The major art museum project that Schneider, Cox and Bryan are working on now? It's my understanding that your son has been with SCB Associates for a couple years, and he's principal for that project."

"Yes."

"So he could have gotten crosswise with someone. He's way young for the kind of responsibility he has. Maybe there's some real resentment there."

"I suppose... I suppose that's possible," Tasha said.

"More than that," Mitchell said. "That's an angle we need to pursue. He's been with them a while?"

"He did some design work for them when he was an undergraduate over at Stanford and worked with them part-time all through his graduate program. And now two years full-time. He was thinking of taking a year's leave to finish his PhD."

"Impressive." Mitchell leaned forward a bit, resting his chin on the back of his crossed hands, waiting. "In fact, it's *way* impressive." He regarded Tasha, surveying the young woman's attractive features—slightly aquiline nose, skin the richest ebony, high cheekbones, and raven black hair secured in a ponytail.

Estelle knew that a decade from now, Mitchell would be able

to write an accurate description of the girl based on this meeting alone—his reports for the Sheriff's Department had always been encyclopedic and accurate.

"The two of you have lived together for going on two years?"

"Yes."

"You're familiar with SCB's office?"

Tasha frowned. "Actually, no. I've never been there. And, anyway, most of the time, Carlos works from home. He absolutely *hates* fighting the traffic into Berkeley."

"How does that work? Remember you're talking to someone from the Stone Age."

"The computers talk to each other," Tasha said. "It doesn't matter where they are. Carlos works with his advanced CAD programs, and he and the other project people conference back and forth."

"Occasional meeting there? In person?"

"Perhaps once a month, sometimes more often."

"You don't go with him to those?"

"No."

"You folks have lived in the current condo for some time?"

"Two years next September."

Mitchell shook his head and looked down at his hands. "What I'm getting at, Tasha, is trying to determine circumstances when Carlos might have gotten crossways with someone, in this case someone at work. Or maybe with someone he met over a drink somewhere."

"Carlos doesn't drink," Tasha said with a faint smile.

"Or smoke, or vape, or any of those other things," Mitchell said. "And when you do go out, you go out together?"

"No to the first, yes to the second."

"Maybe argue with any of the neighboring condo residents?"

"No."

Mitchell pursed his lips. "I'm trying to think of a reason why someone would drive by, see you guys, then turn around and intentionally crash into you. If the truck wasn't stolen, I'd say it *could* have been a spur of the moment thing. Like something right out of the fifties...some redneck bigot who sees the two of you together and flips out. But he *stole* the truck, even switched plates. And then he tracks you down. That's what it looks like to me. He tracks Carlos down, or he tracks *you* down. Was he after the both of you, or what?"

"At night, how could he tell?" Estelle said. "Both Carlos and Tasha wore bike helmets, and the Spandex outfits covered the rest—all but the face, the lower legs, the arms below the elbow. The attacker either knew them so well that he instantly recognized them, or..."

"Or?" Mitchell prompted. "He was just out hunting, looking for a target?"

"That's possible. I would guess that bikers are common around here. Good weather, good bike lanes, well marked."

"Which brings me to this, Tasha," Mitchell said. "Why riding at night?" He held up a hand abruptly before she had a chance to frame an answer. "And don't misunderstand me. I'm not suggesting that this is somehow your own fault. You had proper lights on your tandem front and back, even a set of those high-visibility strobes. You wore reflective clothing, you were riding properly on the right side of a marked bike lane. And in that spot, it's an *extra* lane that's set aside for bikes. But what prompted you two to ride at that particular time? Maybe there's an answer there."

"We often do," Tasha said. "It's a wonderful way to unwind at the end of the day. Until we bought the tandem on Wednesday, we rode separate bikes. That makes conversation kind of tedious."

Mitchell squinted at the young woman, and Estelle couldn't tell if the expression was one of skepticism or just plain bafflement. "You purchased the bike when?"

"Wednesday morning."

"We're talkin' just yesterday, then. A maiden voyage, so to speak."

"Yes."

"You rode earlier in the day as well?"

"Yes. Then on Wednesday—right around noon—we took it back to the bike shop to have a couple of adjustments made."

"How often do you do that? Ride, I mean."

"Almost every evening."

"Almost."

"Well, four out of five weekdays."

"And on the weekends?"

"It just depends."

"On?"

Tasha frowned. "Usually we do something outside. Swim, hike...just about anything to get out of the city. Carlos just joined a hang-gliding group, and he's pretty excited about that. We like to go out to the coast north of the city." She smiled at Estelle's expression. "I'm a ground lover, but Carlos is accomplished. He talks a lot about flying Cat Mesa."

"*Ay, por díos.* That's just what I need to hear," Estelle murmured. An image of Cat Mesa's raw, vertical face just north of Posadas reeled through her mind, and her mouth went dry. It had been easy to keep track of her sons when they were little boys, into little-boy mischief. Now...not so easy.

"He's rigged up a remote camera. He's taken some amazing photos."

Mitchell's eyebrows drifted up. "Maybe of something he shouldn't have?"

"I don't think so. He likes to photograph landforms when the breeze is just right—sand dunes, the seaside cliffs, the surf, things like that."

"While hang gliding." Mitchell sounded skeptical.

"All he has to do is push a button," Tasha replied. "It's no big deal." She ducked her head, almost as if in apology. "You know, with the right updrafts, you can stay up just about forever." She nodded to Estelle. "Carlos talks about the hang gliders who go off Sandia Crest, up outside of Albuquerque. He has photos of several of them hundreds of feet *above* the crest towers, riding up on the air currents. But the hang glider isn't the best camera platform. What he's designed to mount on the ultralight is much more versatile."

Mitchell frowned again, his heavy black eyebrows almost joined in the middle. "So I gotta ask, young lady. Coming back to the moment. The truck makes contact, striking Carlos but missing you. Now the driver would know that." He fell silent, regarding Tasha, his face expressionless. "Might that explain why, after he stopped, he took the time to back up and hit you again? Now, thank God he didn't hit you, but what if he wasn't after Carlos at all, but after you?" Tasha remained silent. "We'll have to think about that," Mitchell said. "So tell me. What keeps you busy, Ms. Qarshe? Do you work from home as well?"

She nodded quickly. "I do. Graphic arts, mostly related to the automotive industry. Lots of interesting photoshopping for special effects."

"For whom?"

"R.K. Benjamin Graphics. Their office is in Livermore."

"And no arguments there? No discord, no disagreements?"

"No."

"*Ay,*" Estelle whispered, but the vibration of her phone interrupted her train of thought.

Call Bill.

Sheriff Bob Torrez's text message was his usual achievement in word economy. No other explanation was included. Nor *when you get the chance,* or *sometime tomorrow.*

"Excuse me for just a moment." Estelle rose, thumbing in former sheriff Bill Gastner's number. She was out in the hallway when it connected.

"Gastner." The eighty-five soon to be eighty-six-year-old's voice was gruff, and so welcome it almost brought tears. She forced her tone to be upbeat and cheerful.

"*Padrino,* we're still out here in la-la land limbo."

"So I gathered. Look, I didn't want to call you because I

figured you would most likely be in the middle of something. I figured Robert could leave you a message that you could ignore until you had a minute or two."

"He just texted me. Two words."

"That's something of an accomplishment for him."

"He's learning. *Padrino,* the news here is wait-and-see. Carlos is still in surgery. He's lost his spleen and is in the process of losing a kidney."

"Well, he's too young for that shit. What's your hubby say?"

"That all we can do is wait. Carlos is in good hands."

"You've been able to talk with the lad, sweetheart?"

"A few words now and then. When he's out of surgery, he'll probably be afloat in a sea of opiates for a while."

"The maestro gave me the same report. He called not long ago to catch me up. He says the Briones cop—is that how you say that place?"

"Brio-niss."

"Whatever the hell it is. Anyway, the cop who met you all there at the hospital is an old friend of ours?"

"Eddie Mitchell. Thank God for him, *Padrino*."

"I'll be damned. What's he say?"

"They're stumped, I think. He's with the SO, but he's working really closely with the Briones PD on this. Right now he's debriefing Tasha."

"She's banged up some, Francisco says."

"Yes. But she's going to be all right."

"So is Carlos, sweetheart." Gastner's calm, gentle tone brought a lump to Estelle's throat. "You'll not hesitate to let me know how I can help." It was not a request.

"Of course. At this point, we just don't know."

"Well, keep yourself occupied and productive. Give Mitchell as much help as you can. Standing around waiting in smelly hospital hallways doesn't do much good." The old man chuckled. "There I go, huh. Mr. Helpful. But it's true. You and I have both spent plenty of time in hospitals, and a more awful place is hard to imagine. Put that wonderful brain of yours to work. And, by the way...next time Carlos surfaces and can talk, tell him I'm focusing all my incredible mental powers on his getting well. Okay?"

"I'll do that, *Padrino*. We all thank you, *mi corazón*."

"You're entirely welcome. Is Tasha within earshot?"

"She's just next door in the snack bar."

"Let me talk to her a bit. Will she agree to that?"

"Of course. Hang on a moment." Back in the snack bar, Tasha arose from her wheelchair with slow caution, more like a ninety-year-old than the graceful young lady that she was. She accepted the phone and made her way out to the hallway, free hand running along the wall railing.

"How's the boss?" Mitchell asked Estelle. "He's as old as the hills by now, for sure."

"Eighty-five," Estelle said. "He'll be eighty-six in a week or so. He's not what I'd call exactly spry, but still active, still interested. Still working on a cold case or two, believe it or not."

"The Posadas Legend, that guy. Any words of wisdom from him that you care to share?" Mitchell looked as if he meant it.

"Just to get to work. Not to sit around and worry." She managed a weary smile. "All easily said. It's not my case, and certainly not my jurisdiction."

Mitchell nodded slowly. "He never gave a lot of advice when I was working in Posadas, but on the rare occasions when he did, it was worth listening to."

Chapter Nine

The overhead lights in the Quonset building came on with a loud snap of circuits. "Oversized and awkward stuff," Captain Mitchell said. "We share some space here with the PD." He snugged the heavy door closed behind them, and then pointed with both index fingers together at the older model Chevrolet three-quarter-ton pickup parked on the building's center line, facing the roll-up door. It was in front of three other vehicles—a Bug Eye Sprite, a dust-laden older Mercedes sedan, and in the back where its tailgate must have been touching the far wall, an International light-duty dump truck.

"The owner is pestering to get this back, but that isn't going to happen any time soon." He chose one of the walkways bordered by brightly painted orange lines on the concrete floor. "We ask that visitors stay between the lines. It's kinda like a giant barn sale, with the temptation to wander around picking up stuff." He turned in place and nodded at the vast collection.

The 80-by-140-foot Quonset was divided by heavy chain-link fencing into lockable bins, most of them crowded with a vast assortment of items—bicycles, yard implements, an enormous four-wheel-drive ag tractor, a matched pair of fabric-covered airplane wings, a selection of kayaks and canoes, kitchen appliances, lawn mowers, ATVs, even a couple of camper trailers. One entire bin was crammed with televisions and stereos.

Mitchell turned to the uniformed officer who had accompanied them. "Oscar, if you want to head back, I'll take it from here."

"That's all right, sir. I'm fine."

Mitchell grinned and glanced at Estelle. "Their policy is that no one's alone out here. Always signed in, always chaperoned. That way, there are no surprises. But I'm preachin' to the choir, right?"

Estelle held up both hands. "You'll remember that we make do with the county's maintenance boneyard...and none of it under cover. This is pretty swank." She turned in place, and Mitchell laughed.

"'Swank' isn't a word I've ever heard applied to this place. Contra Costa County is huge, so we have several facilities like this."

"And this is the truck." She stepped up to the Chevrolet before Mitchell had the chance to reply. Her eyes locked on the massive grill guard and broken right headlight. The black guard had bent backward until it crushed into the light, scarring the fender as well. She'd seen the same sort of damage after deer or antelope strikes.

"It's been carefully photo-documented. If you want a set of photos to take with you, no problem. Our friends at the PD will be pleased to oblige."

Estelle reached out a hand and pointed to an area of discoloration on the dented fender, behind the outboard curve of the grill guard, behind the quad headlights.

"And that was collected and typed," Mitchell said. "And, yes. It's a match to Carlos."

Her stomach wrenched. "I need to see that."

"'That' what?"

"I need to see the clothing that Carlos was wearing."

Mitchell looked hard at her. "You don't need to do that, Estelle."

"Yes...I do."

The captain hesitated, then nodded. Choosing another key, he opened one of the wall cabinets and withdrew a small bundle secured in a plastic bag. Moving with it to a steel table, he reached out and pulled off several feet of white butcher paper to cover the table's surface. "Cap, jersey, shorts, socks, shoes," he said.

Donning a pair of latex gloves from the wall dispenser, Estelle unfolded the jersey, its white and blue nylon decorated with various designs, including the familiar U.S. Postal emblem and logo. The bloodstained garment was ripped and mangled in several places. She tried to ignore the odd, cloying coppery smell, now concentrated by time in the sealed bag.

Mitchell reached past her and pointed to an area that would have covered her son's left torso. "We think this may be from the tire tread."

She realized that she'd been holding her breath, and Estelle tried to relax. "That's a stretch, Eddie."

"Yeah, it's a stretch. Wishful thinking, even. But it's what we have, and we'll go with it."

"You have good photos?"

"Sure. I'll get copies to you if you want."

"I'm not sure just now what I want, Eddie."

"We've work with the clothing, and we've covered the truck from one end to the other. In fact, I've got Blair Ulibarri coming over from the San Francisco PD, probably tomorrow. Not that our guys aren't excellent as well. But she's an artist with fingerprints. I've gotten to know her well over the years. I think she could lift prints off a melting ice cube. She's agreed to go over the whole truck again to see what she can find, especially the cab area." He smiled. "She reminds me a little bit of you, as a matter of fact."

"You have several jurisdictions vying in this," Estelle said.

"Hopefully not vying, my friend. Hopefully working together. The assault actually happened on the county's turf, so we're the lead agency. Your son and his fiancée live in the city, the truck was found in the city, so there you go. The PD is involved."

She walked along the truck's broad flank and then stood still, looking down at the Wyoming license plate with its bucking bronco figure. "This is an eighty-four Chevy or thereabouts?"

"Exactly."

The plate was held in place with one round-headed, slotted bolt, the remaining three bolt holes empty.

"I don't understand this thinking," Estelle said. "I understand stealing the truck. It was apparently easily available and easy to hot-wire..." She swept a hand forward, indicating the entire vehicle.

"We didn't find any signs that it had been jumped," Mitchell said. "I mean, it's not uncommon for thieves to leave a dangling wire...something. But everything is tight and snug."

"The thief found a way," Estelle mused. "Anyway, it's a good choice for a hit-and-run truck. It's certainly lethal enough. New enough to be dependable, beat up enough not to draw lots of attention, dark color to blend in with the night. Everything spells intent." She knelt and stared hard at the Wyoming plate. "So why this? What do you know about it?"

"The car that the license plate was taken from was parked on the street in a pretty busy neighborhood," Mitchell said. "The owner wasn't paying any attention to it. He was watching football, he says."

"How long has he been in California?"

"Not long enough to reregister the car with local plates."

Estelle reached out and came within a fraction of an inch of touching the single attachment bolt. The traces of black print powder were evident. "Maybe a print there. It's hard to dink with a fastener like that with gloves on."

"Maybe. Blair will do it again, I'm sure. I'll make sure that she does."

Estelle glanced up at Mitchell, interested in the familiar way he referred to Officer Ulibarri. "How was the plate originally attached to the Subaru?"

"Four plastic threaded retainers. All left behind in the gutter."

"Whoa." Estelle frowned. "The thief brought along his own plate screws?"

"The owner of the truck claims he had all four in place. He says they were of this type."

"So the thief used one and dropped the other three? He's getting in a little hurry, then. And he doesn't know much about the Department of Motor Vehicles or police computer networks. He thought this clever little ploy was going to throw you guys off?"

"For about a minute."

Estelle straightened up. "Where was the truck recovered?"

"Over on Berkshire. A residential street over west and runs alongside the college. It was parked in a visitors' area, near one of the admin buildings. About three and a half miles from the scene of the assault."

"And where was it stolen? You said something about a brother-in-law?"

"An interesting coincidence, that," Mitchell said. "The truck's owner is a guy named Jim Wayne. No priors of any kind. He says that he loaned the truck to his former brother-in-law, one Stanley Wilke, last Sunday, so nearly a week ago."

Estelle frowned at Mitchell. "Loaned to who?"

"His brother-in-law. Well, ex-brother-in-law. And like I said... an interesting coincidence. Wilke is a mechanic who works over at Crosby's Cycle Shop on Cutler. Wayne said that Wilke told him he wanted to use it to move an old refrigerator out of his apartment. Maybe some other stuff as well. Apparently, the truck was parked Sunday through Wednesday behind the bike shop. Wayne said he doesn't drive it much." Mitchell made a face. "Makes it easy to steal, right? I mean, who's going to see that?"

"Wilke," Estelle said. The hollow in the pit of her stomach grew.

"Yeah. Stanley Wilke."

"What does this Wilke say?"

"We haven't made contact yet. He hasn't been to work, and we haven't caught him at home." Mitchell stood and stretched his heavy frame. "And now you know just about what we know."

Estelle completed her circle of the truck, lingering at the driver's door. The windows were tightly closed but she could see that the door lock button was fully up. "Will you open this for me?" She held up her hands indicating that she would not touch the truck. Mitchell snapped a latex glove on his right hand and thumbed the black latch button under the chrome door handle, pressing just the edge of the button.

The truck cab carried all the ambiance of nearly forty years of people and service. An after-market horse blanket seat cover, itself on its last legs, was stretched tight. Abundant cracks laced the broad windshield. The truck's owner was evidently a person who believed that flat surfaces were storage spaces. The expanse of dash was covered with a potpourri of junk—small hand tools, a box of Band-Aids, two small containers of automotive fuses, a package of Swisher Sweets with two remaining, and half a dozen books of matches. In the far right corner, a package of Little Debbie brownies would bake in the sun.

Estelle's gaze drifted down past the cracked steering wheel to the enormous stalk of the four-speed gearshift. The brake pedal was missing its rubber pad, and the clutch rubber was so worn that metal showed through.

She took a deep, slow breath. The truck carried a rich perfume of Old Truck, a combination of oil, gasoline, maybe stale food, maybe aftershave or perfume. She took her time, trying to isolate the aromas.

Finally satisfied, she stood back and watched Mitchell close the truck door.

"I'd like to talk with this Jim Wayne fellow, Eddie. Right now, though, I need to get back to the hospital. Maybe a quick look at the bike."

Mitchell gestured toward one of the enclosed pens and at the same time beckoned to Officer Oscar Benevidez, making a twisting motion with his right hand. Benevidez produced a bundle of keys and opened the heavy padlock, then swung the chain-link door wide.

The tandem bike was suspended from stout plastic hangers attached to the chain-link wall of the pen.

The front wheel was out of line with the handlebars, but Estelle couldn't tell if it was actually bent. The lower frame member was crimped just forward of the front set of cranks, the fancy turquoise paint scuffed.

"I'm surprised at how little damage there is," Estelle said.

"The riders got the worst of it, that's for sure." Mitchell pointed at the damage to the frame. "We think that this happened when the driver backed up and struck them for the second time." He reached out and pointed at the scuff marks on the frame. "This is tire rubber, and we don't think it's from the initial strike."

She took a deep breath and held it.

"You okay?"

"No, but yes."

Benevidez took his time securing the bin lock as they stepped out.

"Anything else we can do, anything I can tell you, don't hesitate," Mitchell said.

"Well, I appreciate that offer, but I'm a little hesitant with that. It's not my intent to barge in here and play cop, Eddie. My badge isn't much good here. You have your own crew. The county, the PD, whoever else is assisting."

Mitchell gave her that dark, puckered brow glower she remembered so well. "Lemme tell you, Undersheriff, we welcome all the help we can get. And let's talk about jurisdiction. I could not care less about the frickin' jurisdiction. Anybody questions it, we'll take care of it. The way I see it, you *are* a cop, whether in Posadas, or here, or in outer Mongolia. We...*you*...

are in pursuit of a felon. If you have ideas or theories, I want to hear 'em. It'd be stupid for me to think otherwise."

"Right now, I confess that my mind isn't too focused," Estelle said.

"I can appreciate that, but work on it, my friend."

She started to walk away toward the steel entry door where Officer Benevidez waited patiently, his clipboard poised. She signed out, nodding her thanks to the officer. Once outside, she flinched against the harsh and hazy late afternoon sun.

"Two things," she said, turning to Mitchell.

"Name 'em."

"I want to talk with Tasha some more. I want to see the collection of photos that my son took from his hang glider. Have you looked at those?"

"No." He frowned. "You're thinking there's a possibility he saw something that maybe he shouldn't have? Is that where you're headed with that?"

She gave a little helpless shrug. "Any possibility." She first fanned her hands so her fingers pointed every which way, then she held up a second finger. "And you know, I'd like to talk with Wayne, and then I'd want to visit the bike shop. Just by myself, if you can arrange that."

"Tell me what you're thinking, then. I've got guys going over that place with a fine-toothed comb."

Estelle thought for a moment about how to respond. "Maybe I'll buy the kids a new bike as a get-well present."

"Uh huh." Mitchell's deadpan expression said that he believed that as much as she did. "But you're right. There has to be a link. That's a hell of a coincidence. The kids are active bike shop customers, the attack truck is stolen from the bike shop. That's the direction we need to go."

Two hours later, Dr. Tobias Baines-Smith beamed as he met with the Guzmans and Tasha. "He's strong, otherwise healthy, and came through the surgery beautifully," Baines-Smith said, a strong note of triumph in his voice. "The best news is that the bleeding has been entirely controlled. There were some surprises, I have to say. I won't kid you there. But he's doing as well as anyone could expect or hope."

"Surprises?" How could there be anything about what had happened to her son that was *not* a surprise, Estelle thought.

"From the bruising, it appears that one of the rear tires of the pickup actually backed over Carlos, or at least partially so. The tire struck him from about here," and he held a hand against his abdomen in line with the umbilicus, "to about the level of his fifth rib. He was not free of the bike when that happened, so there's ancillary damage—crushing injuries, if you will. Those are almost always elusive. But..." The physician nodded toward the ICU center. "He's asleep now, and that's what he needs... about a week's worth of uninterrupted sleep. He's sedated, but the less of that, the better for him."

Estelle squeezed both of Tasha's hands that she had somehow grasped with both of her own.

"The second kidney is undamaged?"

"It's fine. With the other torso injuries under control, one of our major concerns now is the leg," and he held up his index finger. "There's going to be more work needed there." He bent down the index finger. "And an area of extensive bruising of the colon. We're going to proceed carefully with both."

Estelle closed her eyes. After a moment, she said, "Francis was meeting with one of the other physicians?"

"Your husband spent some time in consult with two of the orthopedists at Norse-Kaseman, where Carlos will be transferred for the advanced ortho work, as a matter of fact." He smiled. "We're very proud of what we do here, but I have to tell you...it's been a real boon to have your husband at hand." His smile widened. "You know, if you folks should ever consider moving to California..."

"Thanks for that thought," Estelle said.

Chapter Ten

"I need to roam a little," Estelle said, and Francis looked up at her. He was scrunched down in what passed for an easy chair in the ICU lounge, reading yet more papers generated as part of his son's medical history. He raised an eyebrow quizzically. The shadows under his eyes were dark. Neither he nor Estelle had slept well since leaving Posadas, and neither of them had slept the night after the surgery.

"Roaming?" he asked.

"I just need to get outside for a while. I want to talk with the owner of the stolen truck, for one thing. Then I'm going to drive down to where the assault happened, and then swing by the bike shop. I won't be long."

He gazed at her for a moment. "And then, and then," he said, the crow's-feet around his eyes deepening. "There's nothing you can do out here, you know."

"I know that, *querido*."

"Unless they're planning to hire you on, heaven forbid. Then…"

She crossed over to him and bent down to hug him. "If I can do something to answer some of the questions, that's all to the good. Right now, I just need a change of air, *Oso*. A change of scenery."

"I'll be here."

"And so will I be—in about an hour. Maybe by then *hijo* will be awake."

That earned her an encouraging smile. "My phone will be in hand."

"Be careful, *querida*."

"Always."

"If you want company, one of the cops would be glad to chauffeur you."

"No. I want to drive myself. It'll give me time to think."

A long, lingering kiss, and then she headed toward the nearest EXIT sign and the stairway. Outside, she was astonished at how good the early morning air smelled, despite the jets, the traffic, the watered lawns, the exotic trees and shrubs, the too many people. Even the interior of the Toyota was bearable, new enough that it didn't need any of those perfumed evergreen danglies.

She fumbled the GPS menu, having never used the Global Positioning System in Posadas County, where she knew every sage, cactus, arroyo, coyote, or human. The tech screen was enormous in the Camry, its technology frustrating. Finally, she succeeded in breaking through the menus, and the screen flashed the address of the destination, Crosby Cycle, and presented a little icon that represented her car, its nose pointed somewhere out there.

"Stay in the right-hand lane," the gadget instructed in a voice that sounded as if recorded in the Philippines "In eight hundred yards, turn right." The helpful voice continued to weave her through traffic, heading generally east, until the happy computer announced, "Destination." Sure enough, Crosby Cycle Sports was perched at the intersection of Lexor and Cutler, a tightly packed, older neighborhood that had seen ownership of stores and shops change with the tides.

The concrete block cycle shop building showed signs of the pharmacy it once had been but was now decorated with a couple of bike frames perched on the edge of the roof overlooking the sidewalk. They partially blocked a clear view of the well-worn Rx mortar and pestle painted on the facade. The display bikes' front wheels, sans tires, hung over the sidewalk.

The parking lot shared by the bike shop and the prosperous-looking real estate office next door included a half-dozen vehicles, one a compact car with bike racks on the back bumper. A Nissan pickup truck was nosed in behind the bike shop.

Estelle parked the Camry in the slot nearest the sidewalk and sat quietly, the engine idling almost silently. She shut off the GPS display. Clearly, she had no jurisdiction in this state. She had no badge, no commission, no gun. But she did have Captain Eddie Mitchell's words: *"I could not care less about the frickin' jurisdiction. You're a cop."* She could imagine that line echoing through a crowded courtroom, could imagine the defense attorneys chortling with delight.

Odds were good that Mitchell had said that as a polite nod to old times' sake. What did she expect to accomplish? She didn't know. The confines of the hospital, with its aroma, its stuffy air, its unrelenting hustle and bustle, its hushed conversations, had set her nerves on edge.

Had she been home in Posadas, she would have driven out into the tawny countryside, found a desolate two-track leading off into solitude, and idled the county car far away from even the tiny village of Posadas, with its three thousand familiar inhabitants.

Here, finding time to think without interruption was an endless challenge.

She startled so hard it twinged her back as a knuckle rapped on the driver's side window. She craned her head around to see Sergeant Jake Kesserman, looking entirely too thin, almost emaciated, like an Ichabod Crane in khaki trousers and soft yellow golf shirt. It was warm enough that he'd shed his jacket. If not for the automatic on his left hip and the cuffs and badge adorning his belt, he'd have looked like a starving pro golfer.

He ducked his head and offered an almost embarrassed grin, then took a step back as Estelle lowered the window.

"Good morning, Undersheriff Guzman."

Estelle switched off the engine. "Good morning, Sergeant." She smiled at him. "Are you officially following me or just stalking?"

He considered the question and instead said, "I heard that the kidney surgery went well."

"Yes. 'Resting comfortably' is the euphemism that they use for drugged senseless. My husband is sitting with him." She frowned. Why did she feel the need to explain herself?

He looked sympathetic. "Is there someplace in the city that I can help you find, or is this it?" He nodded toward the bike shop.

She pensively tapped the steering wheel with her wedding ring. "I want to talk with the truck's owner...Jim Wayne? I have the name of the construction company he works for, but I'll have to talk with them, I suppose."

Kesserman grinned. "L and L Bonded," he said. "Right now, they're doing a water main project over by the college. Wayne would be there. He's one of their excavator operators."

"Well, then," Estelle said, "that makes it easier, for sure. I had Crosby's name, and the GPS brought me here." She looked up at Kesserman. "My county car at home has one, I think. Somewhere in its little brain. I never use it."

"I'm not surprised. The captain has told me a few tales about working over in that country. From what I hear, it gives the word 'rural' a whole new meaning. Coming here must be something of a culture shock for you. I think that's why he suggested that maybe I could offer some assistance."

"I appreciate that, but you know what? Now that I'm here," she gestured at the bike shop, "I don't know why I wanted to see it."

"Well, your first job is to figure out what you are—mom or cop. It's hard to just turn off the cop instinct, isn't it?" He straightened up. "So, Undersheriff Guzman, what we know is that your son purchased the tandem here just Wednesday morning. He and Ms. Qarshe dealt with the owner of the place, a guy by the name of Todd Stringer."

"Not a Crosby?"

"Nope. Emmett Crosby started this business when it was a big fancy place over in one of the strip malls on Tucker. Stringer was his son-in-law. He went to work for the old man, put in a year or two, and then Crosby dropped dead, right in the showroom, right in the middle of a conversation with some customers." Kesserman shrugged. "Enough to make a guy take up a different hobby, I'd think. Stringer tried to take over the business but had his share of troubles. Lost that big, fancy place, moved, lost that, found this place."

Estelle opened the car door, and Kesserman stepped to one side as she got out of the car. His gaze traveled down Estelle's graceful figure and then snapped back to her face. Estelle noted the scrutiny, a common reaction from the males of the species. "You sound as if you've had cause to deal with him from time to time."

"I ride," Kesserman said. "Probably too much. A lot of us around here do. Great country for it. You could spend a lifetime exploring Briones Regional Park, up north a little. If I had all the money I've spent on bikes, and sometimes on medical bills after crashes, I could retire to the Maldives tomorrow. As it is, I count down the remaining six years of my tenure with the cops, and *then* I'll head for the Maldives."

Estelle glanced at her watch, and Kesserman took the hint.

"Do you want company going in there, or are you okay?"

"I appreciate the offer, Sergeant, but I don't want to be mistaken for a police officer." Estelle smiled. "That would be their natural reaction if I were with you. Not that I wouldn't enjoy the company, but I don't want to have to explain who or what I am."

"Understandable, and probably a good plan. You have my card?"

"I do."

"And a phone?"

"Yes."

"Then if you need anything, there I am. Right in the neighborhood. All right?"

"Yes. Thank you."

"If you learn anything interesting, we'd like to know. The evidence room visit went all right?"

"I appreciated that opportunity," Estelle said.

"Of course."

He gave her a three-fingered salute. "I'll be at the hospital to relieve Dinsman. So I'm nearby."

She watched him step out into the street and circle around to the driver's side of the unmarked Taurus, and a moment later, when he pulled out into traffic, she turned toward the bike shop.

A life-sized picture of a multi-winning *Tour de France* champion stood in the window, one hand on the handlebars of his fancy bike. He looked gaunt and exhausted, both mentally and physically. Kesserman shared the gaunt look—perhaps some sort of badge of honor for pro cyclists.

Three other bikes were crowded into the window display, including a weird little folding bike that looked as if it were designed to be airline carry-on luggage. She tilted her head, read the price tag, and winced.

The glass door opened with a musical series of cowbells and she stopped in mid-entry, trying to decide which way to step. A sea of bicycles spread across the floor, divided into clusters. Some were fat-tired creations that looked heavy and ponderous. Another group, including a racing bike on a center pedestal, was clearly competition-ready. Brightly colored posters of cyclists in lush countrysides lined the walls and hung from the ceiling.

The place smelled of rubber tires and fine oil. On one wall, a sixty-inch flat screen played a bike racing video, the sound muted. On screen, the peloton wound through a European village, half a hundred bikes nose to tail as they flowed like liquid around a right angle corner, the roadsides packed with spectators. The view changed to a helicopter shot of a pair of riders, one tightly drafting the other, in concert with a couple of motorcycles carrying camera crews. The screen banner announced that the breakaway pair was one minute, thirteen seconds ahead of the peloton.

"Be right with you," a voice shouted from behind a glass partition to one side of the television. She could see the top of his head, carrot-colored hair chopped short. When he left his chair, he didn't bother to remove the granny glasses but peered over the tops at Estelle, giving her a thorough up and down as if assessing that she had the physique to power a bike.

"Well, for heaven's sakes," he said. He stepped around the partition, and Estelle noted the wind-cheating form perfect for a pro cyclist—shoes whose sole pedal clamps clicked on the floor, thunder thighs that stretched the Spandex riding shorts, nylon U.S. Postal–emblazoned jersey that clung to his ribs, the close-cropped hair, piercing blue eyes, narrow face, and a beak of a nose that would cleave the air like a hatchet.

He stopped by one of the displayed racing bikes and rested a hand on the handlebars. For a moment, he said nothing, letting Estelle gather her first impressions while he worked on his. Satisfied that his guess was correct, he said, "I heard you and your husband were in town." His smile was gentle. "You look just like you." Realizing how silly that might sound, he added, "The family portrait in the magazine a while ago?"

He stepped forward and offered his hand, his face falling into an expression of deep concern. "But look, you can't imagine how sorry we were to hear about Carlos and Tasha." He read Estelle's expression correctly. "In many ways, this is a very small town," he said, and stepped closer. His grip was strong, more holding than shaking.

"I saw you outside talking with Jake Kesserman a bit ago, so I put two and two together. I heard it was a hit and run? I hope they're making progress with the investigation." He ducked his head in apology. "I'm Todd Stringer, by the way. Carlos and Tasha are good customers of mine. They're the best, those two." His smile widened enough to reveal a flash of gold. "The sergeant is another. The cops have been here a couple of times."

"I'm sure," Estelle said, and let it go at that. The notion of Briones and its environs as a "very small town" was a difficult concept to swallow. There were times when even Posadas, New Mexico, with its three thousand residents, seemed on the verge of being a city...when three or four cars were stacked at an intersection. Although they were well inland of San Francisco, Berkeley, and all the surrounding suburbs, Briones traffic was dense and frenetic.

"You've been at the hospital, of course. How are the kids doing?" His forehead crinkled with concern, but the last thing Estelle wished to do was discuss her son's condition with a stranger.

She settled for, "Yes. They're making good progress," and let it go at that. She glanced around the showroom. On the far wall, an enormous poster depicted one of the mountain stages of the *Tour de France,* where the struggling peloton caterpillared up the endless switchbacks of a ragged mountain in the Pyrenees. In what she understood now as a typical strategy, two cyclists had broken away from the main crowd of riders, charging far into the lead.

Stringer followed Estelle's gaze. "That's a rare photo from several years ago," he said. "Lance in the lead up on the Col du Tourmalet." His voice grew excited. "That's the highest climb in the Pyrenees

Estelle had heard enough of Sergeant Thomas Pasquale's excitement over bike racing, had heard him waxing eloquent after the results of each stage of the famous French *Tour* during July of each year that the names Stringer mentioned, even without the surnames, were familiar to her.

She knew that Posadas's own Thomas Pasquale had tried his best to invite some of the big name cyclists to the Posadas 100 mountain bike race he'd organized. He'd had partial success—a popular former New Mexico governor had tried his luck with Cat Mesa's steep, rugged, almost suicidal descents.

She moved beyond the poster and stopped at two tandem bikes, both looking long and unwieldy with their two of everything.

Stringer patted the nearest one affectionately. "This is a nice machine, kind of an entry-level model, but it's a click or two down from the one Carlos purchased."

She idly turned a small price tag hanging from one of the brake levers—$2,679.95.

"How much was his? No, wait." She abruptly held up a hand. "I don't need to know about that. If Carlos wants me to know, he'll tell me."

"Uh, you know, I haven't seen it since the accident, but we can fix just about anything."

She almost smiled at him. "Fixing the riders is the issue," she said.

"Well, of course. Of course." He frowned with puzzlement. "Was there something in particular that I could help you with? I mean, I think I've told the Briones officers everything that I know." He paused. "Which isn't much. I know the neighborhood where the accident took place. I know that they were riding in the late evening. I know that they were wearing all the lighting gadgetry that's appropriate. And I *know* that both your son and his fiancée are responsible riders who always keep an eye on traffic." He thumped the handlebar of the nearest tandem.

"I say that because we—Carlos, Tasha, and I—had a long discussion about riding these. It's something that Tasha, in particular, really wanted to do. Just learning to be coordinated together for stopping and dismounting, for example. A tandem is big, it's heavy, it's clumsy." He smiled. "I'm not making much of a sales pitch, am I? But tandem riders have to be aware, they have to practice, they have to be in coordination with each other. It's a question of real teamwork."

"And it's your sense that Carlos and Tasha did all of that?"

"Absolutely, they did all that. That was part of the attraction for them, I think. I made sure they had all the available literature. We had some training sessions here as well. They rented a bike a couple of times over the past few weeks to make sure it was something they wanted to do. Last week, they went on at least one tandem ride with another couple who has been on tandems for years. They bought one of the videos that we sell. In short, I think we did everything we could."

Estelle heard the worry, the self-defensive posture, in Stringer's recitation, and she had no difficulty imagining the first lawsuit-itis symptoms he was no doubt feeling.

"Who did you hear about the crash from?"

"Who?"

"Yes."

Stringer frowned. "I guess...I guess that it was actually the next morning. On Thursday, it would be. Emily came in to work and asked me if I'd heard."

"And Emily is..."

"Emily Gere? She's one of my team here, a part-timer. She doesn't usually work during the week, but she had a few things to catch up on." He frowned, looked as if he was going to say something else, but let a shrug suffice.

"I'd like to talk to her," Estelle said.

"The reason being? If it's about the bike, I don't even know if it's worth fixing. We won't know until we see it. And right now, the cops have it."

"It's not about the bike."

"Then?" Stringer looked skeptical, and he held out a hand. He looked hard at her. "Oh...of course. About the truck. That was the damnedest thing. But look, I understand a little, Mrs. Guzman. One thing I understand is that the cops are all over this tragedy, believe me. Another thing I understand..." and he hesitated, unsure of how to continue. He dropped his voice to almost a whisper. "I understand that this is a whole time zone out of your jurisdiction, am I right? If Dinsman or Kesserman want you in on interviews, they'll tell me, right? The last thing I want is to have a hand in screwing up their case, you know what I'm saying? They've already talked to my staff, although why, I don't know. They grilled Emily, of course. And I know they want to talk with Stan Wilke…he's my full-time shop guy, although he took yesterday off, and he hasn't been in yet this morning. And I'm hearing that it was his truck that was somehow involved. Well, sort of. He borrowed it, I understand. He had it parked here behind the shop for a few days. Not much parking space around his apartment complex. Or maybe he thought it would be more secure here." He stopped abruptly, as if realizing he'd been running on unchecked. "But they'll talk to everybody, just to be thorough, I guess." He nodded, then added, "Look, I can imagine that as a mom, this must be a nightmare for you."

"Is Mr. Wilke due in soon?" Estelle persisted.

"We're open, so he should be. But he's had some issues at home. I don't know what he's doing. Moving stuff, I guess. I presume that's why he borrowed the truck. We offered help, but he said he didn't need it. But like I said…"

Estelle stepped to the counter where the large PARTS AND SERVICE sign hung. The parts department featured a series of freestanding floor-to-ceiling shelf units, laden with parts neatly boxed and arranged. A workbench with a scatter of tools, bike parts, and two strangely shaped vises ran along one wall, back to what was most likely a bathroom and a back door, both of which stood open a few inches—but no Stan Wilke. Off to the right, a series of framed eight-by-ten photos decorated the wall, including one of Todd Stringer presenting a large trophy to a cyclist. Another was a promo photo of the bike shop showroom, with three men and a woman grouped around two bikes that had been arranged nose to tail.

"And these folks?"

"Well, that's yours truly." Stringer pointed to his own image on the left. "And then Stan, Barry Whitaker and Emily Gere.

That was taken at Christmas, I think." He flashed a quick smile. "We all clean up pretty good, don't we?" In the photo, Stringer was in a full complement of Spandex riding togs. Beside him, Stan Wilke was nearly a foot shorter, his head shaved to a bullet. With no discernable eyebrows or facial hair, and slim of build, he would be a streamlined rocket on a bike.

"Well, sure enough," Estelle thought. "A new life for himself."

Barry Whitaker on the other hand, looked as if he *needed* to put in some serious miles to whittle down his considerable paunch. Following the streamlined motif, though, his thick blond hair was slicked back in a ponytail. One ear stood out nearly perpendicular to his skull, while the other looked as if it had been superglued flat.

Emily Gere was caught by the camera with her eyes at half-mast, looking as if she were dozing off. Her Spandex duds accentuated her curvaceous body, and black accents on her gold jersey complemented her jet-black hair—also smoothed back in a ponytail.

"Oh, you know what? There *is* something you need to see." He stepped over to a framed poster, a huge enlargement color photo of a tandem bike and its two riders vaulting off the rim of the Grand Canyon into hopeless deep space. He grinned broadly. "Three guesses."

"I wouldn't know where to start."

"Tasha. She does a lot of photo massaging like that. She gave me this when they were first thinking of buying the tandem."

Estelle examined the photograph with more than polite interest, then said, "All right, then. I hope this doesn't give Carlos any ideas. He's got enough healing to do."

"Just a gag photo. But beautiful superimposition nonetheless, don't you think?"

"Indeed." She turned back to the parts counter. "Mr. Wilke would normally be here today?"

Stringer glanced at his impressive watch. "If he's not here by now, probably this afternoon. Hey, look, Mrs. Guzman, if you'd just come out and tell me what it is that you're looking for, maybe I can help."

Estelle turned and regarded Stringer, but he had a hard time holding her gaze. "It's pretty simple, really," she said.

"Well, no, it isn't. Just tell me straight out."

"I want the driver who tried to kill my son."

Stringer let out a gust of breath that might have been an attempt at sympathetic laughter. "Well, don't we all. But that isn't anyone here, Mrs. Guzman. We sell bikes. We give training tips. We organize tours and rides. We sponsor competition. *That's* what we do. Stan borrowed his brother-in-law's old truck to move a fridge or something over at his place, and bingo, apparently it was stolen from right here behind the shop. Go figure this world."

Estelle visibly forced herself to relax and directed a warm smile at Stringer. "It's a frustrating time for me, Mr. Stringer. I hope you can appreciate that and not take offense at all the questions."

"Of course not."

"I'd like to speak with Mr. Wilke whenever he comes in."

Stringer took a couple of steps to the counter and slipped a glossy business card out of the holder. He extended it to Estelle. "His cell is on there, as well as the store's. Feel free to call just whenever. And if you like, when he does return, I'll let him know that you were asking about him. You have a cell?"

"Of course." She slipped a card from her pocket and handed it to Stringer, then turned in place, looking around the store. "Do you think it would be all right if I took a couple of photos? This is such an impressive display."

"Well, sure."

"Can I get you to stand beside Tasha's Grand Canyon photo?"

"Me? I'm not very photogenic."

"Just for scale. You look fine."

As she was arranging the photo carefully, the front door chime jangled. Sergeant Jake Kesserman entered the bike shop and offered a salute to Todd Stringer. "Yo, Todd. Look what she's got you doing."

"Yeah, well, what can I say? Fame is fleeting. We have to grab it while we can. Sarge, good to see you again."

Kesserman frowned at Estelle. "About finished up?"

"Yes. Just about." She snapped a couple more photos, including one of the huge *Tour* poster, and then two or three generic store portraits, finishing with a close-up of the staff's Christmas photo. "Now I'm finished," she said. "Mr. Stringer, thank you." She walked along the wall that displayed jerseys and other cycling togs, cleat-soled shoes, and several dozen helmets. She stopped by the jerseys and ran a hand over the slick fabric. Stringer was so close behind her that she could feel his breath on her neck. She didn't recognize most of the sponsor's names, but the U.S. Postal logo stood out.

"After the seventh Tour win, I ordered a whole raft of those jerseys," Stringer said. "And then the doping scandal, and U.S. Postal backed away, and here I am, with an inventory that's going to fade before it sells." He pulled one jersey off the hanger. "Make you a hell of a deal, Mrs. Guzman."

"He even foisted a bunch off on me," Kesserman added.

"Thanks for talking with me," she said.

"Todd, we'll catch you later." He followed Estelle to the parking lot. "You look a little upset."

She sighed and opened the Camry's door. "I'm just tired, Sergeant."

"I can imagine. May I buy you a cup of coffee or something? There's a quiet little place about three blocks from here." His expression and tone of voice both signaled concern and nothing else but still prompted a smile from Estelle.

"Sergeant, I appreciate the offer. But right now I'd like to go back to the hospital and be with my son."

"Sons," Kesserman corrected with a grin. "Your high-speed world traveler is back. I hear that about half the hospital's nursing staff wants to work overtime." He held the Camry's door open as Estelle slipped into the seat behind the wheel. "Did you learn anything in there?"

"I don't know." She frowned. "I just don't know. Stringer is an interesting sort, isn't he?"

"He is that. And I guess I don't blame him for feeling just a little bit defensive just now." He glanced at his huge, multi-dialed wristwatch. "I can save you a few minutes and some traffic aggravation. Just follow me back to the hospital. I know shortcuts." He flashed a smile. "Then you can tell me and the captain what you think."

Chapter Eleven

Nurse Patton held a finger up to his lips and mouthed, "Sleeping." And indeed they were—Carlos with all his tubes and monitors, Tasha leaning forward from her wheelchair with her forearms resting on the side of the bed near the patient's right hip, her head cradled on a small pillow, and Dr. Francis zonked out in one of the hard plastic armchairs that had been brought in, his chin resting on his chest.

Patton crooked a finger, and Estelle backed out around the curtain. She joined him out in the hall. "Your older son and his wife were here just long enough to wear out my patient. Francisco, isn't it?"

"Yes. Francisco and Angie."

"And William Thomas. He's a cute kid. A real charmer. But look, someone from the *Examiner* discovered that they were here, and caught them downstairs when they first arrived. I understand that the reporter talked them into a fancy lunch somewhere."

Estelle shrugged helplessly. "He's...*they* are in charge of themselves, I guess."

Patton nodded and added a wink. "You look as if you could use a fancy lunch yourself."

Estelle laughed. "That's the second suggestion I've had in less than ten minutes."

"Well, there you go. Your children are beautiful, and it's a no-brainer to see from whom they inherited their looks." His compliment was more a clinical observation than a flirt. His expression said that he wasn't expecting an answer.

Down the hall, elevator doors opened, and Eddie Mitchell appeared dressed in casual civilian clothes, both hands thrust in his pockets. His lips twitched in what might have been a smile as he stepped around a pair of nurses.

"Anyway," Patton said, "rest is what they're doing, and that's good. It's looking like we'll transfer your son out of ICU tomorrow or the next day, if all goes well. There's still some surgical intervention needed on that left leg, so I believe the plans are to transfer him to Kaseman for that." He waggled a finger. "I won't kid you. It's going to be a long road."

He turned and reached out a hand to Captain Mitchell. "They're sleeping, so we're out here, Boss."

"Give us a few minutes, will you?" Mitchell's brows were hooded, his dark eyes expressionless—a look Estelle remembered well from his Posadas days.

When Patton was out of hearing range, Estelle said, "I was a little surprised that the sergeant followed me over to the bike shop, Eddie."

"And I was a little surprised that you *went* there." The left corner of his mouth twitched a little, a tell of amusement. "I knew you wanted to tour here and there, but I wasn't expecting you to go running off by yourself." He grimaced. "That sounds like I'm some kind of parent, trying to keep the leash short."

"I got stir-crazy. I needed some fresh air."

He nodded one slow up and down. "He didn't exactly *follow* you, like a surveillance follow. He was cruising the area and saw your rental. He's just being careful." Mitchell frowned. "You're going to tell me?"

"Tell you what, Eddie?"

"The bike shop. Why the sudden interest? It's where the kids bought the bike. It's where the truck used in the attack was stolen. And so? Anything more than that?"

Estelle leaned against the tiled wall. "Just a little nagging thing," she said. "I don't like coincidences. The truck coming from there is a big, fat coincidence."

"When we visited the evidence yard, and you saw the bent-up bike, as I recall you mentioned that you wanted to visit the bike shop." He nodded. "So, all right. That's what you did. And you know what? This reminds me of what our old friend said on more than one occasion. Bill Gastner would shake his head and mutter something about the 'inscrutable' Estelle Reyes-Guzman." He grinned. "Actually he didn't say 'inscrutable.' He said, 'goddamned inscrutable.'"

Estelle remained silent, and that prompted an even broader smile from Mitchell, who added a 'gimme' motion with his right hand. "Other than the stolen truck, what's the coincidence you don't like? Let's see how it all lines up with ours."

After regarding a wall poster that suggested patients should *Know Your Rights,* during which Mitchell waited without comment, she said, "Eddie, they bought the bike early this week. All right? On Wednesday morning, Carlos says. That's when they picked it up, after a few prior visits, window shopping and test riding. Then, this attack on them? There's nothing about chance encounter involved. Not that I believe, anyway. Somebody *knew* my son's habits, knew that he rode in the evening. Now, they've—Carlos and Tasha? They've lived out here for more than two years, five or six if you count all his college time. Why the sudden attack? With the tandem, the *target* had changed. Taking out someone on a bike is no challenge. Taking out two bikes, a little more so. And more risk of a witness. Suddenly Carlos and Tasha are on a tandem bike, riding by themselves. A nice, handy package."

"Okay."

"If we're looking for who knew—who knew they were riding tandem now, who knew that as beginners on that big bike that they might still be a little shaky? A little slower, a little clumsier, to react? Where would we look for that person?"

"Okay."

"And who knew their riding habits, Eddie? That they bought all the fancy safety stuff for nighttime riding. During the sessions when all that stuff was purchased, what are the odds that the kids would chat about their riding routes, their riding habits?"

"Of course they would. And you talked with Stringer, right? The shop owner? What's your intuition tell you?"

"That he's afraid he's going to be sued, for one thing."

Mitchell grimaced. "Well, of course. That's what happens in this day and age. I'm sure being visited by the victim's mother didn't soothe his nerves any. But there are no grounds for a lawsuit. He should know that."

"I suppose not, but in these times, who needs grounds?" She shook her head. "And I don't see him as the assailant either. Unless he's a very good actor."

"The trouble is, there's nothing that points to anybody from that place, Estelle."

"What about this guy Wilke? The shop's bike mechanic."

"He borrowed the truck last week from a relative to move some furniture. Other than that, it was parked behind the bike shop."

"Handy, that."

"Well, yeah. But it makes no sense to me that Wilke would have anything to do with the assault. I mean, using his own truck?" He looked at her closely. "We'll talk with him."

"Sooner rather than later," Estelle said, and that brought another frown from Mitchell.

"Sure. Today."

"What I'd really like just now is access to a computer and a printer."

"That's not a problem, if you let me in on what's rattling around in your head."

"I have some photos on my phone gadget, as Bill Gastner

calls it. I'd like to enlarge them and make prints. You know… just touristy things."

The expression on Mitchell's face said that he didn't believe a word she said, but he nodded patiently. "Tell you what. There's a BPD substation about a mile from here. I would think that they would have what you need. When did you plan to do this?"

"How about now?"

"All right." He took a deep breath and glanced at his watch. "Give me five minutes to make some contacts, and then I'll run you over there."

Back in the ICU, her husband was standing beside her son's bed, the two of them in quiet conversation. Tasha was still asleep.

"There she is," Dr. Guzman whispered when he saw Estelle. Estelle moved close to her husband, circling his waist with one arm while taking her son's hand in hers.

"Are they keeping you comfortable, *hijo*?"

"I wouldn't go that far," Carlos whispered. "But all things considered, which I'd rather not do just now…" He flashed a quick, somewhat weak smile and glanced down at Tasha, who shifted uneasily but didn't awaken. "You guys need to take in a good dinner somewhere." He pulled in a long, slow breath. "Antonio's Seafood. We go there a lot. Maybe you'd bring me back some crab cakes or something."

"You must be feeling better," Estelle said.

"Oh, yeah. Just great. But all they feed me is what goes through all these damn tubes."

"There's good reason for that, *hijo*," Francis said. "Something goes down the wrong pipe, and you start a coughing fit, it ain't gonna be pretty. You'd pop stitches right and left."

Carlos grimaced at the thought. "Yeah, I guess. Pretty isn't me just now." He started to slide the sheet aside, his arm moving in slow motion. "You gotta see this. I'm black and blue from one side to the other." And sure enough, the side of his torso that wasn't bandaged was a rainbow wash of colors, spreading out from one side to the other. "Ma, you oughta take a portrait so I have a souvenir. Or maybe in a little bit when they change all the dressings and adjust the tubes. You'll be able to see all the carving they've been doing."

"I can't wait." She heard a stifled groan from Tasha, who slowly pushed herself away from the bedside and the pillow that had cradled her head. Estelle moved across and hugged the girl, then massaged Tasha's long, slender neck as she tried to work out the kinks. "This is not a very comfy place to sleep, *hija*."

"I just conked," Tasha said. She closed her eyes and let Estelle's strong fingers work the tendons, ligaments, and muscles. "That feels sooooo good." Without changing position, she reached out and clamped a hand on Carlos's uninjured right toes and gently twisted. "Can't you do something constructive instead of lying around in bed all day? Like wash my car? Fix dinner? Something like that?"

"I'll get right on it."

Tasha stood carefully, a full two inches taller than Estelle, and turned so she could surrender to a prolonged hug.

"Francisco suggested dinner," Tasha said. "And Carlos knows a great place."

"Antonio's. I already told her. You're going to bring back crab cakes."

"Not. A napkin soaked in crab juice that you can sniff, maybe."

"You are a cruel woman." The young man's voice croaked a little, and he frowned at Nurse Patton, who had slipped into the ICU and stood with one hand companionably on Dr. Guzman's left shoulder.

"Gang, time to vanish and leave my man alone." He looked at Francis. "You wanted to know about tomorrow's schedule, and I have that information for you."

"I want to know too," Carlos said.

"I'll be back in a few minutes to talk with you," Patton said. "We'll see how things are going."

"Pictures," Carlos whispered. "I want pictures."

“What are you going to do, sell them to one of those gore sites on the internet?” Patton scoffed.

“Don’t knock it. There’s a lot of money in that.”

“You’ll be a star, I’m sure.” Patton reached across and jostled Tasha’s arm. “You can stay, love. Try to make sure he behaves himself.”

“Impossible mission,” Tasha said.

Outside in the hall, Estelle drew close to her husband. “I need to run an errand or two,” she said. “I’ll be back in time for our dinner engagement.”

Francis glanced across the hall where Captain Eddie Mitchell leaned one elbow on the nurses’ station counter, hands clasped, reading a newspaper that lay folded on the counter. “Is Eddie going with you?”

“Yes. I need to use a computer and printer. Nothing more adventurous than that. He’s going to run me over to one of the substations for a minute.”

“I’m sure there’s such in one of the doctors’ offices right here.” He reached up and put a hand on each side of Estelle’s face, holding her so they looked eye to eye. “You’re following up on something? Is this a chain-of-evidence sort of thing?”

“Yes.”

“What’s Eddie say?”

“He doesn’t know yet.”

“Yet.”

“I’m not sure what I have.”

“Let’s focus,” Francis said. “Our son is in a lot of pieces. He’s going to need help to put himself back together. His rehab is going to be a long, rough road.”

She held up two fingers, tightly crossed together. “He and Tasha. We can be thankful for that.”

“And I agree…thank heavens for that, *querida*. You know, I even thought for a little while about asking them to live with us during his rehab. I mean, we have room. Francisco, Angie, and the baby will be coming by now and then, now that their additions to the Gastner place have been finished. That's something to consider."

"There's a catch, *Oso.* Their home, their work, their friends... they're all out here. I wouldn't intrude on that. If they ask, then that's a different story."

"A gentle suggestion to them, made once?"

She smiled. "Made once."

"And maybe I should be the one to make it. An appeal with free medical services, perhaps."

"You know, *that* might work. That way, they couldn't accuse me of being a doting, smothering, controlling mother."

Captain Mitchell was busy with his phone, and stepped away from the nurses' station.

"Let me get this done, *Oso,*" she said. "It won't take long."

He swept her into a fierce hug. "Go get 'em, *mi corazón.* I can see that look in your eyes. So be careful."

"Oh, *sí.* One little step at a time. And this may be nothing."

"We're shooting for dinner at six with the kids," Francis reminded her.

"Absolutely. I won't be long."

Chapter Twelve

The Floyd Paddock substation looked exactly like the single-story library it had once been before a bond issue had built a new library, and neighborhood policing made a new satellite cop shop efficient, even necessary.

"Your office is here?" Estelle asked as the captain glided his sedan into a vacant slot between two Briones cruisers.

"Nope. I'm downtown in Martinez. I get to buck the traffic every day. Both Dinsman and Kesserman work out of here, though."

"This is probably an unnecessary question, but what brings you to this case, then?"

"Yep, it's unnecessary." He laughed. "The firm that Carlos works for? One of their satellite offices is about a block from mine downtown. So I see him once in a while. I'm serving as sort of a liaison between the SO and the BPD." He flashed a smile. "Primarily because I know you, and I know Francisco, and half the world is going paranoid about this assault on the maestro's brother. Anyway, word of this crash spread pretty fast. Folks get nervous about headlines, you know. Fame rubs off."

"I think we've been lucky so far. Francisco has developed skillful paparazzi-avoidance techniques."

He shrugged and opened his car door. "Yeah, well, Carlos has made a few headlines himself with some of the firm's projects. And with all this happening, I knew you'd be out here lickety-split. It's good to see you guys again. And if this turns out to be something more than just an unfortunate accident—if there's intent involved? Watch what happens then with the media. Your son's face, well, no doubt *both* sons', will be on every supermarket tabloid in the state...or the country." He looked over at Estelle and shook his head. "Yours, too, my friend. But, hey, you get what you get. Go with the flow."

Inside the substation, an older man in civilian clothes manned a horseshoe corral of desks behind a low, gated room divider. He looked up as they entered. He held up his left index finger as a request for them to wait for him to finish whatever it was that he had been typing. Estelle took a moment to survey the rotunda-like lobby, decorated with a Wall of Honor, a display of Officers of the Month, even various politicians, including the governor and the mayor of Briones.

Just behind the man's desk, shielded by the bulk of a copier, was a small, framed poster that read in part, "*I'm surrounded by stupid people...*" The poster was a spoof of the famous line from the film *The Sixth Sense,* in which the boy complains that he sees dead people in his visions.

Mitchell followed Estelle's gaze. "I love that poster. PC or not, it stays up until someone tells the chief here that it has to go. So far, so good. I think it fairly reflects most of our customers, one way or another."

The civilian was wearing trifocals, but he let them drift toward the end of his bulbous nose and peered over them at Mitchell and Estelle. "Well, howdy, Cap."

"Howdy to you, Sig." Mitchell turned to Estelle. "This is Sig Roland, one of BPD's civilian workers, without whom the whole shebang would collapse in on itself."

Roland shook Estelle's hand, his grip moist and limp. "Flattery like that, I figure the captain wants something, am I right? Howdy to you, Miss."

"Undersheriff Estelle Reyes-Guzman, in from Posadas, New Mexico," Mitchell prompted.

Roland's sparse eyebrows shot up. "Undersheriff Guzman? Don't tell me you're related to the Guzman boy who was hurt in that biking accident a couple of days ago?"

"Yes."

"Mother?"

"Yes."

"Well, I see the resemblance. Nice to meet you. Sorry about the difficult circumstances. How's the young man doing?"

"Slowly but surely," Estelle said.

"The surely part…that's good." Roland leaned back from his computer and locked his hands behind his head. "Sergeant Kesserman happened to mention that he and Dinsman are sticking close to the hospital for a while."

"We all appreciate that."

"So, what can I do for you at the moment?"

"We need access to a decent computer and a color printer," Mitchell said. "If Kesserman's is handy, we'll use his."

"Sure enough. Right now?"

"Right now. We'd appreciate it."

"Hey, *Mi Capitán* Mitchell!" A plainclothes cop who looked like a stereotypical California surfer dude appeared from a nearby office, clad in faded yellow chinos creased just so, yellow polo shirt, and fancy running shoes. But the typical plethora of cop stuff weighing down his belt belied that notion. His yellow hair, tinged through the sideburns with gray, was slicked back into a ponytail. He took hold of Mitchell's left arm and shook it. "Ooh, wow. The Sheriff's Department's got you lifting weights, or what? What a brute."

"Or what. Sid, this is Undersheriff Estelle Reyes-Guzman from Posadas County in New Mexico. Her son's the one in pieces over at Temerly. Estelle, this fashion plate is Lieutenant Sid Beaumont."

Beaumont extended his hands and took both of Estelle's in

his, looking hard at her, brow furrowed. He would have looked good hanging ten, Estelle thought. The color of his eyes would have matched the surf, his strong jaw thrust forward to cleave the air. "Nice to meet you. Difficult circumstances, but welcome. Is Kesserman taking care of you folks? Is there anything you need?"

"We're doing fine, Lieutenant. Relatively fine, anyway."

Beaumont smiled slyly. "I'll keep Kesserman on a short leash, Sheriff. He can be sort of a wolf at times, if you know what I mean."

"Not to worry, sir."

He laughed again. "Well, we know a couple undersheriffs out here, and they sure pale in comparison to you. Ain't that right, Cap?"

Mitchell offered his trademark glower. "Look, we need the use of a computer and color printer for just a few minutes. I know Kesserman has a fancy new printer, so we'll use his, if that's okay with you."

"His or mine, whatever," Beaumont said.

"Kesserman's is fine."

"Then follow me."

More of a cubbyhole than an office, Kesserman's space didn't need to be unlocked since it had only three walls. For some semblance of privacy, the sergeant had his desk turned so that the computer's back was to the cubbyhole's entry. Beaumont consulted a small notebook. "His password is *Kesser9182730."* He snapped the book closed as if someone were looking over his shoulder.

"You have everyone's password?" Estelle asked.

"Oh, sure," Beaumont said, adding his electric grin. "Just in case. Something happens to one of our guys, we don't want to waste time trying to access recent computer use. Not that breaking a password like that is rocket science." He tapped the little book against his chin. "If somebody wants totally secret files, let 'em do it at home on their own equipment. I'm sure you do the same thing."

"Light years," Estelle said.

"Ahead?"

"Behind." She tried to imaging Bob Torrez with secret files—or any computer files at all, for that matter.

Beaumont laughed, an expression he did easily, but one that didn't extend to his surfer blue/green eyes. "Help yourselves." He lifted the printer's paper tray. "Good to go. You use an iMac at home?"

"Sure."

"Then knock yourself out. Captain, I'll catch up with you later. Undersheriff, it's super to meet you. I hope everything turns out well. Believe me, we're workin' on it."

"Thank you, Lieutenant."

Beaumont flashed one final grin and ducked out, and Estelle could hear him in conversation with Sig Roland.

"So..." Mitchell said. He watched as Estelle popped out her phone's photo card and reached around to insert it in the back of the computer, then quickly typed in the password.

The screen filled with the card's contents. She leaned forward, cupping her chin in her hand, and examined the tiny icons. After a moment, she selected one. The photo filled the screen.

She leaned back, regarding the photo—in this case, a photo *of* a photo.

She reached out and tapped a face. "This man."

"Uh huh." Mitchell pulled out his phone and stroked its face for a moment. He found what he wanted and said, "That would be Barry Whitaker, one of the mechanics at the bike shop." He reached across Estelle's shoulder and touched the image on the screen. "Left to right, Todd Stringer, Stan Wilke, Barry Whitaker, and Emily Gere. Both Gere and Whitaker are part-time. That's my understanding, anyway."

"What do you know about Whitaker? He doesn't exactly fit the cyclist profile."

"What do *I* know? About nothing. He works at the bike shop

part-time. He obviously enjoys eating. With the full beard, it's hard to tell what he actually looks like. I know that he has no record."

"Your men checked that?"

"Sure. You're not the only one who doesn't like coincidence. Why are you zeroed in on him?"

Estelle didn't answer and touched the screen with the pencil eraser. "What about her?"

"Ms. Gere is a transplant from Eureka. She has a rather lengthy list of moving violations, we noted. Another point or two, and it'll be a good thing that she has bicycles available for her use."

"Just a lead foot?"

"Yes. All speeding violations with one stop-light episode thrown in. Kesserman says that she rides a bike the same way, for what that's worth. Ducks lights, runs between lanes when the traffic is choked—things like that."

"She has a death wish?"

"Who knows."

Estelle moved the pencil pointer. "And Wilke?"

"Stan Wilke is one of Briones's bottom-feeders." Mitchell shrugged. "Unmarried, lives in an economy two-room apartment over on Cherny, rides in every bike event that comes along. He's one of those guys who loves nothing better than working on a heart attack trying to pedal up the steepest hills he can find."

"And he's full-time at the shop?"

"The only full-timer, as far as I know. Other than Todd Stringer himself, I mean. He's missed a day or two here lately, if you like thinking about awkward coincidences."

"I'd like to talk with him."

"So would we. I'm assuming that he wasn't at the shop when you stopped by?"

"No."

Mitchell cocked his head, his expression appraising. "A

connection with the bike shop. I can see why, but we haven't been able to establish anything."

"That Wilke's truck—the truck that was supposedly borrowed—was the one stolen and used in the assault is the troubling connection. That doesn't mean Wilke is in any way connected, Eddie, but I'll go down that road until I'm sure it's a dead end. Until I have a chance to really talk at length with Carlos, just to see if there's some other link somewhere." She sat back from the computer. "I just can't imagine that someone randomly driving by sees a couple riding a tandem and takes it into his deranged head to chase them down and deliberately smash into them...and then back up and give 'em another smash for good measure. That's homicidal, and it's been my experience that most homicides have some fundamental reason—however twisted. The percent of homicides that are perpetrated just for fun and thrills is pretty low."

"Remember—this is California, not Posadas," Mitchell said. "We have more than our share of interesting people who think drive-bys should be the national pastime On top of that, don't ignore the obvious."

She looked up at Mitchell in surprise.

"Tasha Qarshe is black. *Really* black. Your son is white." He hesitated and smiled. "Or if you're a fan of the new politically correct anthropology, he's *brown.* Anything except peach-belly white offends some people. I know this is the liberal twenty-first century and all, and California is home for all kinds of...well, as I said, interesting people. But still, there are freaks out there."

Estelle shook her head impatiently. "How could the attacker tell, at night with the riders wearing concealing clothing? I mean, they both even wear gloves. Helmet, gloves, bright Spandex that draws the eye. Other than their faces, which would be hard to see, the only exposed skin is from mid-thigh to ankle." She smiled tightly. "Good looking legs, both kids. But at night? Tasha is dark, and Carlos is swarthy, a good long ways from peach-belly white." She smiled. "He played an Ethiopian king in a high school Christmas production of *Amahl and the Night Visitors,* and a few members of the audience thought a new family had moved into town."

"Yeah, I remember that. And that was Posadas. But this is Briones, after all," Mitchell laughed. "If you happen to be xenophobic, there might be easier places to live than here."

"Oddly enough," Estelle said, "bigots don't seem to do that. They live where they get the most stimulation for their half-wit ideas." She leaned back and cupped her hands behind her head. "You may recall how many folks live in Posadas who hate Mexicans. I always found that odd. Which leads us around."

She let her chair slide forward, reaching out to trace a circle with her pencil eraser around Wilke's face.

"You want that enlarged?" Mitchell asked.

"This will do. The whole gang." She printed a copy, and nodded with satisfaction. "It's clear enough." She glanced up at Mitchell. "May I have another?"

"You can have as many as you like," the captain said. "Especially if you'll tell me what you're thinking."

Estelle took a deep breath as she regarded the computer's image. "You know, everyone in that shop knows Carlos and Tasha. They had time to discuss bikes, gear, personal riding habits, apparently long before they bought the tandem. There's been plenty of time for feelings to fester, if there's somebody there who has it in for mixed races, or is so xenophobic that when they see someone with a Middle Eastern or African name, they make all the worst kinds of assumptions. If that's the case, I'd think that Carlos and Tasha would have picked up on those vibes. Most xenophobes that I've met aren't really skilled at hiding deep-seated hate. It just bubbles to the surface. It's that all-consuming."

Estelle reached out and told the printer to make a second copy. "It's just hard for me to imagine someone actually meeting Tasha and Carlos face to face and wishing them harm."

Mitchell puffed out his cheeks in frustration. "That may be

one of the problems. Both your son and his fiancée are gorgeous people. Handsome. Striking. Talented. Choose any adjective you like. That generates its own resentment, sorry to say. We don't know that's what happened, but it's something to explore."

Estelle heaved a mighty sigh. "And here I am." She looked up at Mitchell. "My son's in the hospital intensive care unit, and I have to admit it...here I am, indulging myself thinking that I can somehow run around behind the scenes and bring his attackers to justice."

"Just keep thinking, Undersheriff. If your questions and probings force us to take some route we're missing, that's all to the good."

She held up the photocopies. "Thanks for these, Eddie."

He offered a broad smile. "And I can see the wheels turning, Undersheriff. So fair trade. Clue me in sooner, rather than later, and anything else we can supply, just say the word. In the meantime, I'm going to ask that my guys work every angle of the bike shop. We'll see what's going on. We're as eager to solve this as you are."

"I bet not, Captain. When you talked with the truck's owner, what did you think of him? Any vibes?"

"I know where he's working. Let's make a quick run over there before he's gone for the weekend. You need to make up your own mind."

Chapter Thirteen

The waterline trench was straight enough to have been cut by a laser. After a brief consult with the project superintendent and listening to his litany about thirty-year-old failed infrastructure, he directed them to an expanse of quadrangle behind the college library, where he said they'd find Jim Wayne on board his excavator.

Jim Wayne obviously remembered Mitchell from their previous conversations about the truck, and he settled the bucket, chopped the throttle, and switched off the noisy little diesel. Instead of a greeting, he simply raised a hand in half-salute, then pushed back his tan baseball cap.

"Jim, you've about got 'er whipped," Mitchell said.

Wayne turned and looked over his shoulder toward the next marker. "Little bit yet." He raised a bushy blond eyebrow, his gaze giving Estelle the once-over.

"This is Undersheriff Estelle Reyes-Guzman, from Posadas, New Mexico, Jim. She's giving BPD and the SO a hand."

Wayne stretched a little and relaxed his hands on the excavator's joysticks. That was the extent of his greeting. "Any news on my truck?"

"We're working on it," Mitchell said. "That's why we stopped by. We have a question or two."

"Sure enough." Wayne looked appraisingly at Estelle, a slow smile revealing too many teeth for his narrow jaw. "Long way from home?"

"Yes."

"That wall thing keeps you busy?"

"The 'wall thing'?"

"That fancy wall that's supposed to stop the illegals from crossing the border." He dug out a little round can from his shirt pocket and pinched a generous wad from it, taking his time settling the tobacco behind his lip. "Never did understand how that was supposed to work."

"It has its share of problems," Estelle said.

"I just bet it does. But I'm guessing you didn't come here to talk about that."

Estelle smiled. "Mr. Wayne, when Stan Wilke borrowed your truck, did he say what he needed it for?"

Wayne frowned as if it were a complicated question. "He wanted to get rid of an old freezer and an old set of box springs. Maybe some other stuff."

"He's your wife's brother?"

"Former wife," Wayne said, and shifted the chew.

"He didn't ask for help with the move?"

"Nope. He's got neighbors he could ask, but all they drive is those little faggoty cars that don't carry diddly. See, the way I'm thinking is that one of them took the truck after Stan was through with it. I was going to ask him about that, but I didn't get around to it. That little squid is hard to catch sometimes."

"But you reported it stolen?"

"No. I knew Stan had it." He shrugged. "He's borrowed it before. Usually pretty careful with it. And then the cops found it where somebody left it parked over by the college. That's when I found out about it." He nodded at Mitchell. "He claims that it was used in some kind of hit-and-run. I don't know about that. You'll have to ask Stan, 'cause I just assumed he still had it."

"You didn't talk with him?"

"No. I was going to. I mean, I use that truck now and then. He's going to have to come up with a way to fix it if it was broke. Don't know where he's going to get the money to do that. I mean," and he patted the right joystick, "how much can you earn fixing other people's bicycles? He needs to get him a real job."

"But you haven't seen him since."

"Nope. But then again, I ain't exactly looked, Sheriff." He looked meaningfully at his watch. "I've had a few visits from you guys, and I was hopin' here before long to get the truck back. And somebody is going to have to pay to get it fixed."

"You've seen it, then?"

"No. But I don't guess you can come out of a collision with a couple of bikers without doing some damage. That was a good, clean truck."

"After you heard about the crash from police, you didn't call your brother-in-law to find out what was going on?"

"Nope. Well, that ain't exactly true. I tried his cell but didn't get an answer." Wayne twisted his face into a comical expression as if remembering something distasteful. "You know, I gotta be honest. Him and me don't talk much."

"But you loaned him your truck."

"Well..." He shrugged. "Yeah, I did. Maybe not the smartest thing I ever done, but he always returns it filled up."

Mitchell nodded and looked at Estelle. "Anything else?"

"Not at the moment."

"Then we'll get out of your way, Jim."

They had not walked a dozen steps before they heard the excavator fire up.

"Not a lot of love lost there," Estelle commented. "It puzzles me that he hasn't been pestering the cops for a look at his impounded truck. And I've got some questions for Stan Wilke, too. Was the truck locked? Was it hot-wired, or did he make the mistake of leaving the keys in it?"

"Add to the list," Mitchell said. "When we find him, we'll find the answers."

Chapter Fourteen

"It's one of those 'it's who you know' kind of things." Francisco Guzman was interrupted in mid-thought. He leaned a bit to one side, giving the attentive waiter room to maneuver. They had followed his brother's suggestion and arrived at Antonio's shortly after six that Friday evening. Estelle had been in no mood for a heavy dinner, but the quiet, intimate ambiance of the restaurant, along with the heavenly aromas, changed her mind. The menu was a substantial book, and she took her time, enjoying the presentation.

Alphonse the waiter bowed between little William Thomas and his father. "And, Maestro, the little one? What would he like to drink?" William Thomas peered at the waiter as if wondering why the man was wearing such a funny penguin suit.

"A light but playful Cabernet, no doubt," Francisco said with a perfectly straight face. "In a sippy cup." Before the waiter could react, Francisco grinned. "Actually, a chocolate milk...in a sippy."

William Thomas said something that could have been "choco-muh" and beamed.

"I'd like lemon water," Francisco continued. "Would anyone like a glass of wine? A carafe? A bottle? A jug?" They all settled on water, some with lemon, some without. Francisco shrugged and looked up at the waiter. "We're a boring lot, Alphonse."

"You may be many things, Maestro, but boring isn't one of them."

"Oh, ho," Francisco said. "Thank you. I was told that the seafood platter was a good way to go?"

"Despite the rather inelegant name, yes. The platter offers a broad selection of our best. It is served on a somewhat modest platter that is easily passed, and endlessly refilled."

"Whaddaya think?" Francisco scanned his dinner companions.

"If it's not enough, we can always go out for hamburgers afterward," Dr. Guzman said, and William Thomas looked excited. Alphonse smiled benignly.

"Trust me, Dr. Guzman," he said. "That will not be necessary."

Alphonse vanished, and Estelle relaxed a little, one arm outstretched across the back of Tasha's wheelchair, the other hand playing with the long black hair on the back of William Thomas's head. "So you were saying, Maestro?"

"Yeah." Francisco lowered his voice, although there wasn't another occupied table within their small, intimate dining room. "It turns out that Alphonse enjoys classical music, Angie's cello artistry in particular. And he reads. He saw the article in *Stone,* the one that had that nifty family portrait? So, there you go. He's met us all in print, so to speak. Knowing his customers is one of his talents."

Estelle remembered flinching at seeing the 'nifty family portrait' in the national magazine. It was actually a photo that department photographer Linda Real Pasquale had snapped at the scene of a house fire and ruptured propane tank. In all the mayhem, Linda had been nearby with the camera during a moment when Estelle paused to talk with her husband, also at the scene because of a plethora of injuries and cases of smoke inhalation.

Linda had caught the instant when Dr. Guzman's right hand reached out to Estelle's left shoulder, at the same time her hand found her husband's left. Their faces, etched in soot and anguish, were inches apart. Dr. Guzman and EMTs triaged at the scene while Dr. Alan Perrone worked the emergency room. Later, when Linda had asked Estelle if she minded the photo being submitted, Estelle had agreed without giving it much thought.

The magazine had run the photo in a collaged group with two attached photos of the boys—Francisco and Angie performing together at the Kennedy Center, and Carlos caught in midair in a photo snapped by Tasha as he launched in a high dive from Black Rock at Ka'anapali in Maui.

Francisco leaned back as a young man in solid white arrived with the shimmering glasses of water...and one polished sippy cup.

"As it turns out, a friend of mine from the conservatory days now is in the music department at UC-Briones," Francisco said. "He heard...and that's probably an interesting story in itself... he heard that Angie and I were in town. He'd heard, or read, about Tasha and Carlos being hurt. Being the opportunist that he is, he reached me at the hotel and begged and pleaded. He wasn't about to let this opportunity slide by."

"Not wanting to intrude on the family's privacy," Estelle muttered.

Francisco held up his hands in surrender. "What he really wanted was a full-blown master's class, but I said no, nobody is prepared for that, least of all Angie or I. But maybe we'd like to hear what the students are doing. Just like that," and Francisco snapped his fingers, "he put together this mini-smorgasbord of...what did we have?" He looked at Angie.

"Twelve advanced students," Angie said. "Four on the piano, four on violin, one cello, one French horn, two flutes."

"Two hours' worth," Francisco added. "My favorite was the comedian—kind of like a modern-day takeoff on Victor Borge. If he can't make it in show biz, he wants to be an elementary school music teacher, and he'll be wonderful at it. We've already got plenty of comedians, and probably nowhere near enough music teachers."

"You didn't play?" Estelle asked. "I mean, if your conservatory friend is going to be presumptuous, he might as well go all the way."

Francisco made a face. "No. What he asked for didn't seem presumptuous to me, Ma. Just talk and a little entertainment to help us feel at home. But it didn't seem appropriate for us to play. I mean, if it's a genuine Master's Class, sure. Yeah. That's one thing. You show 'em things, ways to improve. And they come to the class prepared for that. But this was different—just an impromptu visit. We gave 'em feel-good pep talks and were an encouraging audience. One guy was so nervous he could hardly hang on to his violin."

"And good evening, all." Sergeant Jake Kesserman appeared—almost materialized—from behind the ocean motif of the room dividers. This time, Estelle saw, he was dressed more formally, with an impeccable dark-blue suit, light-blue button-down collar shirt, and dark blue tie. The suit added just enough additional bulk that he didn't look like an anorexic teasing himself with a restaurant visit.

He held up a hand. "I don't mean to intrude, but I heard you might be here, so I just wanted to check in." He looked hard at Estelle. "I missed your visit to our office a little bit ago, Sheriff." As he spoke, he waved a hand at Francisco and Dr. Guzman, who both had made moves to stand. "Please, don't get up."

"Good evening to you, Sergeant. As your source probably told you, I needed a printer, and yours was offered. I'm sorry if that caused a problem."

"Oh, no, no," Kesserman said quickly. "No problem at all. I just wanted to check with you when I had the opportunity. Anything else you might need?"

"I don't think so. Captain Mitchell was very accommodating."

"Yes, he is." Kesserman's gaze lingered on Estelle, then flicked across to Tasha Qarshe. "You're doing better, young lady. That's great."

"Thank you, sir." Tasha's smile was brittle as his gaze lingered.

"Well, anyway, have a grand dinner. I just wanted you to know that if there is anything you need, don't hesitate to let me know. All right?"

"We appreciate that, Sergeant."

He didn't offer to shake hands, but ducked his head deferentially, offered a friendly pat to Francisco's left shoulder, and departed the same way he'd come.

Francisco laughed and twisted around to look after the departing officer. "Why does it feel as if we're under surveillance?" He turned back and looked questioningly at his mother. "How did he know we were coming here?"

"I suppose Eddie—Captain Mitchell—told him. No matter," she added dismissively, and rested her hand on Tasha's forearm. "This is a high-profile case—at least the press thinks it is. The cops are sensitive to that. They're trying hard."

"I talked to Carlos for a few minutes before we came over here," Francisco said. "He said that both Dinsman and Kesserman have been keeping close tabs on who goes in and out of ICU. They've talked to him a couple of times." He looked at Tasha. "They've been seeing you, too?"

"At the very beginning. Not since then." She stretched her back, shifting in the wheelchair. "'Who did you see? Did you see the driver?' That's what they wanted to know. That seems to be *all* they want to know."

"Stands to reason," Dr. Guzman said. "They have the truck. They don't know who the driver was. So...that's what they're going to be looking for."

The food—a vast smorgasbord of the ocean's bounties from shallow reef to deep sea creatures—arrived on a huge platter, with Alphonse justifiably proud of the presentation. At the same time, the young man in white delivered the individual plates. A silver tray of condiments arrived as well. Alphonse held the platter and maneuvered it from plate to plate, turning it this way and that to bring all the samples within reach.

William Thomas's eyes were huge as he gawked at the giant array. He rapped his sippy cup on the table. "Chocomuh," he said with satisfaction.

Chapter Fifteen

Estelle's phone vibrated sometime during the perfect filet of sole and the second helping of creamy avocado-and-lime-spritzed shrimp. She mock-glared at the tiny hand that was crabbing across the tablecloth, its target one of her shrimp. William Thomas had his own, of course, but his grandmother's plate was too much of a temptation. He looked up at her, his handsome little face a comical combination of guilt and stealth.

"Leave me one," Estelle said and winked at him. The little hand darted, and Estelle pushed her chair back a bit as she palmed her phone. "Guzman."

"Estelle, Eddie Mitchell. You're still at Antonio's?"

"Good evening, Eddie. Yes, trying to eat myself into a coma."

"That'll be the day. Look, sorry to bother you. We found Stan Wilke a little bit ago."

"*Found* him?" From Mitchell's tone of voice, Estelle knew exactly what the captain meant but was still unprepared for the jolt.

"In one of the dumpsters behind Jessie's Produce. One of the employees went out to dump some refuse, and opened the dumpster top just a little too far. There's Wilke, sleepin' among the corn husks and rotten sweet potatoes."

"*Ay.* COD?"

"He's wearin' a third eye. Single GSW, entry, exit."

Her grandson's tiny hand was advancing again, and Estelle nodded permission. Her own appetite had vanished.

"Anyway, your intuition about Crosby Cycle is spot on, Undersheriff. That's what I'm thinking. We have Jessie's shut down, cordoned off, and we're working the scene a square inch at a time. So here's the deal. If you want in, just say so."

"Of course." The words came out automatically, before she had a chance to give it a second thought. She could have just as easily have added the single word "not" to the response, but her instinct was to be included.

Mitchell remained silent, as if determined to give her that chance for a second thought. After a moment, he said, "How much time do you need?"

She met her husband's steady gaze, his expression mirroring her son's face.

"Is the ME there yet?"

"ETA ten minutes, I'm told. And it'll be easier for us just to pick you up right there at Antonio's."

"All right." She glanced at her watch. "I'll be out front at seven oh five."

"That'll work. Make sure the officer gives you your ID. "

"Thanks, Eddie."

"Don't thank me yet, ma'am. You always got to be careful about what you wish for."

She hung up, and Dr. Guzman's expression included a long-suffering sigh.

"This is like having a giant snowball starting downhill, gathering momentum," she said.

"Seven oh five? You're going to miss dessert."

She looped an arm around William Thomas's shoulders. "This guy can have mine."

"If it concerns you, it's gotta mean that they found a body," Francisco said.

"That was Captain Mitchell," Estelle explained. "They found a man dead, dumped in a trash receptacle behind Jessie's Produce, wherever that is."

"I have no idea," Francisco said.

"I do," Tasha added. "It's over on the other side of the airport, kind of out in the country, away from everything. In that hilly country not far from the road up to Briones Park."

"They're going to pick you up, then?" Dr. Guzman asked.

"Yes."

"There's a connection, isn't there? Is that what they're saying?"

"Maybe so."

"Do they know who the victim is?"

"Yes." She glanced around the room, but they still had it to themselves. "Stan Wilke."

Tasha gasped. "He works at Crosby's." Her right hand flew up to cover her mouth.

"Yes. He did."

Chapter Sixteen

Francis walked Estelle out to the patio that fronted Antonio's. They stood near the multitiered fountain, and during a long hug, neither spoke. Finally, Francis said, "This is all somehow related? Is that what Eddie is saying?"

"Somehow. We don't know how yet."

"We."

She nodded, her hand cupped around the back of her husband's neck. "If it's related to what happened to our son, then, yes…it's *we.*" She tightened her grip a little. "We're fortunate that Eddie Mitchell is the lead in this. He's made no bones about wanting, even welcoming, my help—whatever it might be that I can do." She smiled grimly. "Even if it's just listening to my intuitions."

"And this time, what does your intuition tell you?"

"I wish I knew. Stan Wilke worked at the shop that sold Carlos and Tasha the bike. He's always at the shop, I'm told. It's his life. An then he borrows his former brother-in-law's truck to move some furniture, and all of a sudden, he goes missing. And now we hear that he's been murdered." She pulled her hands away and cupped them together into a tight ball. "It's a tangle of coincidences, *Oso.* And I can't… I can't just turn my back on it. I can't just wave a hand at Eddie and Kesserman and all the rest of them, wave a hand and say, 'Well, it's not my turf. You guys figure it out.'"

"Because it's Carlos. It's *his* turf."

"That's exactly right, *querido.* And if I can help, I will." She reached up and caressed his short beard. "You've been an invaluable resource for the medics here, I'm sure. Now it's my turn. I'll have someone give me a ride back to the hospital."

A marked Briones patrol car swung into the restaurant's roundabout.

"My ride," Estelle said. Their kiss lingered. "Keep the kids close," she whispered.

"*Sin duda, mi corazón.* Take care."

At first glance, the uniformed officer behind the wheel of the lavishly appointed Charger looked to be fifteen years old. His polished name tag read *O.S. Scott.* He watched Estelle slide into the passenger seat, the undersheriff mindful of all the projecting, sharp corners threatened by radio, computer rack, shotgun, even Scott's aluminum clipboard. When she had buckled in, he held out a gold chain with a laminated ID attached.

"Captain Mitchell instructs that you wear this at all times while you're with us," he said. She took the ID, a fancy card that announced that she was an *Official Police Consultant.* It bore the signature of the Briones chief of police, as well as the Contra Costa County Sheriff, and Eddie Mitchell.

"As opposed to *unofficial,*" she said soberly. "I'm impressed with how all you folks are working together. I haven't seen a single turf fight yet."

That prompted a smile from Officer Scott—a nice, warm smile that perhaps he'd find useful when responding to domestic disputes.

"Are you carrying a weapon, Undersheriff?"

"No, I'm not."

He grinned again. "I know this is California, but...Captain Mitchell wants you to know that there's a Sheriff's Department–issue Glock 23 in this center console." He patted the console near his right elbow, then reached out and rested a finger on the muzzle of the pump shotgun that was clipped vertically against the dash. "Ithaca Model 37, a great old antique. It's holding three double-ought, followed by two slugs. Nothing in the chamber. The electric release is down here on the control box." He paused, making sure her eyes had found the shotgun release.

"Probably the same as in my own unit," Estelle said, and the kid looked relieved.

"Then we're good to go." He hesitated. "I probably don't need to say this, ma'am, but I've been instructed to, so I will. If there comes a time that I or any other officer instructs you to remain in the vehicle, you will do so. Any questions about that?"

"Of course not. I've told a few civilians that same thing from time to time."

He nodded enthusiastically. "I don't anticipate any issues, but," he shrugged, "this is a crazy world. We all want to be able to go home at end of shift."

"Absolutely."

"I'm honored to have you on board."

"Thank you." *We can actually move now,* Estelle thought with amusement. Officer Scott obliged by pulling the car into gear.

"I hear your older son was featured in national magazines."

"That would be true. Both he and his wife."

He glanced at Estelle. "I'm really sorry about what happened to your other son and his girlfriend. It's hard to figure why anyone would want to do something like that."

She regarded the young cop as they maneuvered through traffic. "How long have you been with the PD, Officer Scott?"

"I'm the token rookie," he laughed. "Four months come next week. Between this and the National Guard, they're keeping me busy."

"Good for you. You've been around the block enough times to know that there are people out there who don't think like we do. Who don't hesitate to do awful things, sometimes just for kicks."

"Or people with a screw loose in their wiring, people who short out and can't control themselves," Scott said. "Yes, ma'am, I know they're out there. So how long have you been with the Sheriff's Department over there in New Mexico?"

"Too long, my friend. Too long."

"So how many years, then?"

"Thirty-three."

He shot a quick look of astonishment her way. "Geez. That's amazing. You don't look that..." He stopped, and Estelle took the opportunity to provide the word that had tripped him up.

"Old?" Estelle said.

"I guess. I mean, no. You really don't. Have you ever wanted to do something else?"

"No. Well, actually that's not quite true. I'd like to be a full-time grandmother, without interruptions."

"*That's* even more amazing."

"I've been fortunate. I've always worked with people whom I admire." She smiled. "One big happy family."

"Well, that's good." Scott concentrated on his driving, changed lanes abruptly, and reached down to toggle on the red lights. "Let's get through this mess." In another few blocks, four lanes narrowed abruptly to two, and rolling hills stripped with vineyards framed the highway as they headed southeast. Just beyond Dixon's Tractor and Implement, after the last row of shiny ag machines, he braked hard and pulled into a police parking lot. Estelle counted eleven police units, including an enormous black-and-white crime-scene RV. Yellow tape blocked most of the Jessie's Produce property.

Scott deftly swung through the maze and then braked hard. "This is as close as we get." He looked at Estelle. "You're wearing a belt?"

"Yes."

"Then now would be the time to hook up with the Glock." He opened the center console and hefted the Kydex-holstered pistol toward her. "Fifteen in the magazine, nothing chambered."

She looped the gold chain of the ID around her neck, accepted the pistol, and slid out of the car. It took an awkward moment to snug the heavy clasp of the holster over the leather belt of her pants, but once in position, with her suit jacket concealing the weapon and the ID hanging from her neck, she looked just like what she was—a plainclothes cop.

"I can't believe it's necessary, but did Sarge or Captain Mitchell explain the jurisdictional concerns to you?" As Scott made his way around the car, she saw that he was clearly not the skinny kid he'd first appeared. Broad and heavy-shouldered, just breaking six feet tall, and given his articulate ways, Estelle guessed that Scott had already started down the long road to some future command.

"The captain made his position, and mine, quite clear," Estelle said.

"Then you know that even with the chief's blessing," and he nodded at her ID, "we're skating on kinda thin ice here."

"Yes." She wondered if Officer Scott was enrolled in night law classes at UC-Briones.

"Okay. Just so you keep that front and center. And remember you're not wearing a vest. I have an extra in the trunk for you if you'd like."

"I hope the killer is long gone," she said, at that instant realizing how dumb that might sound. Of course, killers never returned to the scene of the crime… "I'll borrow the vest, thanks."

Like all ballistic vests, this one was uncomfortable and confining, not designed with a mature woman's curves in mind. After struggling into it, she tossed her suit jacket into the car.

"Okay." She stood by the car for several minutes, taking in the scene, trying to imagine the place without squad cars, crime-scene vans, milling people, gawker traffic slowing on the highway. Why would the killer pull in *here,* to this particular spot? The dumpsters were not visible from the highway, so the killer knew—or correctly assumed—that they would be tucked in behind the building, with a drive around for the trash collection truck.

"Number five," Estelle said, and Officer Scott raised a blond eyebrow. "Over the years, I've done my share of dumpster diving. In not one of the four Posadas cases did the victim climb into the dumpster under his or her own power. I'm guessing this one didn't either?"

"I have to admit that I haven't toured the crime scene, ma'am. I'm on taxi duty." Scott chuckled with light sarcasm. "That's why we should be paying you the big bucks, Undersheriff. So maybe this is the old story. Somebody pulled in, popped the trunk, hauled out the body, and in he goes. The victim had no choice in the matter."

"If that's the way it happened," Estelle mused, more to herself than to Scott. When she showed no sign of advancing into the crime scene, Officer Scott prompted her. "Ready?"

"In a minute." Half turning, she surveyed the neighboring expanse of Dixon's Tractor and Implement. It would be unlikely—even in broad daylight—that anyone standing inside Dixon's showroom could look across the half-mowed field of late-season alfalfa and see details of activity next door at the produce market. They'd be too occupied looking at all the wonderful ag machines on display, especially the red behemoth taking center stage, hooked to an eight-bottom plow unit, which in turn trailed triple harrows—fifty lineal feet of linked equipment blocking the view.

Even if the dumpster were steel and opened with its heavy, flapping top making the usual clang, anyone nearby would hear it, if they were paying attention. The body tipping into the cavernous interior wouldn't make much noise. A muffled thump. Then clang the lid shut and away he goes to the county landfill or incinerators or ocean dump—whatever seaside communities were doing these days.

The crunch of boots on gravel drew her attention. Eddie Mitchell held out a hand as he approached. "Thanks for coming."

His grip was firm and businesslike "Check-in is over by the van." He released his grip and then punched a heavy index finger into the center of her chest, nodding at the vest. He turned to Scott. "Good man."

"Officer Scott, thank you," Estelle said.

"You're most welcome, ma'am. I'll be here when you need a ride back."

Mitchell accompanied Estelle in silence and watched as she signed in, the clipboard offered by a young officer who might have barely cleared five feet tall. Her name tag read *N. Rubenstein.* Her uniform appeared as if it had just been unwrapped, fold creases still obvious on pant legs and shirt sleeves.

Mitchell said, "This is probably a waste of your time, but I thought what the hell. You're in the neighborhood. Any ideas are helpful. Depends on your definition of 'neighborhood,' of course."

Jessie's Produce was a simple prefab structure, with generous porches added on three sides. Plywood weather beaters were lowered to close off the porches during off-hours, each panel adorned with artistically rendered paintings of everything from corn to carrots, rutabagas to radishes...and of course, various renditions of bunches of grapes.

"That's Jessie Contreras," Mitchell said, nodding toward a compact, rotund woman engaged in animated conversation with two officers. Ms. Contreras caught sight of Mitchell and raised one imperious hand as she cut short her conversation with the two cops.

She strode toward Mitchell and Estelle, her boots scuffing gravel. The denim that she favored—jeans, shirt, ball cap—did nothing to hide her pudgy figure. Her face was amazingly round, Estelle saw—full, plump cheeks down to a round chin, no harsh outline around her jaws. Someone's pleasant grandmother.

Without a greeting, she raised a heavy black eyebrow at the captain. "You're Mitchell from the SO, right?"

"Yes, ma'am." He started to say something else, but Contreras interrupted him. She turned her gaze to Estelle.

"And you're new." She frowned and leaned forward a bit to read the laminated pass. "What's an *Official Police Consultant?* We don't have enough cops around that our taxes have to pay for you too?"

"Whoa, whoa, whoa," Mitchell said. "Turn off the charm, all right?" Her eyes narrowed and snapped back to Mitchell when he said that, but he continued on. "Undersheriff Guzman is working another case that may or may not be related to the body you've got stashed in your dumpster. The more cooperation we get from you, the faster we'll wrap this up."

"If I knew who stashed it, he'd be in there with 'em."

"I'm sure. In the meantime you're just going to have to put up with us, like it or not."

"Well, I *don't* like it. And I sincerely hope you all are out of here by morning because this ruckus is sure as hell going to play hob with my business. I mean, we're open until nine o'clock, usually. So you've already cost me some hours."

Mitchell smiled, but it didn't reach his eyes. "We'll do our best. And I'm sure you'll cooperate with us." He beckoned to one of the officers, a burly, older man with lots of sleeve stripes and too much waistline. "Sarge, Ms. Contreras wants to give a statement. Meet with her inside for a few minutes?"

"Who said I wanted to give anything?"

"You did. Thanks for your cooperation. It's citizens like you who make our job easier." Estelle noticed that Mitchell managed to say that with a straight face.

"Ma'am?" The sergeant held out a companionable hand.

"This is such a mess," Ms. Contreras snapped. Mitchell watched her trudge off with the officer.

"Notice the overflowing concern for the victim in the dumpster," Mitchell muttered.

As they crossed the parking lot, skirting around behind the building, Estelle got the sense that Eddie Mitchell was expecting something from her. She didn't need to identify the body—she'd just be matching the victim's remains with his image in a single photograph. Someone else would do the identifying, had no doubt already done so to the local cops' satisfaction. There was nothing inherent in the scene itself that required her expertise—if in fact her limited knowledge of bodies in dumpsters could be considered expert.

The body had been removed from its gruesome resting place and was now zipped inside a black body bag on a gurney. Several people whom she assumed were plainclothes officers were gathered around the shrouded corpse. A man and a woman, both with stethoscopes around their necks, were engaged in earnest conversation with Lieutenant Sid Beaumont and Sergeant Jake Kesserman, who must have headed over here directly from Antonio's restaurant.

Mitchell stopped well out of earshot of the group, braking Estelle's progress with a hand on her arm. "You know what's coming?"

She frowned. "Meaning what, Eddie?"

He thrust his hands in his pockets and regarded her. "We worked together for what, a dozen years or maybe more, back in the day?"

"Yes."

He nodded. "In all that time, I never knew you to do something without a purpose. Something clearly defined in your head, or something that you were *trying* to clearly define." He nodded again. "That's an interesting trait, Undersheriff."

"Or a curse," Estelle said.

"Yeah, well maybe. But it makes you a hell of a detective, flattery intended. So let me ask you flat out before they do." He had been standing with his back to Kesserman and Beaumont, and now turned to look their way. He lowered his voice. "Tell me what you know about Stan Wilke, Estelle." He regarded her evenly. "From way back when."

She didn't answer right away. Mitchell said, "Because with a little prodding, *I* could pretend that I remember him." He almost smiled. "I remember the incident, though."

Estelle felt an odd surge or relief that the memory that had nagged her had finally surfaced and could be dealt with. The photo in the bike shop had started the process, and with enough time since then, the memory had percolated to the surface.

"He gave grand jury testimony in the case against Andy Browers."

"Andy Browers. Not a name you're likely to forget, is it? Even after twenty years or so."

"No."

"When you went into that bike shop, did you know that Stan Wilke was employed there?"

"No."

"But then you saw his photograph."

"Yes. It's one of two or three on the service counter wall. I wasn't sure right away. Something nagged. I took a photo of it to help."

The evening shadows were growing long, but Mitchell showed no signs of impatience. "How long ago was that with him, anyway? Fifteen, twenty years ago when that all went down?"

"Twenty-four."

He smiled at her prompt, exact answer. "So your son Francisco was three...three*ish*...when he was kidnapped by Browers. He and another little boy."

"Cody Cole."

His gaze searched her face. "You *have* been thinking about it. You know, back then, I was just on the periphery of that case, ran a few plates, did some blood work. Was in on the chase at the end. But it was a big deal at the time for Posadas County." He smiled. "I still recall, with considerable pleasure, that moment when Tom Pasquale drove the electric company's truck right through the border fence into Mexico to apprehend Browers." He chuckled. "So much for jurisdiction, eh? And I think everyone agrees—it was Bill Gastner, you, and Neil Costace of the FBI at your cooperating finest. With an assist from the Mexican authorities."

He waited for a moment, their gaze locked. "As I remember it, the scam was to take the two kids down to Mexico and sell them." He made a face. "Interesting scheme. Every parent's dream at one time or another, maybe."

Estelle remained silent, and Mitchell hooked his thumbs behind his gun belt. "So let me see what else I can remember to fill in the gaps." He held up one finger. "Stan Wilke was a close family friend of the Coles—the parents of the other little boy involved. Little Cody. I remember the negotiations to get Wilke to testify at the grand jury. He was able to confirm that the family went on a camping trip, and claimed that their son had wandered off from their campsite. A 'missing child' case turned into a kidnapping. Do I remember the reports correctly?"

She looked over at the shrouded figure strapped to the gurney. "You do. He knew… Stan Wilke knew…that the Coles' report of their son's being just a walk-away from a vacation camp was bogus. He knew from the very beginning. But he didn't come forward to say so until Browers was in custody."

Mitchell nodded slowly. "Fear, maybe." His expression turned questioning. "Was there going to come a time when you were going to trust us with this information? Or were you content just to have us dig it up, sooner or later. 'Cause I have to tell you, we were on the way. Kesserman was already running background checks on all the bike shop employees. He feels the same way that you do, about coincidence. And when he found out that Wilke is actually from New Mexico, way back when, that jarred *my* memory."

Estelle thought about that for a moment, and Mitchell gave her the time. "It's not a question of trust, Eddie," she said finally. "Don't think that for a minute."

"What is it, then?"

"I wasn't absolutely sure about Wilke when you first mentioned his name. I mean, 'Stanley' is common enough, and I've known other Wilkes. And the issue with this particular Stanley was twenty-four years ago. There's been a lot of sand down the arroyo since then. But then I had a good, long look at the photo in the bike shop." She held her hand out indicating height. "I recognized his stature, his roundy-shouldered hunch, his little moon face. I looked at that, and in my mind, tried to age the kid I knew back then with the middle-aged man now." She shrugged.

"Kind of a forgettable kid back then," Mitchell added. "Kind of a schmoo."

"And after the grand jury hearing, he left town. Apparently traded quiet little Posadas for hectic points west, maybe because he had a sister out here already. I saw that photo at the bike shop, with the employees all relaxed and full of holiday cheer, and I recognized him. You had mentioned the name to me, and I wasn't absolutely sure. But then the picture?" She nodded. "He's changed some, of course, like all of us. But then Stringer gave me all the names."

"But you looked at the photo and couldn't bring yourself to say, 'Hey, Eddie. Or hey, Kesserman...I think I *know* this little rat.'"

"And I should have. But I wanted to be sure. I didn't want to send people from your two departments off on some wild goose chase. I mean lots of people look sort of like lots of other people. What I really wanted was the opportunity to talk to Stan Wilke in person, to make sure...to make sure. I never had the chance, Eddie." She fell silent, and Mitchell gave her time. "I have to wonder," she added, "did Wilke put all the pieces together? Did he figure out that Carlos was my son when Carlos and Tasha visited the bike shop?"

"How could he not?" Mitchell scoffed. "You two share a whole library of mannerisms and facial expressions. You're thinking that Wilke was satisfying some kind of wacko old grudge against you by attacking your son?"

"I don't know what I'm thinking at this point, Eddie. Except that twenty-four years ago, we spent a lot of time across the table from each other. Face to face. I was in on all the plea bargaining with Wilke, during all the interviews. He's not going to forget me, any more than I'd forget him."

Chapter Seventeen

Stan Wilke didn't look peaceful, or asleep, or any of those other euphemisms for stone cold dead. There was enough of him left to bring back memories for Estelle, though. He'd been a skinny, scared kid back then—not particularly good-looking, not self-assured, not ready to tough it out with the cops. He caved without hesitation and told them everything he knew.

Estelle remembered having to slow Wilke down during his blurting of what he knew as the facts of the Browers-Cole kidnapping plan. He wanted to tell the cops, both local and the FBI, everything, just as quickly as he could.

That was twenty-four years ago. Nothing of his youth was left for him. He'd buried himself in the world of competitive cycling, sweating out the memories. Kesserman unzipped the body bag and stepped aside, beckoning Estelle. The bullet that had ended Wilke's life had struck him on the left side of the bridge of the nose, likely smashing his glasses, driving through his skull to explode out just over his right ear, leaving an exit wound the size of a quarter. His fists were tightly clenched on his chest as if trying to protect himself from being punched. His right eye was wide open, his left eye half closed and dotted from close range unburned powder granules.

"You want to take a look?" Kesserman offered.

He watched as Estelle knelt beside the body. Wilke was wearing a white T-shirt with the cycle store's logo over-printed on a head-on view of a hard-charging biker, the man's head down, elbows akimbo, teeth bared in a finish-line sprint. Wilke's right shoulder was bloody and gore-soaked, front and back, from the head wound.

Estelle turned to Dr. Pete Carduro, the medical examiner. Carduro had accepted the introduction to Estelle with a dismissive nod. He was a short, pudgy man on the uphill side of sixty, wearing a summer-weight white linen suit…just the thing for dumpster diving. He held his gloved hands in front of him as if he didn't really want to claim ownership of them. He certainly offered nothing other than the nod. No warm handshake, no elbow bump, no little punch with closed fist.

"Were there any other wounds?" Estelle asked.

"Nope." His reply was clipped, but then he added, "Unless something really bizarre shows up in the postmortem."

"Were any fragments of his glasses recovered? The impressions of the eyepiece on either side of his nose would hint that he wore them all the time." She directed the question to Kesserman.

"Nothing," Kesserman said. "I'm assuming they were blown off at the scene of the shooting. I don't think that happened here."

"TOD?"

Kesserman said nothing but nodded toward Carduro.

"I'm guessing, but we're talking a couple of days here. Maybe a little less, maybe a little more," Carduro said.

The dismissive tone prompted Estelle to turn and look hard at him. "It's going to matter, Doctor."

"Matter, schmatter," Carduro snapped. "Of course it's going to matter, my dear." He tilted his head so he could bring the appropriate portion of his glasses to bear on Estelle's name tag. "I'm sure you know as well as I do that the range for rigor varies for all kinds of reasons. Most of that rigor is now gone. It would be nice if some fly buzzed in and set up a nice predictable population of larvae in the body, like we see in the TV shows. But that hasn't happened. Be nice if a witness would tell us that the bullet entered the man's skull at 11:02 a.m. right on the dot. But we don't know that, do we?"

"I'm sure you'll do the best you can."

"Well, I mean, why wouldn't I? For forty years, that's what I've been doing. The best I can." He squinted at Estelle's ID again, as if he hadn't been sure of what he'd read the first time. "And you are with whom?"

"Posadas County Sheriff's Department."

"Never heard of it."

"I don't doubt that."

He sniffed like a little old lady might, and nodded abruptly at Kesserman. "Are we finished here, Sergeant?"

"Thanks, Doctor." Kesserman sounded almost sincere, then turned to Estelle. "So?" According to Eddie Mitchell, Kesserman had found the connection between Wilke and Posadas County. At the moment, it wasn't information he was willing to divulge.

"Layering of the trash in the dumpster will come close to telling us when Wilke took up residence there."

"Yeah, I guess it would." Kesserman didn't sound excited. "The pick-up schedule for this area is Tuesdays and Saturdays. Used to be Fridays, but then they changed it because of some petition by the residents."

"The power of the people." She looked up at the sergeant. "That makes me wonder if the killer was aware of that."

"It's no mystery." He shrugged. "But you have other things to do. I'll get the team working on that. We'll figure this out."

She held up both hands, palm to palm. "We know within minutes, maybe seconds, when my son was hit by that truck, Sergeant. We know exactly when I visited the bike shop on Thursday. We know that Wilke didn't show up for work that day or today. Was that because he'd taken up residence here?"

"Possible. What we do know for sure is that at about five

o'clock this afternoon, Wilke's body was found in this dumpster by one of the employees here."

"So, yes," Estelle continued, speaking as much for Dr. Carduro's benefit as anyone's. "It matters when he was dumped. It matters a whole lot."

Chapter Eighteen

"How about you try talking to her?" Eddie Mitchell said. "She's scared to death and not getting good advice."

Jessie Contreras, the owner of the fruit stand, had that "you're going to have to go through me" look, burly shoulders squared, hands on her hips. Sergeant Thomas Sanchez, who had been tasked with taking a statement from Contreras earlier, hadn't made much progress. Instead, he looked as if he wished his last day of work before retirement was yesterday.

And now, the woman was sure it was well within her rights to block interview attempts with her employees. If anything, Captain Eddie Mitchell's looming presence only fueled her ire.

The frightened girl, Judy Patchett, was sitting in Contreras's orange crate-decorated office, hands between her knees.

"I think you can go home now," Contreras said to the girl. "They've had enough time."

"It's interesting that you wait until you have an audience to say that," Estelle observed.

Contreras glared as she demanded, fists balled pugnaciously, "What did you just say to me?"

"You heard me." Estelle kept her tone low and pleasant. "Now, I can either talk to the young lady here, if you'll excuse us, or we can talk out in the car. Either way. It doesn't matter to me. Judy, it's your choice, no one else's."

"Listen...you cops have been here for two *hours*," Contreras snapped.

"Seems like a lifetime, I know. "

"Oh, you *don't* know."

Estelle leaned against the corner of a desk that looked as if it had seen a lifetime of service outdoors, the oak veneer cracked and curling. The girl looked up at her nervously.

"It's Judy Patchett, am I right?" Estelle asked, and the girl glanced first at Jessie Contreras before nodding. She was an attractive blond, her ponytail reaching down to the small of her back. Ponytails seemed to be the general working fashion in this part of the world, Estelle thought. "Judy, there are some things we need to know, all right?"

"Judy, you go home now," Contreras said.

Estelle laughed gently, turning to meet the woman's glare without flinching, and without borrowing one of the cops' tasers. "Bullying has always worked pretty well for you, hasn't it?"

Contreras turned scarlet, her jowls bouncing. Then she did an astonishing thing. Her eyes welled up, the tears overflowing and tracking down her plump cheeks. Estelle hooked the desk chair out from behind the desk with her foot and pushed it toward the woman. "You'd better sit down before you fall down," she said.

The woman floundered back, her weight making the chair squawk. Estelle noticed that Eddie Mitchell hadn't moved from his spot in the doorway, seemingly content to watch his crime-scene consultant's technique.

"Judy, at the moment, this is the only thing that's important, and you're the only person who knows for sure. I'm led to understand that you discovered the body in the dumpster when you went out this afternoon to dispose of some trash. Is that correct?" The girl nodded, and Estelle saw that Mitchell had thumbed on his mini-recorder. "We'll need a spoken answer, Judy. We record all our interviews."

"Yes, ma'am."

"What time was that?"

"Five oh two."

Jessie Contreras dabbed at her flooded eyes with a tissue from the dispenser on the desk, but other than a snuffle, remained silent.

"Five oh two. That's very exact, Judy."

"Yes, ma'am. I looked at the clock."

"*Well, duh,*" Estelle almost said, but instead settled for, "The trash run is part of your afternoon routine."

"I...I go home at seven," Judy said. "I was running a little late, with lots still to do. On the way out the door with the can, I looked at the clock." Her spine stiffened a little and she squared her shoulders, releasing her hands from the knee-lock that had held them. "That's how I know."

"Tell me what happened."

"I walked out with the can and opened the dumpster lid. Its sides are tall enough that normally I wouldn't see down inside. But some of the trash wouldn't come out of the can, so I stood on my tiptoes and thumped it, kinda, on the edge. That's when I saw him."

"What did you see when you did that?"

"All I could see was the top of his head, and one foot. From the ankle down, against the back wall of the dumpster. The rest was covered with flattened cardboard boxes and a whole bunch of rotten corn."

"*Mexican* corn," Jessie Contreras interjected, making the adjective sound somehow second-rate. "I think it got wet somehow during shipment."

"Did you put that in the dumpster? The rotten corn?"

The girl nodded.

"When did you do that?"

"Just after ten in the morning."

"You didn't happen to stand on your tiptoes then."

"No, ma'am. I didn't need to. Just three black trash bags full."

Estelle looked back at Mitchell, one eyebrow raised. He nodded, knowing what she was thinking. *When I visited the bike shop, it's possible that Wilke was already in the dumpster.*

"Did you know the victim?"

Judy shook her head quickly. "But we get a lot of people every day here. He might have come in before, and I wouldn't know."

"Have you ever had occasion to visit Crosby's Bike Shop? It's not far from here, over on Cutler."

"No. I don't ride. I see groups ride by here all the time, though. We carry a couple brands of juice that they like. And energy bars, stuff like that."

Estelle held out the photo of the bike shop staff. "Do you recognize any of these people, Judy?"

The girl frowned, peering closely at the photo. "I don't think so. I'm not sure. Maybe him?"

The "maybe him" was Stan Wilke.

Chapter Nineteen

"I'll keep you posted," Eddie Mitchell said, and shortly after that, Estelle settled in the front passenger seat of Officer Scott's squad car. She knew that there was nothing else for her to do at this scene except to execute a thorough staying out of the way. She counted Lieutenant Sid Beaumont, Sergeant Jake Kesserman, and eight other officers from the two departments—five uniformed and three plainclothes—taking the dumpster evidence apart, one molecule at a time.

No matter how skillfully athletic, it would be difficult to hoist a dead body—even one as slight as Wilke's—clean over the rim of the dumpster without leaving something incriminating behind. Corpses were uncooperative and awkward to handle. One-hundred-thirty pounds of dead weight, up and over the tall rim of the dumpster would have been a challenge, no matter what. And not something to be done silently. One person might be able to manage, given sufficient strength. Two people were more likely.

The investigators might recover a strand of clothing fiber, perhaps. A tiny smear of tissue and blood where the sharp edges of the dumpster scraped a wrist or the back of a hand. For the detectives, it would be a long night.

Officer Scott waited patiently for her to say something, and it was several minutes before she realized, as lost in her thoughts as she was, that he was watching her.

"I'm sorry. I'm wasting your time." She offered an apologetic smile as she slipped the holster off her belt and ripped the Velcro fasteners loose from the ballistic vest. After a contortionist's struggle, she pulled it off, folded it neatly, and laid it on the center console, placing the consultant's ID on top. "I've never done this before."

"I don't follow. Never done what? And you may still need that ID, ma'am."

She patted the laminated plastic, content with its place in the return pile. "Leaving a crime scene like this, Officer. Were this back on my home turf, were my son not in a California hospital, I'd work this case all night." She nodded at the squad of police around the trash container. "Just like these officers."

"I'm on until two," Scott said helpfully. "Then we can find you another driver. You can work all night if you want to."

"I don't want to. I mean I do, but I've already been away from the hospital too long. That's where I need to go."

"You got it. Did you sign out?"

"Yes."

"Good deal." He pulled the car into gear and backed away from the police tape.

"I understand you worked with Captain Mitchell in years gone by."

"Yes, indeed. He was with our department."

"Oh, wow." He glanced sideways at Estelle. "He's cool."

Estelle laughed. "Yes. Eddie Mitchell is certainly that."

By the time they reached Temerly, it was as dark as it was ever going to be with the myriad lights—street, parking lot, entryway, and vehicle headlights—diluting the night. Out of habit, as she got out of the car she looked up into the night sky and saw illuminated haze from horizon to horizon. Traffic on the various neighborhood arterials was a constant, muted roar.

"Officer Scott, thank you for your courtesy, your good

nature, your professionalism." She bent down, one hand holding open the Charger's passenger door. "If you ever tire of sunny California and feel the urge to move east, stop by and see us."

He frowned. "My sister is in school in Las Cruces. How's that for the small world department? That's near you, right?"

"Sort of."

"Yeah. I was going to visit when she graduates next June...a year from now. You never know. I might show up on your doorstep."

"Easy to do, Officer. Take the Posadas exit from Interstate 10. You can't miss us. A good dinner and free lodging."

He offered a broad smile and touched the brim of his cap. "Good night, ma'am. My best wishes for your son's recovery."

"Thank you."

For several minutes after he drove off, Estelle stood under the portico of the main hospital entrance, hands in her pockets, deep in thought. The two rental cars were tucked in their spots side by side, meaning that her husband, son, daughter-in-law, and grandson were all inside, keeping Carlos awake far too long.

She glanced at her watch. If Carlos was asleep, maybe it would be a good time to pay Todd Stringer a visit. His residence shouldn't be hard to find. He would know about Stan Wilke's death—Stan Wilke's murder—by now, and it would be interesting to hear what he had to say.

Estelle drew a deep, shuddering breath and shook her head. "Just stop it," she said aloud, and turned around to activate the hospital entrance's electric eye.

Chapter Twenty

Dr. Francis Guzman's hands were cupped in front of him, as if he were holding an invisible football. Reese Patton's forehead was crinkled in a deep frown, his head slowly nodding in agreement. Patton saw Estelle first, and his face relaxed into a warm smile.

"She's back," he said. "A good time was had by all?"

Estelle slipped an arm around her husband's waist. "Not so much."

"We're discussing the looming PT," Francis said, nuzzling the top of her forehead just below her hairline. As per habit, he didn't ask about the investigation.

"PT so soon?" Estelle groaned. "That's when all the sadists gather, no?"

The nurse laughed gently. "It's never too early, my dear," Patton said. "Were it not for that damaged leg, we would have had him on his feet by now."

"It's never too early to pop stitches," Estelle grimaced.

"No, no. We don't do that. But the real intensive rehab starts when we move the young man out of here. *When* we move him, and that's not just this minute. But it's never too early to plan. We've found him a spot over at Schuyler Orthopedic. He's stable now, or close to it. They'll take him from here."

"I've got names and contacts," Francis added.

"But..." Patton held up a hand. "He's not going anywhere for several days. As I was just discussing with Dr. Guzman, with as many leak issues as the young man is facing, we want to be very sure about each step. *Maybe* out of ICU to one of our other rooms in a couple of days. But, as I'm sure you're aware, it's too easy just to lie there and puddle. We have to make sure that the body's core keeps up, you know what I mean? So even lying here, half-drugged out of his mind in ICU, there are some things that your son can work on. Things that address those core needs."

"A long, long road," Estelle whispered.

Patton nodded. "I won't kid you there, my lady. A *long* road." He consulted his clipboard. "A young woman named Nettie Osmond will be in to talk with Carlos in the morning. She'll be his PT specialist at Schuyler Ortho, and she always makes contact with her patients early on. Very, very good at what she does. She'll talk him through some simple regimens that he can do while he's flat on his back." He waved a hand in the general direction of Carlos's bed. "No popping of stitches, but always keeping a close eye on the monitors. We've got him headed in the right direction now, and we don't want anything to interrupt that."

"I know you're not with physical therapy, Mr. Patton, but you know about these things. What's your best guess for his rehab?"

He nodded vigorously. "You're right. I'm not the one to say. I'm the bedpan person, the drug guy, the monitor... I don't do PT."

"But you know," Estelle pressed.

"Sure. Let me put it this way. If Carlos is discharged from Schuyler Rehab in eight, ten, twelve weeks, he can count himself very lucky. That's followed by a *long* stint of rehab at home, with frequent visits back to Schuyler for progress checks. With that shattered leg, with the ribs, with the internal injuries, look to Christmas to see him on his feet unassisted." Patton grimaced in sympathy. "As you said, a long road. If he beats my pessimistic guess, we'll all be delighted."

"Ay."

"Yes. A year from now, he'll have unpleasant reminders. Aches, pains, ghost twinges."

"I know about those."

He smiled benignly. "Your husband shared some of your history. All very hush, hush, highly confidential. But when I'm dealing with a patient like your son, it helps *me* if I understand his background. So, for the next few days, the important thing is for him to be careful. Not to get impatient. You folks can help with that."

"I know it's late, but I'd like to talk with him for a few minutes."

"I'm sure he's awake. His brother brought him a stack of reading material, along with music for his phone and earbuds. Who knows what he's listening to. Tasha was with him for a while, then she ran out of gas. One of the aides wheeled her back to her room and put her to bed."

"The crush of relatives," Francis quipped.

"But the company is good for both of them." Patton looked at his watch. "I'll give you about ten minutes, Mom. Then he and I have some work to do."

When they were alone, Francis put a hand on Estelle's shoulder and drew her close, his voice a husky whisper.

"The guy from the bike shop? What was his name?"

"Stan Wilke. We knew him years ago in Posadas, *Oso.* He testified against Andy Browers."

"For sure I remember *that* name. And then Wilke split for California," Francis nodded. "That's not a period in our lives I'm likely to forget. Wilke thought he'd be safe out here, I guess."

"Except." He raised an eyebrow as Estelle spoke. "I don't think—I *can't* believe—that whatever troubles he had in Posadas County two decades or more ago have anything to do with his murder out here."

"A bizarre coincidence?"

"That's exactly what I think. He was executed, *Oso.*" She rested a finger on the bridge of her nose. "One shot, right there. Blew his glasses off. Significant powder tattooing indicates the gun was close." She moved her hand and touched behind her right ear. "The bullet exited his skull right there."

"No sign of a struggle?"

"No. And no sign that he was killed at that spot. No blood splatter, no fresh bullet holes in the container. Everything points to his being brought to the dumpster already dead, and tossed in." She pulled a deep breath. "I didn't stay for the whole sorry inventory, but I don't think the cops are going to find anything."

"It's probably likely that his death has nothing to do with the bike accident."

"*Probably* is a tricky word, *Oso*." She bumped his chest with her forehead. "And it was no bike *accident*."

He shook her shoulder gently, and she whispered, "Our ten minutes is ticking."

"Yes, it is."

"Where are Francisco and Angie?"

"Back at the motel. Little guy needs to wind down and get some beauty sleep. We all do."

"Just a few minutes."

"You're going out again tonight?"

"No."

Francis waited a few seconds for her to add a qualifier, and when she didn't, he pulled her into a hug.

Chapter Twenty-One

The patient could have been sound asleep, except he held up a single finger when his parents drew close to his bedside. Then he reached up, his arm still moving slowly as if powered by hydraulics, and removed the earbud.

"Have you listened to Angie's Hawaiian concert yet?" His voice was scarcely a whisper.

"About a hundred times, *hijo,*" Estelle said.

He let the hand holding the earbud relax against the pillow. "I think it's her most amazing work yet. It's going to go gold." He shut his eyes. "Did you enjoy Antonio's?"

"Too much. That was a great suggestion."

"And then bro said you had to go out with the cops."

"For a little bit." She watched as he tried to shift a little, a movement that brought a twitch of his heavy black eyebrows. "Are they able to keep you comfortable?" *What a dumb question,* she thought the instant she uttered it.

Still, her son's whispered response was cheerful, almost triumphant. "For the first time, I successfully managed a bedpan. You know what General Patton said?"

"Here we go," Dr. Guzman chuckled.

"He shouted loud enough for most of the ward to hear, 'Hey, no red stuff!'"

"I suppose that would be good?"

"I guess so."

"Absolutely wonderfully good," Francis added. "Most patients at this stage couldn't even manage to lift a bedpan, let alone dribble into it."

"The bad part is that I hurt everywhere from the top of my head to the tip of my toes. The good part is that I keep falling asleep, so it doesn't matter. And nobody brought me a crab cake." Carlos grinned. "I'm crushed. But that's okay. I'm tough. I can handle the rejection. So..."

He opened both eyes and looked at his mother. "I'm guessing you've been out and about looking for bad guys."

"Sort of."

"And Big Bad Bobby must be getting impatient."

"Ask me if I care, *hijo*."

He closed one eye in an exaggerated, slow wink. "Do you care?"

"Not even a tiny bit. If Bobby gets impatient, he can take it out on the wild hogs that he loves to hunt so much."

"You know..." and he stopped. Estelle could see that he was holding his breath, and then slowly relaxed. "Wow," he whispered. "I think that when they opened me up, they forgot to put some important things back. Or put 'em in backwards or something." He squirmed a little, trying to find a comfortable position.

"So, I can see it in your eyes, Sheriff. What did you want to ask me? And before I forget...there must be some jurisdictional problems with you working with them, no? How's that work?"

"I stay careful. And they keep the leash short."

He nodded slowly. "Glad to hear that."

She moved closer and bent down, nose to nose, then thought better of what she had been poised to say. She kissed the end of his nose instead. "Sleep lots, *hijo*. Listen to the music, trust what Nurse Patton and your doctors tell you." She held right thumb and index finger a quarter inch apart. "Every day will be this much better."

His eyes crinkled with amusement, and he held his own thumb and index finger a good two inches apart. "Especially with that much help from my little friend." His hand moved to touch the morphine drip remote. "But you wanted to ask me something."

"Yes." She watched his face, debating. "The body of Stan Wilke was found in a dumpster behind Jessie's Produce, a fruit and vegetable stand next door to the tractor dealer a ways out east of here. You've ridden that way on occasion, I'm guessing."

"Wilke?"

"Yes. The Wilke who works at Crosby's."

"Dead?" He gave his head a little shake. "Well, of course *dead.* He's not going to be sleeping in a dumpster, is he?" Carlos stretched carefully. "How did that happen?"

"Judy Patchett discovered the body. You've met her?"

"I think maybe I have." He looked as if he was still trying to swim against the currents of his drug. "I guess. That's the big fruit stand place? Brunhilda owns it?"

"Yes. Judy discovered Wilke's body."

"Yuck."

Estelle nodded. "You knew Wilke pretty well?"

Carlos closed his eyes, and his right hand strayed toward the morphine drip. He didn't touch it. "Not pretty well, Ma. Just in terms of his job at the bike shop. I knew who he was, he worked on my fat-tire bike a couple of times, ordered some parts for me. He set up the tandem for us. So I knew him well enough to call him 'Stan.' That's all."

"Did you know that he used to live in Posadas?"

That prompted a deep frown. "How's that possible?"

"*Hijo,* everybody lives somewhere at sometime. It all happened before you were born, but remember the story about Francisco being kidnapped when he was three years old?"

"That was the Mexico thing? The *kid for sale cheap* gig?" He shifted again, screwing his face up into a tight grimace. "This gets old real fast." He reached out and clamped Estelle's hand in his. His grip was insistent. "Not the conversation. Tell me more."

She enveloped his hand in both of hers. "Wilke testified at the grand jury for Browers, the guy who masterminded the whole deal. Wilke made a deal with the DA. After he testified, he fled Posadas and headed for California."

"Ah. And eventually got a job at a bike shop."

"Yes. At least that's where he ended up."

"And then he ended up murdered. It would have to be murder, right? Unless he climbed inside the dumpster and did himself in."

"He was shot once in the head."

"Whoa. That's gross. Somebody came up behind him and popped him."

"No. Someone shot him between the eyes. Close range. Face to face."

"That's cold." He regarded her for a moment. "That tells you a little something about the kind of person you're dealing with, no?" Carlos closed his eyes. "He was such a soft-spoken little guy. It's hard to imagine him caught up in something dark enough that he'd end up murdered. I mean, I could imagine a store robbery or something. Or some wacky love triangle. Some drug deal gone bad, maybe." He suppressed a cough and made a face. "Wow, that hurts."

Estelle sensed another presence behind her and turned to see Sergeant Jake Kesserman whispering to her husband.

"I hear good progress," Kesserman said when they made eye contact.

Carlos squeezed Estelle's hand abruptly, his voice a hoarse whisper. "I don't want you getting caught up in this, Ma. It's not your deal."

"If it's connected to what happened to you, it *is* my deal, *hijo*." She turned to Kesserman, but before she had a chance to do more than nod to the detective, Reese Patton pushed the curtain to one side.

"Way too much traffic," he announced but offered Estelle a smile. "I know there's lots of important stuff going on that maybe can't wait, but"—his gaze shifted to the monitors—"Mr. Carlos and I have nighttime business, so vamoose, you all. Let's let this fellow get some rest." He made sweeping motions as he escorted the three visitors out into the hall.

"Ma?" Carlos raised his voice just enough to be heard, and Estelle stopped and turned back.

"Thirty seconds, Mama," Patton said. "No more."

Carlos beckoned her close, and she bent down, her hand finding his. "You and Papa need to go home now," he whispered. "You don't need to watch over me."

"I know we don't need to, *hijo*. But the seafood is so good here..."

"Yeah, right. Well, go back and take care of Big Bad Bobby and all the rest of your people. I'm just going to be doing a lot of lying around and healing. I don't need an audience for that, much as I love seeing you all."

She patted his hand but remained silent.

"When I'm what do they call it? Ambulatory? When that happens, Tasha and I will come for a nice long visit, okay? Lots of green chile lasagna. That's a promise. Deal?"

He saw her glance toward the others waiting out in the hall and lowered his whisper still further. "Ma, be careful of him." His free hand strayed toward the morphine release, and as if his actions had conjured up the nurse, Patton appeared at the side of the bed. He took Carlos's hand in both of his, blocking access to the dose release.

"Mama, time to hit the road," Patton said.

Chapter Twenty-Two

Tired but unable to sleep, Estelle groaned as Francis worked on her back muscles, one at a time, his deft fingers working through all the old injuries and insults. After spending half an hour limbering her husband's back, she'd readily consented to turnabout being fair play. Dr. Guzman gave special attention to her right side, starting high under her armpit, following the heavy scar down and around.

"Is this ever still tender?"

Her voice was muffled in the pillow. "No. Just when I have to lift a truck off somebody."

He laughed. "It's fortunate that our son inherited his mother's rapid healing genes. I like what I see with him. His numbers are all excellent."

Estelle lifted her head out of the pillow, twisting around so she could see his face. "He wants us to go home, *Oso.*" She then collapsed back into the pillow.

"I'm not surprised. All the company cramps his style. And no matter who you are, it's close to embarrassing—maybe even humiliating—to be the target of all the scrutiny. Now that we know he's going to be okay, it may be a good call. Best for us all to head home. Let him heal in peace."

"He promised that he and Tasha would visit."

"Of course they will. That's something to look forward to, then. Or you can zip out now and then to check his progress if FaceTime on the tube isn't enough."

"My concern..." She paused to groan as he worked his way up over the top of her right shoulder. "My concern is that we're keeping Francisco and Angie tied up. If we go, they'll likely go too. They'll take your word that it's best, that he's really out of danger. It'll be easier on Carlos, easier on them."

"Yep."

"There's a great crew here. At Temerly, I mean."

"They're the best. If I had the power, I'd beam them all up and over to the clinic in Posadas."

"I was a little puzzled that Carlos warned me about Reese Patton."

"Warned you?"

"Just as we were leaving. Carlos called me back and whispered to be careful of him. Patton had just come into the room and put us on notice. I'm assuming that Carlos was referring to him."

"Patton? The nurses run the place, is all Carlos likely meant. Patton doesn't take grief from anybody, and he's right...too many of us in a room where there generally aren't visitors at all. It's ICU, after all. They've made far more concessions than they normally would."

"Or maybe he meant Kesserman," Estelle said. "Mr. Pick-Up Artist. He was there, too." She turned partially on her side. "It's not that I don't appreciate their concessions for us, *Oso*. I really do."

He massaged without comment for a moment, then said, "There are no absolute guarantees, *querida*. Not with any patient. But the odds for Carlos are good. Better than good. He's strong, he received urgent care just moments after the accident in one of the best trauma centers in the state. The staff are all superb. They truly know what they're doing and exactly when and how to do it. If I didn't think so, I'd have raised hell to get him transferred somewhere else."

She groaned again and shifted to flat on her stomach as he worked his way down, first left, then right latissimus dorsi complexes, staying close to the spine, all the way down to the flare of her hips.

"I need to talk with Todd Stringer," she mumbled, and was rewarded with a vigorous but affectionate slap on the rump.

"The guy who owns the bike shop."

"Correct. I'm sure he's been interviewed up one side and down the other, especially after today. But I want to talk with him again. And the two others. The part-timers. Especially the girl, Emily Gere."

His fingers walked up her spine like a stealthy, strong spider. "Why her?"

"First of all, because she's female. Women notice different things. But really, I need to talk with all three."

He leaned over and pressed his lips against her left shoulder blade and blew a long blast of compressed hot air against her skin. "You think?"

"I do."

"Wasn't there a fourth person in that photo?"

"Yes. Barry Whitaker. Big guy, and interestingly enough, he's the only one of the group, of the store's staff, who doesn't ride bikes morning, noon, and night. I need to talk with him, too."

"Mitchell's minions haven't already done that?"

"I'm sure they have."

"You don't trust what they can find out?"

"It's not a matter of trust, *Oso*." Estelle twisted slightly so she could see his face. "You know how when you talk to a patient, it's better than just reading a written report?"

"Of course."

"This is the same thing. I need to see their faces. Read the expressions. Watch the eyes."

"You still think there's a connection, then."

"I *had* my doubts, but then Wilke was found dead. That's too close. Way too much coincidence."

"All of which means we aren't catching a jet home tomorrow." His hands stroked down her flanks. "We're trusting you with this jurisdiction thing."

She shivered at his touch. "I am being careful. And so are Eddie and his staff. I'm not doing anything by myself that would jeopardize the case. And most of the time, I'm accompanied."

"Most of the time."

"I'm not keeping secrets from Eddie or his staff."

"Most of the time." His hands were a warm delight. "Are you ready to turn over for attention to the flip side?"

"You know what that's apt to lead to," she said.

"*Por dios,* I certainly hope so."

Chapter Twenty-Three

Nature girl, Estelle thought when she saw Emily Gere. Strawberry blond hair pulled back in a messy ponytail, flawless complexion buffed rosy by bike-wind but marred by the puffiness around her eyes. The girl was in a little cubbyhole office, concentrating on the open catalogs in front of her. A wadded tissue was clenched in her right hand.

Like the rest of the shop, the walls of the sales office were papered with colorful posters of bike racers, always photographed in impossibly gorgeous surroundings: riding White Sands in the moonlight, through the garden-countryside of Tuscany, up the blood-stirring mountain challenges of the Swiss Alps or the Dolomites.

"How may I help you?" Emily's voice was a nice alto but tempered by her emotions into not much more than a whisper.

"That poster." Estelle pointed at the print of the riders on a tandem, vaulting the Grand Canyon. "That's amazing. I'd like to see the follow-up photo of them landing safely on the other side."

"Yeah, well." Emily managed a faint smile.

"Tasha put that together for you, no?"

The girl's eyes clicked from poster to Estelle, and a gradual dawning touched her face. She leaned back from the catalogs, both hands flat on her desk.

"You're Carlos's mother. You were in the other day. Yesterday, I mean."

"Yes."

"The resemblance is pretty obvious. He's talked a lot about you."

"Uh oh."

"No…all admiring, all good. Is he doing all right?"

"We'll see. It's a long road."

"You're a police officer."

"Back in New Mexico, yes."

Emily dabbed at her right eye. She said nothing more.

"I'd like to talk with you about Stan Wilke, Emily."

The girl's eyes sprang leaks. "The police have been here," she said.

"Mr. Stringer isn't here today?"

"He usually comes in a little later. Either me or Stan will open." She shrugged helplessly. "I opened today. The police were here two minutes later."

"And did they—"

Emily interrupted her with a hard shake of the head. "I don't think I should discuss this…this *situation* with you, Mrs. Guzman. If you want more information, you can get it from the police."

Estelle looked at the girl for long enough that Emily became more uncomfortable than she already was. She worked hard at avoiding Estelle's gaze.

"I'm serious," she said finally. "I don't think I should talk to you about any of this."

"And why is that, Emily?"

She shook her head hard again, ponytail flailing. "I've told the police everything I know. Everything." She looked up at Estelle, winking back tears. "I'm sorry about your son. I am. I really am. Him and Tasha both. And now Stan…"

A well-worn straight-backed folding chair filled one corner of the office. Estelle moved it out a bit, away from the wall, and sat, uninvited.

"How well did you know Stan Wilke, Emily?"

"I shouldn't talk to you. Look, I'm sorry about all of this, but I shouldn't talk to you."

"Why is that, Emily?" The girl was no pushover, Estelle saw, and she kept her voice soft, as if she hadn't asked that same question earlier. When she saw the muscles around the girl's mouth tense, she asked, "Did you know Stan well?"

Emily shook her head slowly. "We worked here together. He was full-time. I work mostly the end of the week and on weekends."

"Can you think of any reason someone would want to hurt him? Was he having trouble with anyone, do you know?"

The girl looked up, her eyes going wide for just an instant as Todd Stringer appeared, announced by the front-door chimes. He started to turn toward his own office, then changed course and approached Emily's cubicle.

"I don't mean to be impolite or inhospitable, but what is it you want?" He looked hard at Estelle. "The police have already been here and raked us over the coals. Look," and he held out both hands, "we don't *know* what happened. I'll tell you what I told the cops. Stan Wilke was a longtime employee, a valued one. He was a hard worker, honest, punctual, lots of valuable initiative. Customers liked him. I don't know what more we can tell you. If he had something going on the side that I don't know about, well...I don't know about it."

Emily rose from her chair without a word and walked out of the sales office. Estelle watched as the girl crossed the showroom and entered the women's restroom.

"Is Barry Whitaker coming in today?"

"No, probably not. He's a part-timer. He usually works weekends, but Emily was able to come in despite...well, despite the rain of bad news. No races this weekend, so Barry took some time off. He won't be in." He held up a hand. "If we had a race going on in the area, he'd come in to work. Seven days a week, we have someone here, one way or another. Bikers like that.

Always sales and service, any day of the week." He tried a game smile. "And, yes, the police talked with him, too." He huffed an impatient breath. "If you have questions, feel free to talk to them. I don't understand what you think we can tell you."

"I appreciate your time and cooperation, Mr. Stringer. I apologize if I've put you in a difficult or uncomfortable position."

"Oh, no, don't think that. It's just that I honestly don't know what to tell you. Your son—your son and Tasha—are valued customers. We're crushed that all of this has happened." He rested a hand on his chest. "But I don't know how that could be related to this horrible thing that's happened to Stan Wilke." His hand fluttered. "Somehow, somewhere, he ran afoul of someone in a most tragic way. How that could be, I don't know. Stan was a gentle soul. As far as I know, he kept to himself. And as far as I'm concerned, I couldn't have had a better employee. He was loyal, industrious, wonderful with customers, a real problem-solver with the bikes…a talented mechanic. He'll be sorely missed. Beyond that, I don't intend to speculate."

Estelle reached out and touched the shop owner lightly on the forearm.

"Mr. Stringer, thank you."

"Sure, sure." He ducked his head. "The best of luck to you. And to your son and his girlfriend." He tried for a bright smile and accompanied her toward the door. Emily Gere emerged from the restroom and skirted past them without making eye contact.

The heat outside was a physical blow after the air-conditioned bike shop, and the hazy sky was harsh. She stopped short. The unmarked sedan was parked ahead of her rental, and Sergeant. Jake Kesserman was relaxed against the front fender, his boots up on the sidewalk and crossed nonchalantly at the ankles. His position was strategic, Estelle noted. He could have simply pulled in behind her car. Instead, he'd parked in front, a maneuver that required forward and back. A nice informal roadblock.

"Good morning, Sergeant," Estelle said. She let it go at that, but Kesserman offered an explanation without being asked.

"Sheriff, good to see you out and about. Captain Mitchell asked that I keep track of you…just in case."

"Just in case what, Sergeant?" She stopped near his car and looked up at him, amused.

"Oh, in case the hospital needs to reach out. Something like that."

"They have my phone. And my husband's."

"Yeah, well. Look…" He pushed himself away from the car and dusted off his butt. "How about let's find some breakfast somewhere?" He turned and pointed down the street. "A nice little café just a few blocks down that way."

"I've eaten, thanks."

"Just coffee, tea?"

"No, thanks. I'm headed back to the hospital."

"Ah, of course." He smiled. "And by now, you certainly know the way."

"I certainly do." She started to move past him, past the halo of his aftershave, or cologne, or whatever it was.

He laughed gently. "You're a hard woman to talk to, Sheriff."

She stopped and frowned at him. "Did you need to talk to me about something?"

"Listen." He closed his eyes and tipped his head back slightly, as if they were about to listen to the morning's work of a songbird. *You are so transparent,* Estelle thought.

"We know that all this is hard on you folks. It's got to be." He opened his eyes and leaned a little closer. "If there's something we can do to make it all easier, I hope you'll let us know."

"Of course. And don't think your efforts are unappreciated, Sergeant. And as a department supervisor, you need to know that I'm particularly impressed with Officer Scott, the young man who oriented me for the dumpster scene last night. Very professional, very helpful."

A trace of something that might have been disappointment edged into Kesserman's expression and just as quickly vanished. "Good to hear that, Sheriff," he said. He frowned a little. "I'd like to hear what you've found out. You had a chance to talk with Emily Gere?"

"Briefly."

"She's taking all this very hard. That' my impression."

"Yes, she is. I would be surprised if she did not. She worked with Mr. Wilke daily. She must have known him well. She's an impressionable young lady, so it's hard on her. She hasn't built up the armor plate we cops work so hard at. But she made it clear that if she has to discuss the case, it'll be with you folks. Not with me. Not with outsiders. She was adamant about that, and I can understand her concerns."

"The 'armor plate.' I like that." He smiled benignly and nodded. "So, now what?"

She kept her own expression noncommittal. "Now my husband and I will evaluate the situation. If Carlos is well on the road to recovery, and if no complications are expected, then we'll need to head home."

He smiled warmly. "This kind of caught you in the middle of things, I'm sure."

"Yes, for sure it did."

"That's a handy jet your son has."

"Yes, it is. It's amazing what's available for rent these days. But he and his wife have commitments that they've put on hold as well."

"Oh. He *rents.*" Kesserman looked amused. He glanced at his watch. "You're sure that you don't have a few minutes?"

"Thanks, but no. Not unless you have something specific that we need to discuss where a sidewalk conference won't do." She watched his expression roam as he apparently debated with himself.

He lowered his voice and inclined his head toward her. "I think at this point, a little R and R wouldn't hurt you," he said. "Long hours, tough time, you know?"

"*Sin duda,*" she said. "Fortunately, my husband is well attuned to our situation here, and to my needs." He couldn't hide the frown. She added, "But thanks for your concern, Sergeant."

He regarded her soberly, and she let the silence between them hang uninterrupted. Finally he sighed and said, “You’re an amazing woman, Sheriff.”

“Why, thank you, Sergeant. You have a good day. If something specific comes up that I need to know, I’ll most likely be at the hospital.”

She could imagine his gaze locked on her back as she walked to the rental car, and sure enough, as she slid into the seat, she saw that he hadn’t moved. She backed the car up a length, and with a convenient hole in traffic did a curb to curb U-turn.

Chapter Twenty-Four

"I would appreciate something else to think about other than myself." Carlos's eyes were clamped shut, and his right fist rested on his forehead, holding his arm so that the patch of road rash below his elbow didn't touch the bedding.

"Dinsman was here, Mitchell was here, Kesserman was here." He opened one eye and regarded Estelle. "Quite the party. Everybody asks, 'How are you feeling?' The number one stupid question of the day." He raised his head, looking toward the door. "Where's my dad?"

"He's over at the physical therapy place, conferring," Estelle said.

"Oh, *por dios*. I thought he already did that. The torture house. I can't wait."

Tasha appeared at Estelle's side, her wheelchair gliding soundlessly on the polished tile floor.

"He's grumpy today," Tasha said.

"It's hard to be cheerful when every square centimeter of my body itches, *querida*. Every hole they poked in me, every incision, every scab, every drainage tube, you name it. Ache and itch."

"That means you're healing, *hijo*."

"That would be good news."

Estelle rested a hand on her son's uninjured knee and keeping her expression sober, asked, "So—how are you feeling?"

Carlos made a face. "Francisco and crew flew out this morning, didn't they? That means you're stranded here until Monday."

"That's a bad thing?"

He made a tiny motion with his shoulders that might have been a shrug, then lowered his hand to cover hers. "I'm glad you're here. And the other good news is that Tasha's folks are due in way late today." He tried a mock glare at his fiancée. "You have to coach them on how *not* to ask how I'm feeling. They need to focus one hundred percent of their worry on you, doll."

"Fortunately, they've never approved of you, guy, so it won't be hard for them to ignore you and all your complaining."

"And to get your mind off all your complaining," Estelle said, "tell me what you know about the folks at the cycle shop."

"Uh oh. The sheriff just entered the room," Carlos stage-whispered to Tasha. He looked at Estelle, puzzled. "Is that where you were this morning?"

"For a while, yes."

"What do I know? I was sorry to hear about Stan. That's one thing I know. I mean, that really sucks."

"Did you get to know him pretty well?"

"No, not even sorta well. I know he rode bikes a lot. He worked hard for Stringer. He was a talented mechanic. A real tune artist with the welding torch. I know that he lived alone, and I know that he worshiped Emily Gere. Unrequited worship, I think. Sort of like a doting uncle."

"What do you know about her? About Emily?"

Carlos lifted his hand toward his eyes and then rested his fingers lightly on the bandage by his ear. He didn't answer right away, but his gaze was fixed on Estelle, amusement touching his expression.

"Any moment now, I expect to look up and see Big Bad Bobby parting the ICU curtains," he said. "In some ways, you know, Captain Mitchell reminds me of him."

"They worked together on many occasions, *hijo*," Estelle said. "And Emily?"

"Emily. I'm supposed to focus now. Emily, Emily, Emily." He looked down at Tasha, who sat quietly. "Correct me if I'm wrong, Tash, but Emily strikes me as sort of a shy flower. Close to wilting. I know that she and Stan got along okay. On a couple occasions, they rode a tandem together. Sort of trying it out, going for a test spin, making sure everything was copacetic. They're about the same size, so it was a good matchup."

Tasha reached out and ran her fingers along the sheet that covered Carlos's right leg. She patted his shin affectionately. "Stan Wilke may have been like a doting uncle... I think that's accurate." She enunciated the word thoughtfully. "But Emily had a crush on Carlos." Her smile flashed broad and a little bit teasing as she gently rocked his ankle. "No, she really did. Every time we came into that store, she'd make a point of talking with us. And every time she looked at Carlos, it was with that sort of little girl wistful expression."

"Oh, come on."

"No, it's true," Tasha persisted. "Were I the jealous sort, I would have minded." She smiled again, a delightful expression that made Estelle want to fold her into a huge bear hug. "It sort of reminded me of the young women in the front row at his brother's concerts. They'd have been up on stage, drooling over the piano and the artist if given half a chance."

"How do you notice these things?" Carlos protested. "Emily just seemed pleasant and friendly to me."

"Duh," Tasha laughed.

"That makes sense," Estelle said, remembering Emily Gere's reaction when Estelle had visited the bike shop. "Emily is having a tough time right now."

She leaned a hip against the bed, and spoke directly to Tasha. "And Barry Whitaker? How does he fit into all this?"

"The big bear," Tasha said. "Big *smelly* bear."

"Come on. Be nice. Maybe his shower at his apartment doesn't work very well," Carlos remarked.

"Well, maybe," Tasha said.

"Her relationship with him?" Estelle asked.

"Emily and Barry?" Tasha frowned. "There's nothing there. That's my guess, I mean." She shook her head. "I don't think he's her type."

"Plus, I don't think they work together much," Carlos said. "Whitaker works Saturdays and Sundays, when most of the events are. Emily rides, I think. Doesn't she?"

"Most events."

"But you can probably guess that Whitaker doesn't," Carlos said. He managed a smile. "He probably should, but obviously he doesn't."

"Did you ever notice any friction between Whitaker and Wilke?" She did not voice it, but Estelle thought it was not hard to imagine the bear-like Whitaker being able to toss the slight-framed Wilke into the dumpster, alive or dead.

"We didn't hang around there enough to notice anything like that. All the times we were there, everybody seemed content and focused on running a good shop," Carlos said. "Who knows what went on off the time card." He raised his voice a little. "And don't ask!"

That last was directed at Reese Patton, who'd slipped through the curtains.

"I don't have to ask." Patton eyed the array of monitors, then moved forward until he was near the head of the bed. He picked up Carlos's left wrist and held it, still watching the monitor as if comparing the two results. "I don't have to ask," he said again, "because I know *everything* there is to know about you." He turned his head and caught Estelle's eye. He waggled his eyebrows.

"I'm told that this young fellow is being booted out of ICU sometime shortly after noon, way ahead of schedule. He'll be ensconced, I believe, in room R-12. That's just down the hall from this young lady, who is scheduled for release tomorrow." He nodded at Tasha. "A trio of nurses, none of them as gorgeous as me, will attend your every need, Carlos, my man. And then, after a time as yet undetermined, when we're sure nothing is going to come apart, you'll be transferred over to the rehab center, where, if I'm not mistaken, your father is in a tête-à-tête at this very moment. So…"

He turned back to Carlos. "The complication is the ortho work on the leg, my friend. That's going to be a long road. Patience. Perseverance. And hopefully, you have an absolutely mighty insurance plan." He frowned. "I know. We're not supposed to talk about things like that."

"Have at it," Carlos said.

"Yep. Later this morning, we have all the usual uncomfortable prepping and testing to do prior to your move. And then," he waved a hand as if it held a silk hanky, "we whisk you away." He turned and nodded at Estelle. "Questions, Mom?"

"R-12."

"Yes. The day boss down there is Mrs. Shirley Franklin, with some cohorts." He released Carlos's wrist and frowned down at him. "One to ten?"

"About a twelve."

"The ribs?"

"Yes. And about a dozen other places."

Patton smiled in sympathy. "That just means you're healing, my friend. The broken ribs are a pesky thing, especially when they've been danced on by a truck. If we could somehow put you in suspended animation so you didn't have to breathe, that might help, but that only works in the movies. I'll join the long list of folks who have told you—putting up with some pain is a lot better in the long run than getting hooked on all the potions. Trust me on that. Day by day, you'll improve." He took Carlos's left hand in both of his. "I'll be down to visit from time to time. I like to harass Mrs. Franklin."

"Thanks, General."

Patton offered his patient a casual salute. "He's yours for a few minutes, Mom."

Carlos's eyes drifted shut, and for a moment Estelle thought that her son had fallen asleep. She took his right wrist, once again feeling a match to the monitor.

"I'm still here." He opened first one eye and then the other. "You have that cop look, Ma."

"A cop look?"

He grinned wearily. "You look as if you'd really like to say, 'You're under arrest, asshole.'"

"I don't say things like that to suspects, *hijo.* Just 'You're under arrest' is usually sufficient."

"You'd like to say that right now to someone, wouldn't you?"

"Por supuesto, hijo."

"Oh, my God. They're back."

Estelle turned as the air currents changed. Eddie Mitchell appeared at the curtain seam, and behind him, she could see both Dinsman and Kesserman, in company with a uniformed female officer—slight of build to the point of appearing downright small compared with her companions. Only a narrow fringe of blond hair poked out from under her uniform cap. Intense violet eyes set too close together bordered a hawk nose. Thin lips didn't quite do the job of concealing a large mouthful of teeth.

Mitchell beckoned the officer through the curtain. "Estelle, Carlos, Tasha, this is Officer Susan Burke." Before the young officer could speak, Mitchell dove in. "But first things first. The bad news is that we gained nothing from the dumpster site. No prints, no residue, no bullet. The wound was through and through." He held up both hands. "A fat nothing. No one has called in a report of gunshots. No reports of anything suspicious. Whoever did this popped Wilke once, carried him over to the dumpster—from somewhere, we don't know where—and tossed him in." He spread his hands wide. "A time window about this big."

He watched Estelle's face closely, but she said nothing. Instead, she reached out a hand and ushered Mitchell back out through the curtain, gathering the others at the same time with an outstretched arm. Once outside the ICU, and well away from the nurses' station, she lowered her voice to just above a whisper.

"Then the only thing left to us is a microscope focused on Mr. Wilke. Something he did, someone he knew, brought him to this tragedy."

"Could have just been some gangbangers out for a good time," Kesserman observed. "Coulda been a jilted lover." He shrugged his angular shoulders. "Coulda been." He looked skeptically at Estelle. "You're still thinking that Wilke's death and the hit-and-run are related?" His expression morphed into a knowing smile. "The intuition thing?"

"If that's all we have."

"Look," Mitchell said, "Officer Burke here is a transfer over to us from the California Highway Patrol a few months ago. Got tired of chasing speeding tourists on Interstate 5." As he spoke, Susan Burke's expression didn't change, but Estelle felt as if the X-ray gaze of those violet eyes was calculating an inventory of everything she saw.

Estelle extended a hand to the young woman. Burke's grip was firm, cool, and businesslike. "I welcome your thoughts," Estelle said.

"Yes, ma'am." Abrupt, no particular warmth, no particular excitement.

I'm not your drill sergeant, Estelle was tempted to say but let the snapped answer pass without comment.

"Here's the deal," Mitchell continued. "I want Burke to be your chauffeur around our fair city, Estelle. I know you've spent some time out and around by yourself, and now I'm thinking that's not such a good idea." He held up a hand. "I know that Francisco and family have left until what, maybe Monday?"

"Yes. But plans change. They may be back sooner."

"That means you have some time before *you* head for home,

am I right? You're not hopping commercial in the next few minutes?"

"No."

"And I assume you have a list of people you want to interview?"

"Yes."

He grinned. "Okay, I'm on a roll so far. Estelle, Officer Burke is good."

"Looking," Kesserman interjected *soto voce.* Officer Burke's expression never wavered, neither questioning whether the comment was a snide remark aimed at her less-than-fashion-model face or a genuine compliment. Mitchell shot a tired look at the sergeant, then continued. "She's proven to be a keen observer. Now look, I have no objection to giving you all the rope you need. I just think you need somebody with you, somebody you can comfortably share your thoughts with. Am I right?"

"I welcome Officer Burke's company," Estelle said. "We don't want to risk a jurisdictional snarl. There needs to be no question about my presence. It would be more accurate to say that I'm tagging along with her, just as a civilian observer."

"Good. Good." He dug into his pocket and pulled out the lanyard and ID card. "You left this with Officer Scott. I think you need to have it with you."

She accepted the ID again.

"Officer Burke has your vest as well."

"Oh, joy."

Mitchell's chuckle was brief. "Wear it. You never know. In the meantime, we're going to turn the screws a little bit. How about you and I get together for dinner? We'll compare notes. Say I pick you and Francis up at six. Would that work?"

"Of course. We'll be at the hotel. I need to touch base with Tasha. She's being released this afternoon, and her parents are coming into town. She might appreciate some time alone with them."

"Of course. Otherwise, bring her along if she's up to it," Mitchell said.

Estelle turned to Burke, who was still studying her impassively. "You all set?"

"Yes, ma'am."

"'Estelle' would work just fine."

"Yes, ma'am." A flicker of something that might have been humor touched the young officer's eyes.

"We'll need a debrief on what Emily Gere told you," Sergeant Kesserman said. He held out his right hand for a fist bump, an awkward, trendy contact that Estelle ignored.

"As I told you earlier, she's shaken by Wilke's death," she replied.

"Well, sure. She would be. Nothing else?"

"As I also mentioned before, she was uncomfortable talking with me. I'm not a cop in this neighborhood, and my nosing around upsets her, I think. I'm not sure why."

"Well," Kesserman sighed, "she'll deal with it."

"I'm sure she will." She turned and passed back through the curtain, moving to the head of the bed and covering Carlos's left hand with hers. "I'll see you a little later, *hijo*."

He saw the ID and lanyard that she held in her right hand. He frowned at her. "I wish I could convince you to leave this alone, Ma. Strange town, strange people—you running around a thousand miles out of your jurisdiction. The Briones cops know what they're doing. Let 'em do it."

She patted his hand, staying well downstream of the IV shunt. "I'm just not wired that way, *hijo*." She circled the bed and bent to wrap Tasha in a hug. "ETA for your folks?"

"They're scheduled at SFO for 7:10. If the flight is on time."

"That works. It's going to be so good to see them." She knelt, both hands on Tasha's right forearm. "Francis and I are meeting Captain Mitchell at six for dinner. Would you like to join us?"

Tasha's smile was bright. "Thanks, but no thanks." She glanced at the curtain and lowered her voice even more. "I'm about done with all the cops, Estelle. No offense." She glanced at the curtain again. "The captain is okay, but Kesserman likes to disrobe women with those bedroom eyes of his. I can do without that."

Estelle chuckled. "I'm with you there. Did the nurses say what time you were being released?"

"This afternoon is as specific as they'd get. But I'll just hang here until my parents come."

"I'll be in and out. You have my cell."

Chapter Twenty-Five

Susan Burke wasn't one for light chatter, and that suited Estelle just fine.

Maybe it was because the young cop's accent sounded as if she'd just stepped off the boat from Sicily—or from a barrio childhood in the Bronx. After they had settled in her unmarked car, an older Crown Vic, she managed two words.

"Where to?"

"One oh nine Sutton," Estelle said, checking her notebook to be sure. "Are you familiar with that part of town?"

"Sure." They rode in silence for a while, Burke driving as if she knew where she was going. Finally, she heaved a deep breath and said, "So tell me."

Estelle glanced over at her. "Tell you what, Officer Burke?"

"Like, what you're doing." She pronounced the word as if it were spelled "DOOO-un."

Estelle lifted the corner of her ID , turning it so she could read the words. "Like it says, I'm consulting. At Captain Mitchell's request."

Burke's smile was twisted. "Yeah, right." Another lengthy silence followed—four blocks' worth. Burke was no speed demon but stayed in the left-hand lane anyway, despite impatient looks from motorists who passed them on the right.

"Consults," and the accent was hard on the first syllable, "don't go wanderin' around the city on their own." She looked hard at Estelle. "That's your son in the ICU, right?"

"Yes."

"And your other son—he's some famous something or other."

"Yes."

"They were sayin' that he's in town. You all came in on a private jet?"

"Yes."

"Sweet deal. So." She shifted her position and looked as if she wanted to add some other remark, not necessarily complimentary. But with a little jerky nod, she changed her mind and said, "What's up with Fat Boy?"

"Fat Boy?"

"You're wantin' to talk with Whitaker, right? That address you gave me is his."

"Barry Whitaker. Yes."

"Fair enough. Good luck with that." *Wid dat.* She glanced at the dash clock.

"Why do you say that?" Estelle looked at Susan Burke curiously.

Burke shrugged. "He ain't the sharpest tool in the box, is all." She shrugged again. "Maybe it's a show he puts on with us cops. He don't like me, and I *re-cip-ro-cate*. So we're even."

"What's not to like?"

"You mean about me, or about him?" Burke shot a brief smile, and when her face lit up, she was almost fetching.

"Him."

"He's just a slob, and I don't get that." She shrugged again. "Stinks, for one thing. Ain't no wonder that he don't have a girlfriend." She smirked. "Or even a boyfriend. Don't think he's even got a dog. Maybe a cat would put up with him."

"And you've come to know him how?"

"Captain Mitchell had me touch base with Whitaker when

all this first went down. Actually," and she twisted to glance over her right shoulder before merging into the right lane, "Mitchell asked Kesserman, and Kesserman passed it along to me."

"Because..."

"Who knows? Maybe Sarge had a skirt to chase that was more pressing. He's kinda wound up that way." She shot a glance at Estelle. "You mighta noticed that about him already." She shrugged, apparently her favorite gesture. "Anyway, Whitaker works at the bike shop on weekends, the rest of the time he works nights at Lozano's."

"Which is what?"

"Bar and grill over on San Pablo." She actually laughed, a rich chortle that ended with a couple of chuffs. "Maybe it's the smell of all the spilled beer and crunched up peanuts that covers for him. Who's to know."

"Maybe he's a dependable employee," Estelle offered. "They're rare enough these days."

"Ain't *that* right?" Burke pointed at a street sign. "Sutton. And maybe he's home. Bike shop is closed for the rest of the weekend, so he ain't workin'." The street wound out of sight up the grade, a snake through the thick vegetation. "One oh nine is that duplex." She let the car drift to a stop, tires crunching in the gravel of the shoulder. The duplex was redbrick, purpose-built to be just what it was—dwelling for two families, with identical front doors, identical windows and trim, identical driveways on either side, identical huge-leafed trees that wouldn't have survived for a week in New Mexico's dry climate.

"Whitaker lives in *B*," Burke said. "A Pakistani family lives in *A*, a dad, mom, and seven kids."

The yard showed no signs of seven kids—no trikes, no sandbox, no swing set, no abandoned toys.

"So tell me," Burke said, shoving the gear lever into PARK. "What are we lookin' for? What are *you* lookin' for?" She pointed up a narrow driveway on the *B* side of the complex. "That's Whitaker's Prius."

"I wish I knew," Estelle replied. "Let's start with friction in the workplace. What can Whitaker tell me about the relations between Wilke and Gere, or Wilke and Stringer, or Wilke and himself? Somehow, Officer Burke, Wilke got in trouble with somebody. Maybe it had nothing to do with the workplace. Maybe it was somebody he accidentally ran into at the grocery store, both grabbing for the same bottle of milk. Maybe, maybe."

"I hear ya. So this is just a fishin' trip."

"Yes."

"So let's go fish, then."

The door to apartment *B* was open behind the storm door, and Estelle could hear music from inside, a nasal oboe trilling, trying to sound like Kenny G. The music broke off, followed by an odd little clutter of noises, and then began again, this time tackling a difficult three-octave scale.

"That's something I didn't know before," Burke said. "Lemme." She reached out and rapped hard on the doorframe, ignoring the doorbell button. The oboe fell silent abruptly. In a moment, a bulky figure appeared.

"Yo."

"Mr. Whitaker, remember me?" Burke's tone and expression were fetching.

"Sure. Officer something."

"Good guess. It's Burke."

"Yeah, okay." Whitaker stepped closer to the storm door. Estelle could see that the man was considerably heavier than he had been when the group photo was taken. A massive fellow from head to toe, Barry Whitaker wore cutoff blue jeans whose waistline was buried in blubber, and a Metallica shirt with the sleeves cut off...the grody raw armpit look.

"You want in or what?"

"You got a few minutes to chat?"

"Chat?" He snorted. "That's something that cops do, all right. Chat." He looked Estelle up and down. "And who might you be? Actually, I think I know. I heard you were in town."

"I'm with her."

"This is Estelle Reyes-Guzman, Mr. Whitaker. *Sheriff* Guzman."

He chuckled again. "Yeah, okay. I can see that. So all right." He pushed the storm door open, and Estelle saw that he was not quite barefoot—bright blue flip-flops were crushed nearly flat by his weight.

"The horn sounds pretty good, Barry," Burke said.

"Probably not, but thanks anyway."

Estelle followed Susan Burke inside, struck first by the locker-room aroma and then by the otherwise absolutely immaculate interior of the small apartment. The living room and what she could see of the kitchen appeared to be a page out of an Ikea catalog. The laminate maple living room floor was visible only around the edges of a huge Oriental carpet, where faint lines from the vacuum cleaner were still visible. Neat, almost dainty curtains were drawn back to let in cheerful light.

"My humble abode," Whitaker said. He stepped to the sturdy black music stand, heavy with sheet music, and moved it back out of the way, making sure that the oboe was secure on the musician's chair nearby.

He stepped toward them, and without asking about the obvious invasion of her personal space, reached out and took Estelle's neck lanyard in hand, squinting at the ID.

"That's a new one," he said, and turned the ID over to examine the back side. "You're a long way from home, Sheriff Guzman." His cultured diction, grammar, were a surprise.

"That's for sure."

"So you know everything about what's happened," Whitaker said.

"I know part of it," Estelle replied. "Not quite everything."

He nodded. "I have some killer iced tea. How about a round?"

"Sure."

He waved toward the Ikea sofa and the Ikea chairs near the Ikea dining table.

"Get comfortable."

Estelle took the opportunity to cruise along the eight feet of Ikea bookshelves beside the sofa, well-stocked with framed photos and a wide variety of books that showed an eclectic taste in reading material, from bird-watching to fly-fishing to transcendental meditation, with an extensive mix of computer books thrown in. What appeared to be a new section included a dozen books on nutrition and weight-control.

Susan Burke had followed Whitaker, and stood in the doorway to the kitchen as he fixed the tea...poured from a gallon jug over a full pack of ice right to the rim, no sugar, no lemon. He handed her two tall glasses and fixed one for himself.

"Sun tea is the best," he said. "Plain old Earl Grey, bleached by the sun. Cheers."

Estelle sat in one of the straight-backed chairs at the table, and Burke settled on the two-cushion sofa, close enough to the cushion border that it didn't invite a companion beside her. Whitaker trailed fumes as he passed by them to the recliner—no doubt his favorite spot, facing the fifty-inch television set on the far wall.

"So." He settled back and sipped a little, then ran a finger up through the patterns of moisture on his glass. "What more can I tell you? I didn't work today 'cause Stringer was going to close the shop at noon for the rest of the weekend. Sad times." He nodded at Burke. "Your sergeant has been here a bunch already."

"When was the last time you saw Stan Wilke?" Estelle asked.

His big face crumpled with anguish. "Shit. Like I told her," and he tipped his glass slightly toward Burke, "and like I told all the cops. I was at the shop last weekend, and Stan was working. I didn't work this weekend, although I could have. I mean, until Stringer said he was closing the place. I was on the calendar."

"And why didn't you?"

"I managed to pull a muscle in my back, so I took a couple of days off. It's kinda slow around here at the moment anyway. I was thinking of going in tomorrow, though...give me some quiet catch-up time. No customers."

"You also work at a saloon?"

"Yup. Lozano's Bar and Grill. Four nights a week. Four to two. Best Italian food you can ever hope to find. A little hole-in-the-wall place." He spread his arms wide and looked down at the vast expanse of his belly. "As you can see, I sample the goods too much." He flashed a smile. "But I'm tryin.'"

"You're the chef there?"

"Associate. Lozano...his name's actually Walter, but that doesn't sound very Italiano, you know what I mean. He has a set way he wants things done, and that's what I do. When he's cooking, I play bartender."

Estelle set the iced tea down carefully on the bamboo coaster that protected the end table. "What's it like working at the bike shop?"

Barry Whitaker grunted in amusement. "One little fire after another. A rider's got this problem, or that problem. We make it right." He leaned forward with effort, squaring his shoulders to take some of the weight off his belly. "It's okay working there. It really is. Stan Wilke is *really* good." He grimaced. "Was really good. You know, a bike isn't all that complicated. It's not rocket science. But he just made 'em tick like a Swiss watch."

"Did he ever argue with anybody? Make any enemies?"

"No, not Stan. Mr. Mellow. Sometimes Em...Emily Gere? We'd play little tricks on him, just to try to get a rise out of him. No luck. Em used to flirt with him something awful. I mean, embarrassed the hell out of *me*." He glanced at Estelle. "But no rise out of him. Like good old dad with her." He half-closed his eyes and appeared lost in thought. "Only times I ever saw him flustered were..." He stopped.

"Flustered?"

"Now don't take this the wrong way, Mrs. Guzman." Estelle waited for him to continue. "When your son and his fiancée would come in. You know that old-fashioned word...*smitten*? That was old Stan. He told me once that Tasha was the most 'naturally beautiful' woman he'd ever seen. And living around here, he's seen his share. 'Naturally beautiful.' That's what he called her."

"And she is."

"Well, yeah. But old Stan, he'd just get breathless around her. When he was making all the adjustments to the tandem for them and had the chance to work around her, I thought he was going to faint." He held up a hand suddenly. "But you know, Stan would *never* say anything untoward to anybody, let alone Tasha." He smiled gently. "He was *smitten*. Love from afar."

"What did Emily have to say about that?"

"It's just an observation. I never asked her. But Stan treated Em like a daughter. You know, all protective and stuff. Even a blind man could see that Em had a wild crush on your son. Kind of like an 'Elvis is in the building' kind of thing. Stan thought her crush on your son was funny."

"Funny how?"

Whitaker looked embarrassed. "Well, you know. Em would say funny little things after Carlos and Tasha left the shop…or when they were outside, out of earshot. Like, 'Hey, I'd ride back seat to him any old time.' You know, talking about being on the tandem." He held up his hand again. "But I gotta say, though, nothing I ever saw made me think that your son was leading her on. Just being his polite self was enough to make her swoon." He grinned. "Another old-fashioned word, that. *Swoon*."

"Emily has a boyfriend?"

Whitaker glanced at Susan Burke as if her question had taken him by surprise. "I don't know," he said carefully. "I'm only at the shop two days a week. When it comes right down to it, I really don't know her all that well. I don't ride," and he laughed self-deprecatingly, "so that's not much of a surprise. And you know, I don't think I'm her type, so there's that."

"Ever see her with anybody? Like at lunch? Anyone hanging out at the store lookin' for her attention?" Burke persisted. "I mean, you got her reactions to Carlos down pretty good, so it seems to me you were paying attention. So who else?"

"At the shop, no. Nobody that I noticed. And I don't ever see her in between times." He circled his hands. "Different orbits. I know the cop was trying to hit on her a while ago, but then again, he hits on anyone who's female and good-looking."

"The cop?" Burke's eyebrows rose with interest.

"Your boss. Kesserman."

"He's at the shop often?"

"Sure. Almost every weekend. He's a good customer, you know? His bikes take a beating. He pushes 'em hard. He keeps trying new things all the time. Change the gear clusters, change the seat post. Change the headstock. Have the frame extended. New wheels. Different tires. The list goes on. And don't forget the fancy duds."

"The duds?"

"You know. The Spandex stuff." He grinned self-deprecatingly. "Not my world, as you probably could guess. But some folks? Wear the right jersey, the right shorts, makes you ride that much faster. Em is super at selling that stuff, and it's a hot, high-profit market." He bugged his eyes. "Gotta have it. Gotta have it."

Estelle frowned. "The mechanical work...Kesserman has to go to a bike shop for that? I thought most riders did their own work."

"Oh, not all, by any means. You get to know somebody like Jake Kesserman and you find out there are folks who prefer never to touch a wrench. Anyway," and he paused and sighed, "there was once or twice when I thought Em would fall for him, you know? I mean, he sure pushed hard enough tryin' to stay on her tail. He'd come in, and if Em was there, he'd always try to get her to go out to lunch with him. Or for coffee." He shrugged. "Hey, he's a good-lookin' guy, right? You don't think I wouldn't like to be as skinny as he is?"

"Anorexic, not skinny," Burke quipped.

"Yeah, well, I could use a little anorexia right now. Anyway. Em wasn't interested. I mean she was polite and all. Friendly with him, just like she is with any good customer. But that's as far as it went." He huffed a big breath. "Then along comes another pretty face, and he's off and running for her." He cut himself off, and Estelle watched Whitaker's eyes dance a little as if he couldn't decide what to say. "Tasha," he added, and shook his head in wonder. "I mean, if you're going to *swoon* over somebody, why not?" He admired his half-empty glass. "Not that Kesserman is the swooning type, I don't think."

"More like somebody in perpetual heat," Burke said. "Like a hounddog that always tries to hump your leg." She shot a quick glance at Estelle as if she realized that she'd stepped out of bounds a little, criticizing a fellow officer to a civilian. "So did his behavior ever get a rise out of Carlos?"

Whitaker shook his head. "I mean, I didn't stand around and watch the whole show. I got things to do, you know."

"It never got to a point where Kesserman and Carlos exchanged words? Argued?"

"Oh, hell no. Carlos is too polite for that. And Kesserman as well. And the few times I happened to watch the salesroom when Kesserman was there? He's careful, you know. I think being a successful cop, he can read the signs." He bit his lip and frowned. "I gotta say, and Mrs. Guzman, this is just an observation. Take it for what it's worth. It's Tasha who's got the quick wit combined with a sharp tongue. She's good with the put-down, you know? I think she made it clear to Kesserman—well, to anybody—that her relationship was with Carlos. And only Carlos." He held up his hands parallel and created an image of tunnel vision.

"Kesserman accepted that?"

He shrugged. "What choice does he have?"

"How did she make it clear to him?"

"A shrug, a frown." His face lit up. "Oh, and once? She was kneeling by her bike—this was back before the tandem, she's on one side, Stan is kneeling on the other, and they're talking gear clusters. Exciting stuff."

"To a cyclist, maybe."

"Right. Anyway, Kesserman was there, and he and Carlos were over by the tandems, talking about something. Then Kesserman comes over, bends down, and puts a hand on Tasha's shoulder, like maybe he wants to tell her something. She turns and looks up at him. Her expression was what I'd call *glacial*. She glances down at his hand and says, 'How about a little social distancing?'" Whitaker grinned. "Kesserman took the hint."

"And where were you standing when all this went down?"

"Right at the parts counter. About ten feet away. Kesserman had come in to buy a new set of brake shoes. I had those out for him and was waiting for him to finish the flirting circuit."

"He was going to put those on himself?"

"Oh, yeah, he can do that much if he puts his mind to it."

"Did Stan say anything? What was his reaction?"

"I don't recall him saying anything. I mean, it was nothing. Just a moment."

Estelle took another sip of the bitter tea. "You're at the saloon nights now?"

"All week. Then at the bike shop Saturday and Sunday. Sometimes on Friday if they need me. I'm their welder most of the time, and right now, things are slow."

She stood and fished out a business card. "If you happen to remember anything else of interest, I'd appreciate a call, Barry."

With a grunt, he lunged his weight forward, then pushed himself erect. "Anytime, ladies. Officer Burke, good to see you again."

"Sure enough," Burke said. "You be careful out there."

Outside, the air seemed wonderfully fresh. After they had settled in the car, Burke lowered all four windows. "I feel like taking a bath in a tub of hand sanitizer," she said.

"I've smelled worse," Estelle said. "Sometimes with diabetes, the aroma goes with the territory. And you saw his ankles."

"Oh, gross."

"That just tells me that his heart isn't going to take much more. He's about a hundred and fifty pounds over, so he's got everything going against him. And working long hours in a saloon on top of everything else is going to kill him, sooner rather than later."

Burke pulled the car into gear. "His choice."

"Sure enough."

"What now?"

"You have some time?"

"Sure. Fourteen more years before I hit my twenty."

Estelle smiled. "You ever thought about getting out of the city?"

"Doesn't everybody?"

"I'm not sure about that. Some folks actually like the crush."

Burke didn't comment. "So, where to?"

"I want to talk with Carlos and Tasha. And I want you with me."

Burke shot her an amused look. "Swoon time?"

"If you're so inclined."

Chapter Twenty-Six

The ICU bed was empty and stripped. Estelle felt a momentary surge of anxiety, then turned to see Reese Patton standing just outside the unit, watching her.

"R-12," he said. "Right next door to Tasha—who's going home in a bit, by the way. Her folks aren't here yet. You're her ride?"

"I think so." She held out both arms and pulled Patton into a long hug. "Thank you for everything, Reese. You truly do make a difference."

"Well, thank you. It's my pleasure, I assure you. He'll be in R-12 now for a few days, maybe as much as a week, before he goes to the rehab facility, so I'll have the chance to duck in now and then to harass him."

"Please be sure to do that. He thinks highly of you."

"Me too, Mom." He nodded soberly. "He's going to be mighty sore for a few hours. So it's good that you can give him something else to think about."

"That I can do."

Patton turned to Susan Burke. "Officer, good to see you again. You keep these folks out of trouble, now, hear?"

"We'll work on it." Burke offered a tight smile.

Estelle took her time using the stairwell to descend the

two floors, and the minor effort at exercise felt good. Burke followed without comment. The doorway to the R-wing opened to another world. Rather than the hushed determination of the intensive care ward, this place bustled with patient and staff traffic. She closed the door gently and they both immediately flattened against the wall as two nurses guided an enormous patient down the hall. One massive hand was clamped to the wheeled IV pole, his other maneuvering a crow-footed walker.

Both nurses, one Asian, middle-aged, and plump, the other a wisp of a girl, barely old enough to have graduated from her candy striper's uniform, offered noncommittal smiles, but their patient was in no hurry. He shuffled to a stop and took a deep breath.

"Good day to you, little ladies." His imitation of the Duke was not bad. He offered a smile that had benefited from megabucks' worth of dental attention. The smile turned down into a deep frown and just as quickly morphed back to an expression of surprise and delight. "I know you from the movies, don't I? There's all kinds of famous folks in this place."

"Yourself included, sir. It takes all kinds," Estelle replied graciously. "Who did you play for?"

His broad smile said that her guess had hit the mark. "Two years with the Seahawks, twelve years with the Raiders." He shook his ponderous head. "But that was back in the Stone Age."

If she stood up as straight as she could, she could look directly at the small cleft between his clavicles. "You must have won a ring or two, then."

He beamed. "Got two! And this is my advice for the day, for what it's worth. Don't drive your Lamborghini into no tree."

She grimaced in sympathy. "I wouldn't think that you'd even *fit* in a Lambo in the first place."

"Barely, sweetheart. Barely."

His term of endearment, used so easily for years by former sheriff Bill Gastner, instantly reminded Estelle that she needed to call *Padrino,* her sons' godfather, to update Gastner on California developments.

"Keep up the good work," she said, including both of the nurses. She glanced at the directions plaque on the wall ahead of her, and at the same time Susan Burke pointed a pistol finger to their left.

"That way," she said. They headed toward R-12. It wasn't hard to find. Officer Dinsman stood in the hallway, in company with Dr. Guzman, who seemed relaxed, with one hand on the back of Tasha's wheelchair. The door to R-12 was fully open.

Her husband extended his free arm and clamped it around Estelle's shoulder.

"*Querida,* you missed the big show," he said.

"That may be just as well." Temerly had the process of moving bedridden patients down to a science, and simple enough: the bed was moved with the patient onboard. She had seen the moves with other patients, with the whole contraption soundlessly wheeled down the spacious hallways. "This is Officer Susan Burke, *Oso*. She's my escort for the day."

"Leaving no stone unturned," Francis said, and shook Burke's hand. She nodded a greeting in return, together with a little angle of her head as if the view had...had *smitten* her. "Captain Mitchell was here earlier," the physician added. "He wants to talk with you when you can."

"Any time," Estelle said. "No complications with the move?"

"Easy as can be, although he noticed the little joggle over the elevator threshold coming and going." He shifted and held her at arm's length, his gaze direct and unblinking. "Did you and Officer Burke accomplish the impossible?"

She laughed. "Hardly. An interesting interview with one of the bike shop guys."

"Ah."

"And now Susan and I need a few minutes with Carlos, if he's awake."

"He's awake. He'll be happy to see you." He turned and rested a hand on Tasha's shoulder. "Her parents are in Salt Lake City, we're told."

"Some issue with the plane," Tasha said. "They got diverted."

"That's tiresome. Did they know how long that was going to tie them up?"

"Not yet."

"Ay." She frowned at the girl. "You're doing okay?"

"Just sore, is all." She reached out a hand to Susan Burke. "I'm Tasha."

Burke offered a tight nod when she returned the handshake.

"I need to talk with both you and Carlos," Estelle said. "Together would be better."

Francis nodded. "The rest of us out here?"

"Please." She looked across at Dinsman, who so far had been a completely mute witness to the gathering. "Did Captain Mitchell mention how long he'd be gone?"

"No, ma'am. He did not. I can try to locate him, if you like."

"Not at the moment, thanks."

"I talked at length with Bill, by the way, *querida*." Francis spoke quietly as she was turning to go. "He's fine, but worried."

"Sure." That was unusual, since it wasn't in former sheriff Bill Gastner's nature to be a worrywart.

"He said that if you found time to give him a call, that would be good."

"This evening, I think. Chances are I'll know more by then."

"I filled him in on the medical details. He wanted to know every step." Francis smiled and then shrugged. "So I gave him the grand audio tour and explained it all."

"Thank you for doing that."

He held up a hand. "One last thing. The kids will be flying in tonight. Francisco said that they've managed to rearrange things a little bit to give them some breathing room."

"That's good news."

Francis cocked his head a little and regarded her. "You seem preoccupied."

She relaxed against him. "I suppose I am." She turned the consultant's badge this way and that by twisting the gold chain. "In a lot of ways, it would have been much easier if Eddie had never given me this." She looked up at Francis and smiled. "If he would just say, 'Go sit in the corner. Stay the hell out of our way.'"

Susan Burke scoffed but otherwise said nothing.

"He's taking advantage of your strong suit," Francis said. "And he'd be foolish not to, jurisdictions be damned. As long as you can remain objective."

She head-butted his chest gently. "Thank you, *Oso,* but now you're asking the impossible. I've got this one-track mind that won't leave me alone."

"Just be careful."

"Sin duda." She put both hands on Tasha's chair. "Can you spare a few minutes?"

Tasha mock-frowned. "I think I can fit you into my busy schedule."

"Good. Then let's go talk with Carlos. Officer Burke?" She did not invite Dinsman, but he was already turned with his back to them, talking on the phone.

Chapter Twenty-Seven

"I'm one giant step closer to running out of here." Carlos greeted his mother with what she thought was a pained grin. He watched as she shut the private room's heavy door. "You've been up to something."

She stepped close to the bed on the side away from all the monitors and IV tubing and leg framework. She reached out to rest her left hand on his forehead. At the same time, she confirmed from the monitor's read-out what her hand was feeling. "A couple tenths," she said. "That's not bad." A knuckle rapped sharply on the door, even as it opened.

An elderly woman in nurse whites so bright they almost hurt the eyes sidestepped into the room. "Conference time, is it?" Her tone was pleasant enough, but her startling blue eyes, magnified by a set of spectacles attached to a necklace of tiny beads, took in the room's occupants in a single sweep. She managed a smile. "Officer Burke, you're in on this, too?"

"Yes, ma'am."

"And you," and the woman regarded Estelle with a frown, "you must be Mr. Guzman's mother."

"Yes. You're Shirley Franklin?"

"At least so the name tag claims," the woman replied crisply. "We just moved Mr. Guzman in, and we're in the process of getting him settled. So keep it short. Just out of ICU as he is, there are still some issues." She bent down and stared eye to eye with Tasha.

"How's my girl?"

"Eager to go home, Shirley."

The woman patted Tasha's shoulder with a hand cruelly bent by arthritis. "I bet you are." She straightened. "So...officers." She cocked a finger at Estelle. "I understand you're the high sheriff, or something like that, although a little out of your territory."

"Just a little."

"Well, word gets around. You're a very attractive woman, I must say. I see now where this young man gets it." Before Estelle could respond, the nurse continued, "You know, back in the late sixties, my husband and I stayed overnight in your fair town. Posado?"

"Posadas, yes."

"We were on our way home from visiting our son at Fort Campbell. All I remember about that little town was the awful food at the motel. Now Tasha here tells me that the place is beautiful. Posado County, I mean," she said, still tone-deaf. "As a whole, just beautiful."

"It has its own charm."

"True in a way for most places, I suppose. Susan, I assume you're here in your official capacity?"

"Yes, ma'am."

Shirley Franklin actually smiled, showing flashes of gold. She turned to Estelle, still with one hand on Susan Burke's shoulder. "I was working maternity over at General in Patterson, New Jersey, when this young soul joined the world." She beamed again. "How's *that* for a track record? And how's that for the 'Ain't it a small world?' department. Now here we both are." Suddenly turning serious, she said to Officer Burke, "You and the rest of your crowd—keep it down to a dull roar." She turned back to Estelle. "I met your husband, by the way. I'm impressed, and I'm not impressed easily. Especially by doctors."

"Thank you. I think he's a keeper."

Franklin laughed. "Well, good." She held up both hands. "Does ten minutes suit?"

"I think so."

"We have some things to do with this young man, but I can wait ten. The orthopedist is running late, as usual, so that gives me a little time."

"They have to skewer me onto an updated rotisserie," Carlos said.

"I can't wait to see that," Tasha quipped.

Franklin wagged a finger at her and said, "Ten, and then we all vacate. No shenanigans now."

After the nurse had closed the door behind her, Carlos closed his eyes. "I'm ready for shenanigans, whatever they are."

"*Hijo*, just concentrate on healing. That's your only job at the moment."

He patted his left thigh. "Heal, heal, heal." His face brightened. "Tasha goes home today, and her folks will be here. And after a little bit, I'll have my laptop right here with me. I can get some work done. And they can bring in some fancy FOOD!" He took his mother's hand in a hard grip. "And then you and the good doctor can go home and get on with life. I can imagine that B-Cube is banging his head against the wall with you being stuck out here."

"I somehow doubt that." She looked down at her son, her left hand resting on the top of his head, right hand on his biceps. "We talked at some length to Barry Whitaker today, *hijo*."

"You and Officer Burke?"

"Yes."

"Barry impresses me as someone who sees a lot more than he talks about, if that makes any sense. He's pretty sharp, really."

"I think you're exactly right. He talked some about Emily Gere's crush on you."

"Uh oh."

"Own up to it, cover boy." Tasha sat back in the chair and

stretched her arms wide. A joint somewhere popped. She relaxed back. "I could be jealous if Carlos ever noticed her flirting. But he doesn't. Either that or he's a superb actor."

"That's it. Oscar-worthy performances." Carlos said, "No, look, I know Emily is a sweet girl, and I know that she is always very attentive when we're in the store."

"Very," Tasha said. "And judging by the Visa receipts, it works."

"See? She misses nothing. But Emily? A time or two, I thought she was hooked up with the cop. Kesserman? Or at least that's what *he* seemed to have in mind."

"Oh, yuck," Tasha said. "Sergeant Velcro fingers."

"You've had experiences with Kesserman?" Estelle asked, and noticed that Susan Burke moved a little closer to the bed, as well as shooting a quick glance at the door. She, too, was acutely interested to compare Tasha's version of events with Barry Whitaker's.

Tasha grimaced. "Lately, we've been in the shop a lot," she explained, "especially when we were in the throes of getting the tandem...as well as the other road bike that Carlos is having built. There were several occasions when the sergeant was there as well. Once or twice in civvies, several times while on duty. Now and then even in his Spandex so he can show off his skinny butt. I've also seen him at a concert or two. I don't think he's ever skipped a chance to invite me out to coffee or a drink—once, he invited me to go see the sights up on Grizzly Peak. I passed on that. And once, he invited me to dinner. I told him that I didn't think Carlos would be able to break free from work. I don't think he thought that was funny."

"Whoa," Carlos said. "You never told me about that one!"

"What was your reaction to all this?" Estelle asked, ignoring her son's comment. "I know from experience—the sergeant can be persistent."

"I'll say. I've tried to stay polite. Maybe that's why he never seems to get the message. And then he got on Carlos's wrong side, I think."

"Yeah, well." Carlos let it go at that, but Estelle persisted.

"Tell me about that."

For a moment, Carlos remained silent, but his expressive face told the story. "I don't think I want to go there," he said finally. "Come on, Ma...let it go."

"Carlos, I *can't* let it go. The Briones police *won't* let it go. You both were hurt, you could have been killed. The driver of that truck obviously *meant* for you to be killed or maimed for life. What happened was assault with a deadly weapon. And now another murder stacked on top of that."

"You don't know that the two are related, Ma."

"*Padrino* taught me from day one to be suspicious of coincidence."

"What's the coincidence? I'm missing something here."

"Someone knew your riding habits, *hijo*. Someone knew that you and Tasha were out on that tandem, your first day to enjoy it. You had been at the bike shop, and *they* knew something of your riding habits. That's part of the story. Then somehow, Stan Wilke got crosswise with someone. Did that happen at the bike shop? Is that why Emily Gere is so upset that she can't bear to talk with me?"

"It's all just coincidence, Ma."

"Is it?"

"And besides that, I don't see how you can roll Jake Kesserman into this. Just because he's a lecher of the first order. Just because he can't keep his hands off good-looking women."

"Just because he referred to you as 'the Mexican kid,'" Tasha said.

"Well, I *am* Mexican," Carlos said.

"But he said it in the most derogatory way." Tasha turned to Estelle. "Carlos was out trying a bike, and Kesserman came into the store."

"What day was this?"

"Actually, it was the day we bought the tandem. Stan was making final adjustments on it, and Carlos was trying out some radical road bike that caught his eye. Kesserman came into the shop, and it seemed like just seconds after Carlos rode out. That was the question he shot at Mr. Wilke. 'Hey, is that Mexican kid going to buy that bike?' It sounded as if Kesserman had his eye on the bike, too. That's just a guess on my part."

"But see, I *am* a Mexican kid," Carlos insisted with a laugh. "A Mexican something, anyway. You can't blame him for that."

"Right. And you remember what I said happened after that?" Tasha continued. "He starts in on me. Do I want to do this, do I want to do that. I did my best to ignore him without being outright rude. And then he's got his hand on the small of my back, trying out his best confidential manner, directly into my left ear. And that's when his hand slipped a little too far south, and I *did* get rude. 'You need to keep your hands to yourself,' I told him. And that's when Stan Wilke barked at him as well."

"You didn't tell me that part," Carlos said.

"Yeah, well. Mr. Wilke went back into his workshop, and Kesserman followed him. I guess they argued, but they didn't raise their voices, so I don't know what was said. I did hear Kesserman when he was about to leave. He stopped with his hand on the shop doorjamb, turned back toward Mr. Wilke when Mr. Wilke said something, and Kesserman said, 'And you just mind your own business, little man.'"

"And then he left?"

Tasha nodded. "And then he left. He shot a puckered kiss my way just as he walked out the door."

"I've been the beneficiary of that air-kiss myself," Susan Burke said. "That's as far as it went. Maybe fortunately for me, I'm not in the right category to be the target of his charms."

Carlos held up both hands. "Oh, come on. So he's a creep with women. So are lots of guys—and women, as far as that goes."

"Did Stan Wilke speak with you after that incident?" Estelle asked.

"He apologized after Kesserman left. Something like, 'Please don't take offense,' or something like that. He seemed to think that I'd be more steamed than I was." Tasha smiled ruefully. "But lots of guys, and as Carlos says, lots of girls, seem to think it's cute—maybe irresistible—to say something stupid to me." She shook her head in amusement. "Some guy with a nice tan comes up and holds his forearm against mine, and says something like, 'Hey, look. I'm almost as dark as you!'" She poked her finger toward her mouth and made a retching sound.

"Yeah, but look, none of that means that Kesserman had anything to do with the crash," Carlos said. "Or with Stan's murder. I hate to see you going that way, Ma. I mean, it's pretty clear that Kesserman can be a jerk when it comes to beautiful women. He's one of those guys who walks around in a perpetual rut. But that doesn't mean he tried to take us out with a stolen truck." He shifted painfully in the bed. "Or that he had such a grudge against Stan Wilke that he murdered him and tossed the corpse into a dumpster. I don't see a single link."

"That's what we do." Burke's voice was not much more than a whisper. "If there *is* a link, we'll find it."

"If it's there, you'll find it," Carlos countered.

Burke moved closer to the bed. "I have a question that's been bugging me."

"Oh, boy," Carlos said with considerable resignation. "I'm your captive audience."

She reached out a hand, bringing one index finger perilously close to one of the stainless steel support rods around his left leg, but stopping just short of touching it. "The truck that hit you..." She backed up a step, small hands active to help tell the story. "It came in from your left, from behind you. It sort of paced you for a few seconds?"

"No. It never paced us. At least not that I noticed. Just *wham*."

"At no time was it pacing you, you're saying. There was no time when it was just driving *beside* you before the impact."

"Correct."

"You had no opportunity to look over at the driver."

"Correct. I was paying attention to the bike lane and the shoulder of the highway in front of us." He lifted both arms carefully, as if they were made of glass, and rested both hands on top of his head. "I think I've told a dozen cops that same story."

"It was just a sudden, dark shape coming in from the rear," Tasha added.

"In such a way," Burke continued, "that you never actually saw the driver. Not even a glance."

"That's right. I'm sorry, but that's the way it was." Carlos relaxed his arms down and rested both hands ever so lightly on his chest. "It could have been a white-haired old lady holding a Pomeranian in one arm, for all I know." He started to say something else but was interrupted by a knuckle rap on the door, all the warning they were going to get as Nurse Franklin bustled in. "Like this lady, for instance," Carlos added.

Franklin wrapped a hand loosely around the toes of Carlos's right foot and gave them a little shake. "One to ten?"

Estelle glanced at the large, colorful poster on the door that included a graphic description of each level of pain from zero to ten...a poster that presumed that the patient could both quantify and qualify how they felt on a simple numeric scale. Maybe claiming level four got you one drug. Level five kicked in with something stronger.

"Twenty-two." Carlos smiled helpfully.

"Not possible," Franklin shot back, and moved her hand to his right knee. "Where's it hurt that bad?"

He reached up and tapped his right temple. "In here, Shirley. I'm thinking too much. I need my friend, that morphine button."

"And you're not going to get it," the elderly nurse said. "That went away when you left the ICU. If you behave, maybe a little pill now and then. So save your strength to face the orange JELL-O that's on the lunch menu. How are the bowels?"

Carlos managed a weak laugh. "Not with an audience, thanks."

"Well, let's clear out that audience, then." Franklin swept the group with steely blue eyes. "Out, all."

"Tasha can stay," Carlos said quickly, and Estelle Reyes-Guzman felt an odd little pang of loss.

Chapter Twenty-Eight

"Any tidbits?" Captain Eddie Mitchell was in civilian garb—tan chinos with a soft blue polo shirt and racy trainers.

"A few little puzzle pieces, maybe," Estelle said. Mitchell grimaced.

"Then let's find a quiet corner," he said. "Doc, it was good talking with you."

Francis nodded and returned the handshake. "I'll pass on the quiet corner," he said. "I need to talk with the nurse. And Carlos, too. About three this afternoon, I'm told, they're going to turn Tasha loose. We need to be there for that, and help her through the process. For one thing, she has no transportation. So we'll do that."

Estelle noticed and was in full agreement with the implication of the "we" that her husband made a point of using.

"And Carlos is eager for us to go home," she said.

"I don't doubt that. It's hard to recuperate with Mom and Dad constantly hanging around. Francisco wants us to hook a ride with them when they pass through. Probably tomorrow. Maybe the day after." He turned to Eddie Mitchell. "You're about to lose your consultant. So make good use of her."

"You bet."

"Or not," Francis added as he pulled Estelle into a bear hug.

"I need a few minutes with our consultant," Eddie Mitchell said. "Just a few."

A small visitors' lounge about a block down the hall offered vinyl-covered furniture, a carafe of ice water with plastic glasses, and most surprising, a one-cup drip coffee maker, its rack of individual prepared grounds offering a dozen flavor choices.

Estelle settled in a corner chair and shook her head when Mitchell motioned toward the coffee maker. "No?" he said. "It's my drug of choice. I don't know how you get through your day without it. I bet I can scare up some tea, if you like."

"No, thank you." She watched as Mitchell kept surveillance on the machine as it gurgled its way through a batch. Finally fueled, Mitchell dragged one of the chairs close enough that he could whisper his conversation if need be.

"Some surprises," the captain said. "We have one clear partial print, from the license plate retainer." He mimed pushing in a screw with his thumb. "Push it in, spin the nut on the back. Whoever did it didn't bother with a wrench."

"How much of a partial?" Estelle asked.

"Ordinarily, probably not enough. But our guy has a scarred right thumb. An old injury, but the scar extends across the ball of the thumb. Pretty definite." He paused, watching Estelle's face, as if waiting for the obvious question.

"So no glove."

"No glove. Drop something enough times, and he gets impatient. Take off the glove, make it work. He doesn't take time for more than one retainer."

"Do we have a make on the print yet?"

"We don't." Mitchell lowered his voice. "With that scar, it'd be pretty easy for a matchup, since one way or another, they're all on file. But no hit on this one."

Estelle felt as if she'd been punched, and for an instant was glad that she didn't have a cup of hot coffee in her hand.

Mitchell leaned hard on the table, his weight on his balled

fists. "We need to walk really carefully with this. We've got somebody who's never been printed before. There are all kinds of possibilities." *Never been printed before.* Those four little words ruled out a large share of the world's population, Estelle knew. All cops, most folks who had been arrested, most people who had ever applied for government jobs, and even now, most schoolteachers or day-care workers. And no one who had ever applied for a concealed-carry permit.

The expression on Mitchell's face told her that something else was ready to be thrown into the mix. They both were silent for a moment.

"What are those 'other possibilities'?" she prompted.

Mitchell settled back and opened both hands a foot apart on the table. "From the time the truck came into custody late Wednesday night until we got Ulibarri up here from SFPD? A couple of days. If someone messed with the bolt and left a print, and if that print should be a cop's, it would be on file." He shrugged. "No go."

"One anonymous partial print is what we have." Estelle didn't bother to remind Mitchell about her earlier request to watch Ulibarri work.

"Yep. And you can see any number of ways this could be a false signal. But, there's this: Burke did some checking." Mitchell forced a smile. "What a hoot she is. Anyway, she discovered that one of our POIs didn't show up for work Wednesday night."

"Wednesday *night*?"

"Who's the only one who works evenings at a saloon...until closing time, whenever that might be?"

"Barry Whitaker."

"Correct. Tuesday night, yes. Thursday night, yes. Wednesday, no."

"So what's the answer to our obvious question?"

Mitchell held up his right hand and examined his own thumb. "From here," and he touched the right margin of the knuckle half an inch below the base of his thumbnail, "up and around to the middle of the pad. A nasty scar that's three-quarters of an inch long."

"On Whitaker's thumb?"

"Be nice to know, wouldn't it? Before we start fingerprinting half of the city."

"Of course. We could call him up and ask, 'Hey Barry! How'd you get that incriminating scar on your thumb?'"

Mitchell took the first sip of his coffee and made a face. "We need answers. And we don't want to spook him. I have some concerns, though."

"Such as?"

"You talked to this guy. You sat and had a glass of sun tea with him, Burke reports. He's cool as a cucumber, a little self-deprecating humor, absolutely nothing that shows he's nervous. If it turns out he intentionally attacked two bikers, and on top of that murdered a third person—and then sits calmly and sips his sun tea while two cops interview him? What kind of person are we talkin' about?"

"A psycho."

"And, goddamn all this, we have nothing. The bullet went through and through Wilke's skull, so we don't have that. The configuration of the head wound points to a medium caliber gun, say something like a nine millimeter or forty. Maybe as small as a three-eighty. That's potent enough to do the trick under the right circumstances. But there are enough of those around to pave a goddamn street. And that's it." He ticked off the count on his fingers. "We don't know where the killing took place. Nor when, exactly. We don't know the circumstances." He rapped the table. "All we have is a corpse in a dumpster."

"And one thumbprint."

Mitchell held up both hands in surrender. "So give me some good news. You and Burke spent the morning digging. What did you find?"

"Kesserman and Wilke had a maybe-argument on the day

that Carlos and Tasha were in the store. The day they picked up the tandem."

"A 'maybe argument'? What's that?"

"Some words exchanged, but no big blowup. Tasha tells me that Kesserman was putting the moves on her—unwelcome moves, from her point of view. Carlos was out testing a bike, and Kesserman apparently took the opportunity to whisper some sweet nothings in Tasha's ear. She reports that his hand started at the small of her back and then drifted south. At that point, she snapped at him, and apparently Wilke witnessed the moment and added his two cents. Tasha says that Kesserman told Wilke to mind his own business, referring to him condescendingly as 'little man.'"

"Now, to me," Mitchell said, "that's not much." He held up his hands in surrender. "But let's find a path to take. Whitaker is comfortable with you and Burke. I'm suggesting another visit. We gotta know about the thumb."

"I'm willing to…" She frowned suddenly as she interrupted herself.

"What?"

She gathered the gold chain of her ID and carefully raised it to clear her head. She held it out to Mitchell, but when he reached toward it, she shook her head. "No touch, Eddie. When we were sitting with him, he reached out and pulled this close so he could read it. His big fat thumb was planted on the bottom margin. His *right* thumb."

She continued to hold it, the shiny plastic rotating this way and that as she reached back and pulled an evidence bag from her back pocket. That prompted a burst of delighted laughter from Mitchell.

"My God, you always come prepared, my friend." He reached out and accepted the small bag, unzipping it carefully. He held it wide open and Estelle dropped her ID inside. "You have a list of all the folks who have touched this?"

He was half joking, but Estelle rattled off the names.

"Officer Scott was first...first that I noticed. Who knows before him. You? The chief? But then Officer Burke, and myself. And now Whitaker's is mushed right at the bottom."

He zipped the evidence bag closed. "I'll get back to you ASAP." He stood up abruptly. "I gotta take a rain check for our dinner, my friend. Just too much going down right now." Estelle nodded, and he continued, "And one more thing. *Nothing* on your own until I get back to you, all right? Nothing. No interviews, no scouting around, no nothing. Go be with your family."

Mitchell raised an index finger. "And one last thing. As I'm sure you know, Sheriff, we are so far out on a very shaky limb with all this. I mean, we're out there with a whole gaggle of career-enders breathing down our necks. We think that we can control things, but you know as well as I do that a whole smear of things can go wrong." He held up the evidence bag for emphasis. "As of this instant, you're off duty. Make sure you understand that."

"I do."

"Good. I'm glad that you do. Go enjoy your kids. And trust me. The instant that I know about this—if it's a match with the print on the license plate bolt—I'll let you know." He looked grim. "If it's a match, we'll be talkin' to Mr. Whitaker."

Chapter Twenty-Nine

From day one, during her first visit to the kids' Briones condo a year before, Estelle was astonished at the quiet elegance—and the quiet luxury—of the place. The condo included a two-car garage, now with Tasha's purple Volt squeezed in beside Carlos's black Toyota Tacoma, both vehicles sharing garage space with the fleet of bicycles, along with the cocooned hang glider that Carlos cherished. The neat arrangement even made room for a chunky Mexican-style wardrobe that included all the couple's riding togs.

Estelle stood by the open garage door and felt a pang of separation. They might imagine that Tasha and Carlos would move back to Posadas, but their life was clearly here.

Francis had escorted Tasha to the front door and helped her negotiate the three broad granite steps, but Estelle hung back, fascinated by the neighborhood. Lots of deep shade, lots of concrete and asphalt, the place was also a vast parking lot, with every square inch of space taken up by cars with government plates. Carlos had said the neighborhood was favored by faculty and staff at the university, and the university sticker on the back window of the car parked ahead of the Guzmans' rental bore a faculty designation.

Despite the frenetic city surroundings, surroundings that,

Estelle had confessed to her amused son, gave her the heebie-jeebies, once inside the condo the noise pollution vanished. The place was lovely, with the large collection of spectacular framed photos serving to expand the universe for the two young people.

They had been inside less than five minutes when Estelle's phone chimed.

"You're safe and settled?" Captain Mitchell's tone was abrupt.

"Yes. Everything is fine."

"I've got somebody in the neighborhood keeping an eye on things. I've got an arrival time of eight twenty for the Qarshes' flight at SFO. Francisco tells me that his touchdown at Jackson is a little before that. Everybody's rendezvousing at the condo? Is that the plan?"

"So far, that's the plan." Estelle moved to the large window that fronted the living room and cracked open the lattice of teakwood blinds. Sure enough, a squat black Dodge Charger was parked five spaces down on the opposite side of the street, pretending to be a civilian ride. "Who's watching us? I see the car."

"That would be the ever tactful Officer Scott."

"I don't think the surveillance is necessary," Estelle said. "But whatever you think is best."

"I think it's best," Mitchell said. "Think of the officer's presence as friendly company. Until we know. Look, are you headed back to the hospital tonight?"

"Yes."

"About what time?"

"I would guess about nine. Maybe a little earlier if we can swing it."

"I'll talk to you then. Give me a buzz when you're headed that way."

As she switched off, her husband prodded her gently in the ribs. "Tight leash?"

"*¡Caramba, Oso!* Eddie's leaving nothing to chance." She

looked at the prompt for yet another message and saw Francisco had texted to pinpoint his arrival.

"Is something going to break, you think?"

"I just don't know. Lots of people are working overtime on this."

"So you can relax."

"Oh, sure, *Oso*." She looked up to see Tasha standing in the passageway to the kitchen.

"We have some nice red, some awful white, about twenty different kinds of tea, and coffee is the push of a button away," she announced. "What can I serve?"

"Peace and quiet," Estelle said. "Come sit with us."

"I second that," her husband said enthusiastically. He was about to say something else, but this time, with the alarm turned off, Estelle's phone vibrated impatiently enough that he heard it buzz. He put his hand over her pocket, covering the offending little gadget. "Ignore it."

"I wish I could." She slid it out and glanced at the screen. *"Ay."*

Once again, Captain Eddie Mitchell's voice was terse when she connected. "We got a hit," he said. "Thought you'd want to know." In the background, she heard traffic noises.

"Sure I want to know, Eddie."

"Pretty clear match to Barry Whitaker."

"You're kidding." Her hand strayed up toward her neck, where the *Official Consultant* ID had hung before its trip to the crime lab.

"Nope. Some clear prints. Mine, yours. Officer Scott's, of course, since he handed it to you. Whitaker's partial is clear, right down at the bottom edge, where you said he handled it. A clear match to the print on the license plate retaining bolt."

"You're going to talk to him, then."

"More'n that. We're on the way to bring him in. Talk is fine, but it's going to be done here, on our turf."

"I should come."

"No," Mitchell said, "No, you should not. I don't want you

anywhere near the scene. There may be a simple, innocent explanation. So we'll be careful."

"I'm glad to hear that."

"A simple enough explanation about why his thumbprint is on the retainer for a stolen plate on a vehicle used in a vehicular assault and maybe a homicide." Mitchell's chuckle of amusement was clipped. "Sure enough, we'll be careful. Just a second." He interrupted their conversation to attend to some radio chatter, and Estelle took a deep breath. "Maybe," she said to her husband.

"Okay," Mitchell said. "I'll keep you posted."

"Look, Eddie...I want to be part of the interview."

"Again, nope. This is just covering my jurisdictional ass, Estelle. So not only no, but hell no."

"Is there somewhere I can listen in, then?"

A pause, and then Mitchell said with more than a touch of frustration, "Yeah. We can do that. I'll leave instructions up front. They'll take care of it. You remember how to get to the substation? No wait, that's not going to happen. Hold tight for a few minutes." He went off-line for less than a minute and then returned. "Burke says she'll swing by to pick you up after we collect Whitaker. Shouldn't be long."

"Thanks, Eddie."

"I'm sayin' this as an old friend, Estelle. You can't be part of the arrest. Don't be getting in the way. I don't want anything at all that some smart-ass defense attorney can take to the bank. So don't make me sorry I invited you to the party."

"You know me better than that, Eddie."

He grunted another short chuckle. "Yeah. Right." He laughed again. "I know how you're wired, my friend."

Estelle slid the phone back in her pocket and looked up to see both Tasha and her husband staring at her. "Maybe," she said.

Chapter Thirty

Susan Burke pulled window-to-window with Officer Scott's car. "Just Tasha and Dr. Guzman in the house. Her parents are on the way. We're expecting number one son and his family to go to the hospital."

Scott nodded. "I'll be here until they tell me otherwise."

Burke nodded and accelerated away. "That guy rings my chimes," she muttered, and glanced across at Estelle. "Know what I mean?"

"I understand."

"What I need to do is get me a hot tub. That would be half the battle right there." She glanced at Estelle again, as if expecting to ward off a laugh of derision.

But Estelle kept an absolutely straight face. "Kesserman would want to use it."

Burke yelped as if someone had stepped on her foot. "That sure as hell messes up my dream."

"Sorry."

Burke concentrated on her driving for a moment. "Maybe," she said after several blocks, "I should just walk up to Officer Scott and say, 'Hey, man. Why don't you invite me out to dinner?'" She glanced at Estelle again. "That might work."

"It might."

After another long pause, Burke said, "You know, I really hope nothing comes of this. Barry Whitaker is such a pathetic schmoo, you know? If he did all this, then he's going to prison for life. And that life of his is going to be really short in prison. You know what I mean?"

"I do."

"So sad."

"Yes."

Burke laughed, a rich explosion that brought tears to her eyes. "Sheriff, talking with you is like talking to...who was that guy? The marshall in *High Noon*. Gary Cooper. Yup. Nope." She grinned at Estelle. "You must drive your sheriff batshit."

"You would enjoy meeting Sheriff Torrez, Officer Burke."

"Yup."

"Exactly."

Burke did a tire-squealing turn into the substation's parking lot. "Okay, showtime. Believe it or not, we got one of those intero rooms with the two-way glass? Really uptown, just like in the movies. You're not going to be in on the interview, but you can watch and listen. All right? As long as you're not claustrophobic."

"Works for me."

"Sarge and the captain are going to conduct."

"Susan, the apprehension...there were no significant problems?"

"No. Smooth as...fill in your own hyperbolic metaphor. Whitaker was invited to come down for an interview. That's all he knows. He agreed. That's all *I* know."

The interrogation—the *interview*—room was a spacious closet, with barely enough room for an unpainted, heavy steel table that looked as if it might have been a high school metal shop project. No attempt had been made to disguise or hide the four angle irons that bolted the table to the floor. Two steel chairs were painted a bright yellow, stark contrast to the uniform white walls, ceiling, and floor.

"Homey, huh?" Burke said.

"Nice." In the observation booth, Estelle had just enough room to turn around without bumping into her companion as long as she kept her elbows sucked in. The observation window was small, two feet long and a foot high. A single speaker had been hardwired on the wall, and below that, a black telephone. Its twin was recessed into the wall of the interrogation room, well away from the table.

"The phone will buzz once in there if you pick up here, like maybe if you wanted to remind the detectives about something," Burke said.

When Barry Whitaker entered the room, Estelle felt a strong surge of charged, mixed emotions. If Whitaker was her son's attacker, she was glad that he was now off the street. That emotion twisted around the competing, and equally strong, notion that if Barry Whitaker was somehow completely innocent, that bleak little room was the last place he needed to be.

She watched as Sergeant Jake Kesserman unlocked the handcuffs. "Have a chair, Barry, my man." Kesserman's voice through the speaker was plenty loud, but slightly distorted and nasal. Captain Eddie Mitchell's bulk appeared in the doorway behind them. He closed the door and leaned against it.

"This is a dismal little room." Whitaker smiled when he said that. He sat slumped in the chair, hands clasped on the table in front of him.

"Well, we won't be here long," Kesserman said cheerfully. "Just a couple of things. Can we get you something to drink?" Whitaker shook his head. "Nothing? All right. Look, I apologize about the cuffs, Barry. But that's department policy in something like this. Until we have some more answers."

"Okay."

"You're okay?"

"Yeah." He forced another smile. "A little scared just now."

"Well, sure. That's to be expected." Kesserman moved around the table and settled in the other yellow chair. "You've been given your rights, you agreed to talk with us, and that's just normal procedure, too. You understand all that?"

"Yes, but am I under arrest now? When do I call an attorney if I think I need one?"

"You can call whenever you want, Barry. But let's not jump ahead. I'm hoping you'll see your way clear to cooperate...to talk with us without any of that other rigamarole."

Mitchell, still silent, moved away from the door and leaned against the wall near the phone. He glanced over at the one-way glass panel, making eye contact with where he knew Estelle to be. Whitaker said nothing, but his facial contortions said he was thinking hard.

"So tell us about the truck, Barry." Kesserman sounded like a friendly guy inquiring about his next-door neighbor's newly purchased pickup truck.

"The truck?"

"The 1984 Chevy three-quarter-ton that belongs to Stan Wilke's brother-in-law, Jim Wayne."

"Oh."

"Oh. *That* truck," Kesserman said with a smile, more predatory than pleasant.

"Other than that Stan borrowed it to move some stuff, I don't know anything about it. I helped him move an old fridge, and we used that." He stretched a little. "About killed my back."

"This was when?"

"Sunday afternoon, a week ago."

"That's the only time you saw the vehicle?"

"No. It was parked behind the cycle shop for a few days after that."

"What days were those?"

Barry Whitaker frowned. "I think he...Stan...went and picked it up the past weekend. Mighta been Sunday. Yeah, it was Sunday. Sunday morning. Then we used it Sunday afternoon. Then it was behind the bike shop for the next few days. As long as he had use of it, he was planning to move some other junk."

"How long was it behind the shop?"

"Had to have been late Wednesday night."

Kesserman regarded him steadily, as if reading the files in his mind. "That's when you noticed that it wasn't there anymore?"

"I think so. You know, it's one of those things. Don't think much about it, and that makes it hard to remember."

"Sure enough." Kesserman paused again. "That was the last time you remember seeing it?"

Whitaker frowned and pensively picked a fingernail. "I saw it late Wednesday…actually early Thursday. We're talkin' about two thirty or so."

"Two thirty in the morning?"

"Yes."

"Where was this? Behind the shop still?"

He shook his head slowly, still frowning hard. "I was driving to get some groceries over at Country Foods after work. I had just stopped by the shop to check some stuff."

"You stopped at the bike shop, you mean?" Kesserman folded his arms and settled back. "Now why would you do that, at two thirty in the morning?"

Whitaker sighed. "Something so simple. I left one of my tools on charger and forgot about it until later. I didn't want to leave it untended for days and days. So I stopped by to unplug it."

"Didn't want to burn the place down."

"Well, *that* probably wouldn't happen. But still…"

"So then you go to Country Foods, push your way through all the homeless people camped in the parking lot, grab your bananas or whatever, and then?"

"A cantaloupe. No bananas."

Kesserman looked impatient. "And then?"

"And then I headed home."

"And all this time, the truck was parked behind the bike shop."

"No. That's what I'm saying. I saw it when I was on my way home. It was parked over in one of the visitor permit zones by the admin complex on Berkshire."

"Same truck?" Kesserman glanced over at Mitchell and raised an eyebrow.

"Yes. That's why I stopped."

"Now that's admirably observant, Barry. Explain that."

"It was parked on the oncoming side of the street, so it was facing me. I could see that it was damaged. I mean, the deer guard, or whatever you call those rack things on the front, was all bunched up and smashed into the fender."

"Now, Barry...be straight with me. It's dark, you're tired, the damaged side of the truck is offsides to you. How could you see it so clearly?"

"Ah, well..."

Kesserman let the young man struggle with that.

"I couldn't see it too good, you know? Just the very front scrunchy part. So I stopped."

"Being the Good Samaritan that you are."

"Well, I mean it was Stan's truck. His brother-in-law's, I mean. The chromy wheels and the headache rack. I mean, I've seen it enough times. And I'm thinking, what if he's in it and needs a ride home or something? So I parked, crossed the street, and that's when I saw the weirdo license plate. Like Alaska or something."

"Could have been some other state? Texas? Montana? Wyoming?"

"Maybe. Anyway, I'm all, whaaat? 'Cause I knew it was Stan's truck. I bent down to make sure. The thing was all crooked, hanging on by a single bolt. And I'm thinking, 'Now, *that's* weird.'"

"You examined the plate pretty closely, then."

Whitaker shrugged. "Well...I don't know."

"Did you touch it?"

"Yeah, I guess I did. The light wasn't too good. There's streetlights, but you know how they are."

"And then?"

"Then I walked around and looked at the front. Pretty nasty.

I thought, 'Uh-oh, Stan's crunched into something. His brother-in-law is going to be pissed.' And Stan, he's not big on seat belts, so if he crashed into something, maybe he got hurt."

"You called 9-1-1?"

"Uh, no. I mean, it looked to me like the truck hit something somewhere else and then got parked there. I figured you guys would be on it already."

"How do you figure that?"

"It's pretty simple, Sergeant. If he'd hit something right there on Berkshire, like an urban deer or a dog or something, there'd be glass and stuff. It wouldn't just be all neatly parked and stuff like that. Some neighbor would have reported it."

"So what *did* you do?"

"I went home."

"But you didn't go back to the bike shop after that?"

"No."

"Did you know that Stan Wilke wasn't showing up for work?"

"No."

"Stringer didn't tell you?"

"No. He doesn't discuss other employees with me."

Kesserman flashed a smile. "Communicative bunch you guys are. So tell me this. When you saw that same truck parked at the cycle shop, like anytime between the last Sunday that you worked there and then later, what license plate was on it then?"

"I don't know. I didn't notice."

"When you last saw the truck at the cycle shop, it wasn't damaged?"

"No."

"You're sure. You noticed that, for sure?"

"Yes, I'm sure. I had to walk around the front of it to get in the shop's back door. So it's pretty obvious."

Kesserman stood up abruptly. "Give me a few minutes. You want some coffee or something?"

"No, thanks. Are we finished?"

"In a few, my man. Be patient." He beckoned to Mitchell, and the two of them left the room. Estelle and Burke met them out in the hall.

"What do you think?" Kesserman leaned a shoulder against the wall and addressed his question to anyone who cared to answer. His gaze shifted to Estelle. "You want to give it a try?"

"I have no questions for him. I don't want him to know that I'm here."

Kesserman's eyebrows shot up in surprise. "Really."

"Unless something else turns up to change my mind, there's nothing so far that points to him."

"The print?"

"I buy his story. He was surprised to see the truck, the damage, the odd license plate. He takes a closer look, and touches things." Estelle shrugged. "None of the rest is within his ability."

"But he doesn't take the time to check on the welfare of his friend, to see if Wilke is hurt or needs help?"

"As he said, the truck was parked. The accident didn't happen there. So what's he going to do?"

"Oh? Just go home? He's plenty big. No problem with tossing a small victim into a dumpster."

"I don't think so," Estelle said. "First of all, yes, Barry Whitaker is big. But he's not *healthy* big. He's obese. He's flabby. He's unhealthy *fat*. He's not about to dead lift a hundred and thirty pounds, awkward pounds, up and over into a dumpster. And as far as my son's assault goes, I can't picture Whitaker choosing that particular truck, then being that nimble as a truck driver, able to twist around in the driver's seat to back up for the second strike. Most important, though, he *smells*."

Kesserman almost laughed. "I'll sure as shit agree with that."

"It isn't just because he doesn't bathe, Sergeant. Maybe he showers five times a day. But his system is so screwed up that he stinks. Think about this. He climbs into that truck after figuring out how to start it without a key, which with his girth is quite a stunt in itself. Then he drives around, and then assaults the two riders on the tandem, an assault that includes an awkward charge backward? And then parks the truck over by the college. After all of that, what stays behind in the cab? Barry Whitaker's apartment stinks. Tasha mentioned his aroma in the bike shop. How could he spend time in an enclosed truck cab and leave no trace behind?"

"A big can of air freshener?"

"He'd think to use that, when he doesn't use it anywhere else? Strong body odor permeates. A little spritz isn't going to cover it."

"So, you're saying that you gave the truck the old intuitive sniff test?" Kesserman's grin was skeptical.

"Enough to make me curious, Sergeant. We have no evidence, no prints, no nothing, that points to Barry Whitaker driving that truck. Maybe in it, but not behind the wheel, where he'd leave prints. And I don't think he murdered Stan Wilke somewhere, loaded him up, then lugged the body out of the truck over behind the fruit stand, dead-lifted him five feet or more, and tossed his body into that dumpster. None of that fits the man that we see sitting in there. All of that activity hints at somebody with a coordinated, strong body. Somebody used to exertion. That isn't him. Whitaker's a shmoo."

Mitchell, who had been listening to the exchange without comment, rested his hand on the interrogation doorknob. "Let's hear his story one more time," he suggested.

Chapter Thirty-One

"We could have grilled him a dozen times," Estelle said later that afternoon. "The only ones who are getting hot and bothered are us." Mitchell had shed his jacket and rolled up his sleeves, and he was halfway through chugging a bottle of lemon water.

"Nothing," he muttered.

Even the unflappable, smooth Sergeant Jake Kesserman looked disgusted. His polo shirt stuck to his back and ribs, thanks to the substandard air conditioning in the room. "You think we should cut him loose?"

"About two hours ago." Estelle tried her best to sound pleasant. She glanced through the one-way glass at Barry Whitaker. The big man had sunken into a deep slouch, his hands still clasped in front of him, resting on the smooth surface of the metal table. He'd studied the label on his water bottle for so long that Estelle was sure he could recite it from memory. "Turn him loose with a sincere apology for wasting his day."

"You're such a sweetheart," Kesserman scoffed. He leaned down altogether too close for Estelle's comfort. "He'll get a 'You're free to go' and a nudge toward the unlocked door."

"Whatever your procedure is, Sergeant."

"You betcha."

She met his gaze until a smile cracked his veneer. "When you climbed into the cab of that recovered truck and did your investigation," she said, "and now, in talking to Mr. Whitaker and observing him, did you get any sort of notion that it's a vehicle he would have used with such adept skills?"

"What the hell does that mean? 'Adept skills.'"

"Sergeant, Barry Whitaker drives a Prius with automatic transmission. Tiny. Its doors are pretty wide, but still, it's hard to imagine him fitting inside. I don't see him taking a big old clumsy truck with stick shift as his weapon of choice."

"He could have. He might be an overgrown farm boy."

"Could. Perhaps. But he didn't. I'm as sure of that as I can be." She stood up and stretched to relieve the kinks. "I spent a few minutes in that truck, enough to know that Barry Whitaker hadn't been in it. If he had, his aroma would have lingered." Kesserman's eyes narrowed a little. "*You* sat in that truck, I'm sure," Estelle continued. "Because your cologne fragrance lingers there. It's surprising how tenacious things like that can be."

"So you're suggesting we bring in one of the dogs to do a sniff test?" The sergeant laughed.

"Now might be a little late, but it could be worth a try. I'm sure your department has canine search dogs." She opened her water bottle and took a long drink. "And luminol," she added.

"Luminol what? What are we going to luminol?" Kesserman asked, but Mitchell had already followed Estelle's line of thinking.

"I'd be interested to see what shows in the bed of that pickup truck. If Wilke's body was pitched in there and then transported to the dumpster site, there's going to be residue...could be enough to survive even a quick wash down, if the killer thought to do that. Unless the body was wrapped really carefully from the get-go."

"So all of a sudden," Kesserman said, "you're putting the two incidents together."

"Yes. And not all of a sudden."

"Well, lemme tell ya, that's a stretch, and I'll tell you why.

The MO is as different as night and day. Attack with a truck one day, then use a three eighty to the brain the next? I don't think so." As soon as he said that, Kesserman looked a little uncomfortable. He jammed his hands in his pockets.

"You know better than that, Sergeant," Estelle said. "Whatever tool is handy. Use a hammer to bash in a skull one day, stab 'em with a screwdriver the next. Poisoned tea one day, push them over a cliff the next."

"I go along with that, Sheriff." He shrugged. "MOs don't always fit a nice pattern. We're looking at opportunity here." He stretched his right shoulder, the shoulder joint making a loud pop. "I'm tired and I'm frustrated."

"Join the club."

Kesserman looked across at Susan Burke. "You're not saying much, Burke."

"Nothing to say, Sarge. The luminol is a good idea—and we should have done that early on—as soon as we knew that Wilke was a victim."

"Then we do it now," Mitchell said. "We're not that far behind the curve." He frowned at the expression that had touched Estelle's usually poker face. "What?"

"I need to talk with you, Eddie." She nodded toward the door. "Guys, excuse us for a few minutes."

When they were alone, she drew close to Mitchell so that she could speak in a near whisper. "Eddie, we need to know *exactly* when Jake Kesserman had access to that truck. I need to know when he was in the cab. Another look at that sign-in log."

"What are you after, my friend?"

"The fragrance of cologne lingers, Eddie. How long I suppose depends on all kinds of variables. If he just slipped into the cab during the preliminary search, that's one thing. I'm not sure how much the aroma is going to linger if he was there for just a few seconds. Or even a few minutes. But." She stopped, hesitant to take the next step. Mitchell waited silently.

"But...if Kesserman was in that truck long enough to roam around town, then long enough for the assault on the kids, then maybe an incident with Wilkes where he loaded the body, and then drove to the disposal site, then left the truck in a suburban neighborhood...that's a *lot* of exposure, Eddie. A lot of high emotion, a lot of sweating."

Mitchell's right eyebrow drifted up. "Come on, Estelle. You're going off the deep end here."

"He's one of those guys who slathers on the cologne. I mean, I can smell him across the room."

"Just imagine," Eddie Mitchell mused. She looked at him expectantly. "Just imagine what a talented defense attorney would do with that bit of evidence, Estelle. Your smell test theory." He smiled grimly. "I don't think the department owns a smell-o-meter. If you can give me some suggestions for gathering quantitative evidence that identifies types and levels of smell, I'm all ears."

"I can't. No one can. But what if, Eddie? I can think of one simple motive for Wilke's murder."

"I'd like to hear it."

"What if Wilke was a witness somehow to the assault on Carlos and Tasha?"

"You mean in the truck when it happened?"

"That's possible. Or saw the damaged truck moments later. We think that the truck was stolen from behind the bike shop. Okay, maybe it was. And what if, after the assault, it was returned there? The attacker planned to leave it there, but something happened, and he changed his mind."

"You're suggesting that maybe Wilke showed up. Maybe right there at the bike shop. Saw the damage to his borrowed truck. Is that what you're thinking?"

"And what if, during that time, when Wilke saw the damaged truck, he also saw the driver?"

"There's a problem there. Wilke couldn't have known *what* the truck actually hit. He wouldn't have known about the attack on your son. Unless he followed the truck around town. Or unless he was a passenger in it."

"Yes, that's true. But he would have looked closely at the damage. That's a natural reaction. There are streetlights, and there's a light over the back door where the truck would have been parked. He could see the blood on the fender."

"And thought that it was a deer."

"Maybe. But is the killer going to take that chance? By that time, the response to the crash has already been initiated. Maybe he could even hear the sirens. The killer knows that in just minutes, the hunt will be on for the truck. He needs to distance himself from it, and now from Stan Wilke as well. So what's expedient?"

Mitchell leaned back against the wall and stared hard at the floor as if all the answers lay there. "So, in your scenario, the killer shoots Wilke, maybe wraps him in an old tarp from the back of the truck, and away we go." He shook his head. "And you're thinking that Kesserman is involved somehow. All that based on a whiff of cologne?"

"No. I'm saying that's an avenue to explore. It's another possibility."

"Hell, I wear cologne too. And I've been looking around that truck myself."

"You sat in the cab? You drove it? You sweated in it, with your pulse hammering at top speed? Anyway, I know English Leather when I smell it." She smiled. "It's my husband's favorite."

"Good guess."

"In my husband's case, it's no guess, Eddie." She paused, not sure if she wanted to take the plunge. "We don't know what the murder weapon was. Nothing was recovered. No slug, no casing."

"Okay."

"Your sergeant mentioned a three-eighty."

"A manner of speech," Mitchell said. "It's like saying nine millimeter, meaning anything in that generic range. Every gangbanger uses one. And you're forgetting something, my friend. The *why*. Why would Kesserman go to all this trouble, not to mention *risk*, to attack your son?"

"Ego."

"Oh, come on. You can do better than that."

"I've experienced the come-hither looks firsthand, Eddie. The head-to-toe assessment. The constant invitations. And I've seen the look on his face when he's turned down. Ditto for Tasha's experience with him. The one argument we have reported is when she told your sergeant to keep his hands to himself. 'Mr. Velcro,' she calls him. And after that, when he was apparently chided by Stan Wilke, there was some sort of verbal exchange with Wilke, out of earshot, that ended with Kesserman insulting the man. 'Mind your own business, *little man*.' Or something to that effect."

"Thin, Estelle. You're making a quantum leap from a randy bachelor to a psycho who takes a simple grudge to the next level."

"Yes, it's thin. In a normal world, it's thin. In a normal world, people don't try to kill other people when they refuse the offer of a date. Or for five bucks on the street corner. Or for some passing insult that leads to a bar fight." She looked hard at Mitchell. "Someone's going to have to question Kesserman about that incident with Wilke. Neither Emily Gere nor Tasha could hear anything other than snatches of the conversation."

Mitchell nodded. "We got to tread carefully. There's a long, distinguished career on the line here."

"Absolutely. A long, distinguished career of a man who is most impressed with himself."

Mitchell looked highly skeptical. "We'll see what we come up with after the luminol."

"That's important. Be careful who you assign to do the tests."

Mitchell smiled. "Of course. You want to help?"

"No, actually, I don't. I want to borrow Officer Burke's sharp eyes for a little while."

He looked at her dubiously.

"And Officer Scott, if he's on shift."

Mitchell's eyes narrowed. "What, you're playing matchmaker now?"

"You've noticed the attraction there, then."

"Sure. And what are you doing, taking the opportunity to cherry-pick my squad? Taking the opportunity to plunder my staff? Do I want to know?"

"Better you don't." Estelle gave him a warm smile. "Anyway, I imagine that Posadas County pays about half as much as Briones does. One look at one of our paycheck stubs would send them into shock."

"Costs half as much to live there, too. I have every reason to trust you, right?"

"Absolutely. I just need some sharp, certified eyes."

"Is there some reason then that I'm not invited?"

"*Al contrario,* Eddie...join the party."

"I'll keep an eye on the luminol team. You're going back to the bike shop?"

"Your intuition isn't so bad either, Captain."

"We've been over that place, Estelle. An hour after we found Wilke, we checked it out."

"Yes. And now we'll do it again. Just the three of us." She held up two fingers. "The odds say that the two most probable sites for Wilke's murder are his home or the shop."

"Or any place in between," Mitchell added dubiously. "Your ID is in evidence storage now, remember. So tread extra lightly."

Chapter Thirty-Two

The two marked city police units pulled in close behind Estelle's rental Toyota. The neighborhood around the bike shop was quiet that Sunday morning, with just the usual distant hum of traffic from afar, accented by the nearly constant whistling roar of jet traffic. The bike shop itself wouldn't open until ten a.m., if Todd Stringer had changed his mind and decided to open after all.

Estelle squinted up into the pewter sky. "This light might be just right," she said aloud. When the others joined her in the parking lot beside the cycle shop, she pointed toward the rear of the building. The sweep of the parking lot joined first the graveled alley, bordered in turn by a chain-link fence and the broad side of a commercial building that currently housed HomeSafe Insurance Agency in half of the building, and Gutterman's Windows and Awnings in the other. Both businesses fronted on Lexor Avenue.

"I'm guessing that we want to concentrate back there," she said, nodding toward the back of the bike shop. "We have a couple of possibilities. One is that Stan Wilke was shot that night after he discovered the damaged truck and was confronted by the killer. He sees the truck, sees the blood, maybe surprises the killer—then I can imagine that some sort of confrontation followed, and the shooting took place right there.

"The other possibility is that the killer forced Wilke into the truck, and they took a ride. In either case, Wilke wasn't running away when he was shot." She rested a finger on the bridge of her nose. "They were face to face. Remember that. If the weapon used was a normal automatic, the shell casing was pitched either straight up, or out to the right, or to the right and rearward. If it was a revolver, it keeps its empties." She shrugged helplessly. "We don't know what it was, but the entry hole in Wilke's face is consistent with some mid-range caliber. They're all going to look the same going in."

They started at the back of the shop, using the steel door as a focus point, and worked inch by inch outward, like the concentric circles caused by a pebble tossed into a quiet lagoon.

The search had lasted for less than a minute when Officer Scott announced, "Hot damn...a quarter!"

"It's mine, Orlando," Susan Burke said promptly, emphasizing his first name as if it were something seldom used. "I remember losing it somewhere around here the other day."

"You can ID it?"

"Yeah. Washington's bust on the obverse, Acadia National Park on the reverse."

Scott stood up straight, staring at Burke in feigned astonishment. "My God, what are you, some kind of numiracleist or something?"

"Numismatist," Burke said. "And you found it, you can keep it." She never took her eyes off the rough pavement.

They worked in concentrated silence for the next half hour until Estelle said sharply, "Hey?" Caught in a crack in the asphalt, the shell casing winked. "Who wants to be in court?"

"Orlando does," Burke said. Even her short career had been long enough to teach her that a day in court was usually a day wasted.

"Then, Officer Scott, bring your camera and an evidence bag over here," Estelle instructed. "And a marker flag." She waited without moving until Scott joined her. She neither told him what she had found nor indicated its location. In seconds, he saw the empty casing and crouched.

"I think so," he said, making no move to touch the evidence. Instead, he brushed a hand through the top seed heads of the grass tuft rooted in the crack, which had done a fair job of concealing the casing.

"Sure enough. Good eyes, Officer Scott." She knelt and scrutinized the casing. "Little and pudgy, like a three-eighty. Not big enough to be a nine or a forty."

"Well, *I* didn't find it..."

"Yes, you did. Just now." She smiled at him. "We need establishing photos that show the entire parking lot. Officer Burke can hold the reference flag for you. Then close-ups of the casing in situ. Be sure to take the photo so that the head stamp shows clearly." Scott looked puzzled. "On your belly," Estelle instructed. "Sun behind you. Choose your camera's close-up mode."

"Maybe we should call in the crime lab guys," Burke said.

"Good choice. If we find anything else, we will. For right now, Susan, just secure the evidence flag in the crack near the casing. It stays put until we're sure."

"And then?" Scott asked.

"And then we keep looking. There's a lot of parking lot to cover." She turned and looked toward the back door of the shop. "The pickup truck is about what, eighteen feet long or so? Maybe twenty?" She walked quickly to the back door, turned, and paced off the distance. "So the tailgate is about here, *más o menos*." She swung a hand in an arc, ending toward Scott's position where he crouched by the casing.

"The three-eighty isn't a particularly high-pressure cartridge, so the gun doesn't fling its empty cases yards and yards away... not like a nine or a forty. But three-eighties are a common caliber, and each gun has its own individual characteristics." Again, she paced toward Scott. "We don't know for sure where the truck was parked."

"If it was even parked here," Burke added.

"Absolutely right. But *if* it was, and *if* the killer was standing somewhere along here, the shot would fling the casing out there."

"Here, there, and everywhere," Burke sang in a pleasant contralto.

"Exactly. The only known is the location of that casing. We don't know anything beyond that. We've got a world of *ifs*."

"But two minutes ago, we didn't even know that." Scott grunted as he stretched out to bring the camera down to just a couple of inches behind the casing.

"Correct. We don't know how that little casing spun through the air, or how it bounced when it struck the asphalt, or how it skittered along before getting itself lost in the grass. And all that is *if* it was launched from a fired pistol. The other possibility is the same as Susan's alleged lost quarter—it slipped out of someone's pocket. So we search three-hundred-sixty degrees around it."

"And sure enough, it could have just fallen out of somebody's pocket," Burke said. "It's interesting that we didn't find it when we searched this lot before. I thought we were pretty thorough."

"It's an easy thing to miss. Hidden in the crack, hidden by the grass, out a good ways from the building...it's easy to miss. Sometimes too many people were looking—too much of a crowd. And maybe there was no reason. You find the victim in the dumpster, you search there. You search his home. You give this area a shot. Even the neighborhood where the truck was found." Estelle held up both hands. "It's luck, to a large extent."

"My dad used to say that all the time," Burke said. "'I'd rather be lucky than good.'"

"You can make yourself lucky," Estelle said. "So now let's look at assumptions. Assume that shell casing is the one that propelled the bullet through Wilke's skull. Our problem right now is that we don't *know* that it is. But *if* it is, we now have ourselves an epicenter. If and when it was ejected after firing, that casing spun through the air maybe fifteen, twenty feet, maybe farther, depending on what the load was, what the gun was, and depending on how that gun was held." She held out her right hand, pistol fashion, and rotated it from the usual sights-on-top target stance until it lay sideways, Hollywood "gangsta" style.

"And when the time comes," Burke observed, "it isn't rocket science to match the casing to the gun that fired it."

"Absolutely. *If* that time comes." She accepted the camera from Scott and activated the previewing screen on the back. The photos appeared sharp and clear, and even on the tiny screen, she could read the head stamp clearly. "Outstanding. I also would like to see a shot that is more general, Orlando. Even farther back than the ones you have here. One that shows the general layout of the parking lot, the alley, and the backs of those buildings behind the chain-link fence." She handed the camera back. "Remember that you're going to be explaining the crime scene to a jury. Photos help to make things clear."

Once the site was photographed to her satisfaction, Estelle watched as Burke deftly hooked the casing with the tip of her ballpoint pen and lifted it out of the grass.

"Looks fresh," Burke said.

"And smells..."

Burke held the casing close to her nose, closed her eyes, and inhaled slowly and deeply. "I could imagine something there." She offered the exhibit to Estelle, who instead of taking the pen, reached out and held Burke's wrist, drawing her hand close. After a moment, she shook her head.

"Even if this is the case in question, there's been enough time now..." She left the thought unfinished as Scott opened the labeled evidence bag and held it out. "You've signed it?"

"Yes, ma'am."

"All right. Bear with me for a moment." She scrolled her cell phone, found Captain Mitchell's number, and waited.

"Mitchell."

"Eddie, we're over at the bike shop, and your officers have recovered a spent shell casing, a three-eighty PMC. It appears to be reasonably fresh. Officer Scott has photographically documented the site thoroughly, and the casing has been removed, bagged, and tagged." She paused, giving Mitchell a chance to say something. He didn't.

"My question is, given the circumstances, given the *possible* circumstances, how do you want the chain of custody established?"

"Who found it?"

Estelle hesitated. "I saw it initially, but Officer Scott recognized it as well and ran the photo series with it in situ."

"So we can say that you're out of it."

"Yes. I was present as an observer. I offered suggestions on how to proceed with the photos, but it's clear from the results that neither Scott nor Burke needed assistance or even advice from me."

"All right. Under normal circumstances—look, in this case, tell Scott to hold the bagged casing until I get there. At that point, he'll personally transfer it directly to me. No one else. And I mean that. *No one* else."

"Understood."

"If that's the casing, then the actual site of where the victim fell when he was struck is close by. It has to be. I'm putting in a call for the crime-scene squad to respond ASAP. Take another look, see what they can find."

"Good move."

"Let me talk to Scott."

She beckoned to the rookie. He took the phone, still holding the evidence bag in his other hand. "This is Scott." He frowned, listening intently. "Yes, sir." He nodded, and continued "Yes, sir"-ing each time Mitchell reached a period. "Understood, sir. Thank you." He handed the phone back to Estelle.

She turned to speak with Burke but saw that the young woman had returned to her patrol unit and had opened the trunk. In a few minutes, she returned and handed a second evidence bag to Scott. "Sign this," she said. Scott looked puzzled and read the bag's legend, including the fine print.

"'Sub. Ev.' What's that mean?"

"Substitute Evidence." She grinned, but it wasn't a particularly friendly expression. "If someone orders you to hand over the evidence, a someone who isn't Captain Mitchell, demur. When pressed, turn it over." Tapped the bag. "Turn over this one. The casing is from one of my boxes."

"Demur." He was unable to mimic Burke's New Yorkese, which came close to 'dee-mew-ah.'

Burke's grin faded. "Yes. Because the troops will be arriving here in a few minutes, and I understand what the sheriff is saying—we want to make sure that possible legit evidence goes to the right place. We'd hate to see it go missing." She tapped the evidence bag again. "Just a little insurance, Orlando." She turned to Estelle. "And you're one hundred percent sure with the captain."

"Sin duda."

"Yeah, I know what that means," Burke said with a tight smile.

Chapter Thirty-Three

"A hit with the luminol," Captain Mitchell said the moment he saw Estelle. "They'll have the results, maybe by this evening." He held his index finger and thumb a quarter-inch apart. "In the seam immediately beside the right-hand fender."

"Enough to type?"

"I doubt it. The tech is more optimistic than I am. If he's right, maybe we'll be lucky. A match with Wilke will let us say, 'Okay, Wilke was transported in that truck after he was shot.' That makes sense, but making sense and proving it are two different things." He held up the evidence bag containing the pistol cartridge. "Kind of in the same league as this. Prove that it was fired by a certain gun, no problem...if you happen to have the gun for the comparison. Prove that the projectile from this casing killed Wilke? A lot of problems if you don't have the projectile."

"Little pieces," Estelle said.

"That's right. Not enough for a profile yet. Just pieces."

An intensive, organized effort by the crime-scene techs produced nothing for the next two hours, tiny pieces or otherwise. If the shooting of Stan Wilke had happened in this rough, patched and gravel-littered suburban parking lot, it had happened without leaving a trace—other than the possibility of a single shell casing. No explosion of blood, bone, and brains, no convenient bullet hole punched in the wall of the property next door as the bullet whistled onward, no bits of fabric, no bloody shoe prints. No eager witnesses.

For a time, Estelle rested against the fender of a handy patrol car, watching the crime-scene techs work, watching them find nothing. At one point, she counted more than a dozen officers of various ranks and responsibilities—all of them probably just as frustrated as she was.

Across the lot, she saw Captain Mitchell in earnest conversation with Lieutenant Sid Beaumont, Officer Troy Dinsman, and Officer Susan Burke. Off to her left, beyond the ubiquitous yellow tape, Officer O.S. Scott managed the sign in/sign out clipboard, trying to look as if he were enjoying the duty.

In a moment, Mitchell broke away and plodded toward her, hands thrust in his pockets, expression a scowl.

"This is nuts," he announced. "Talk about wasted resources. In that, I agree with L.T." He looked hard at Estelle. "And, by the way, Jake Kesserman carries a three-fifty-seven Sig. Used to carry a forty. He switched to the Sig about three years ago, Beaumont says."

"I'm thinking we're looking at a dead end, Eddie. I want to be the last to admit that, but here we are. That casing might show a fingerprint, and there's a chance that will trigger a hit in records. And just as easily, it could have fallen out of the pocket of some cyclist who has a concealed carry permit."

"And that's not uncommon," Mitchell agreed. "So we'll process the casing and see what we get. A fat nothing is what I'm predicting, but, hey...I admit to being a pessimist. What's next on your agenda?"

"A visit with my son and his fiancée. Some serious think time. And then Francis and I need to think about heading home. I have a grand jury waiting in the wings."

"That bar fight thing?"

"Yes. Now a manslaughter thing." She looked across at the crime-scene activity. "Kesserman is missing the party."

Mitchell glanced at his watch. "He comes on at four today." He looked sideways at Estelle. "He's still on your shit list?"

"We'll see. Everything is kind of muddy and formless, Eddie. I don't know what to think. No sudden flashes of brilliant intuition."

"Maybe when we wrap all this up, something will peek through. The shell casing, the possible blood in the truck. We'll see. You're headed back to the hospital now?"

"Yes."

"Don't forget to sign out, official consultant."

She smiled at that. "Officially useless, maybe."

He nodded. "You're headed straight to the hospital now?"

Estelle looked at Mitchell curiously. "I suppose. Why?"

"If you're planning to poke around somewhere else, you need to have somebody with you." He reached out and tapped the replacement consultant's card. "I know a little about you, Undersheriff Guzman. Tenacity is a good trait in a cop."

"Thanks, I guess." She nodded. "I just get curious. The one key with all of this is the projectile that killed Stan Wilke."

"Off into the dark of night somewhere."

"And I think about that." She leaned back against the fender, arms folded. "Like how far could it go, which is ridiculous, I know. The variables are almost endless."

"We have ballistics experts, and they say the same thing. The path through Wilke's head was left to right, from the bridge of his nose exiting out behind and above his right ear. Screamin' uphill." He thrust his hand forward in an arcing motion. "Lots of loft to the trajectory, if he was standing upright. Virtually no fragments found in the wound channel, so the slug was most likely of a piece. Deformed, maybe, but of a piece. A three-eighty isn't exactly magnum class."

"Opinion, now, Eddie."

"Okay."

"The dumpster scene. How carefully was the ground in that area, the ground *around* the dumpster, searched?"

"The immediate area, pretty thoroughly. But, see, it's a tough call in a spot like that. The dumpster itself sits in a sea…a big mess…of garbage residue. I mean, think on that. How many square inches can one rotten banana peel contaminate? And that fruit stand has been in business for, well, hell, as long as I've lived around here, and then before that. Years of crap being ground into the gravel of that parking lot."

Estelle nodded slowly.

"And if Wilke was standing right there when he was shot, off the bullet goes into the night. His blood and brains and skull fragments mix with the shit all over the gravel. By the time the killer hoists Wilke's body into the dumpster, his heart has stopped beating, and the blood has stopped flowing. Just a little leakage mixing in the bottom of the dumpster with all the rotten rutabagas and whatever else goes in there."

When she didn't comment, Mitchell added, "The killer picked a damn good place for his business, if that's where Wilke was killed. But then tell me this. He's shot there, what's the shell casing doing *here*?"

"I can't answer that, unless that casing is just a stray. A pocket drop." She shrugged. "And the blood in the truck? If it's blood?"

"I don't know about that yet. The lab said they'd work at warp speed, but on a Sunday, you know what that means."

"Who owns the tractor dealership next door to the fruit stand?"

Mitchell frowned. "I have no idea. But I know who would." He palmed his phone, scrolled through the directory, and tapped a contact. "Tom Sanchez lives out that way," he said to Estelle, and waited until the number connected.

"Sarge? Mitchell. Say, look, who owns the ag tractor dealership next to Contreras's place?" He listened intently, nodded, and asked, "Who's the shop manager now, 'cause I know that the old guy died here not long ago." Evidently Sergeant Sanchez knew that, too, because Mitchell nodded again. "That's it. Talk to you later." He paused as Sanchez said something else. "No, I don't think so. Thanks, Sarge."

Mitchell switched off, and traded notebook for phone. "The owner is Carl Johanson, but he kept the old name, Dixon Tractor. That goes back to the war years, Sanchez says. The new shop manager—well, new since last year—is Charlie Stanton." He jotted numbers after both names. "Let me guess what you want to do next."

"Yes."

Mitchell laughed. "And you want to talk with him now."

"Yes."

He grinned broadly, turned, and found Susan Burke, who at the moment was holding the idiot end of a tape measure stretched from fence to where the shell casing had been found. "Mitchell to Officer Burke," he said into his two-way, and Burke jerked around. He beckoned, and she quickly found someone else to hold the tape. When she jogged over, Mitchell extended a hand and clamped it on her shoulder.

"Keep our consultant out of trouble for a few minutes, all right? She has a couple of people she needs to talk to, and you need to be there."

"Yes, sir." To Estelle, she said, "My ride."

"Sure enough." When they were settled in Burke's patrol unit and clear of the other parked vehicles, she explained, "What I'd like you to do is take the most direct route from here to Contreras's fruit stand, out by Dixon's."

"I can do that." She glanced at Estelle's phone. "Who are we after?"

"I need to talk to the owner of Dixon's next door. We'll see." The phone number for Carl Johanson produced the usual infuriating message: "The number you have reached is not available. Your call has been forwarded to a…" She cut off the cheerful voice. "Or not," Estelle added. She keyed in the shop manager's number, and made contact on the fourth ring.

"Hullo!" the loud, commanding voice shouted.

"Mr. Stanton?"

"That's me. Wish it wasn't, but it is." He chuckled.

"Mr. Stanton, this is Estelle Reyes-Guzman, a consultant with the Briones Police Department. I wonder if I might meet with you for a few minutes?"

"Well, bummer. I was about to enjoy my Sunday football. But okay. If it's Sunday, this must be important to you, am I right?"

"Yes, sir."

"Now, clue me in a little. What are we talking *about*? And what did you say your name was?"

"Estelle Reyes-Guzman. I have a Briones PD officer with me. Officer Burke."

"Oh, okay. Where, when, how...right now?"

"I'd like to meet with you at Dixon's. We're on our way, probably ten minutes out."

"Oh, now wait a sec. This is about the dead guy in the dumpster next door?"

"Yes."

"She's open on Sundays, you know. Mizz Grouchy."

"That's good to know, sir. May we meet right in the front parking lot of the dealership?"

"Sure enough. Let me get some clothes on, comb my teeth, and brush my hair, and I'll be with you. Is this about the complaint I filed a couple days ago? Or maybe it's been a couple of weeks. I lose track."

"I'll check that out, sir. Thank you."

"Well, glad to hear from you guys. Sometimes we don't, you know? So let's talk. And by the way, it's Charlie. Enough of the 'sir' business, okay?"

"Can I expect some little ray of light?" Susan Burke said when Estelle disconnected.

"I'm fumbling in the dark," Estelle offered. "Have you ever felt that way?"

"Most of the time."

"Right now, I'm wondering *what if*. What if Wilke was shot out near the dumpster? What if that three-eighty casing in the cycle shop parking lot is in the same class as the quarter that

Scott found—nothing to do with the shooting? What if the killer forced Wilke to ride out there?"

"They checked that area pretty carefully," Burke said.

"Yes, they did. With all the garbage-soaked gravel around the dumpster, I'm not surprised that they came up empty. But I don't remember anyone going over to the tractor place next door."

"I don't see why they would. I mean, that's a ways away."

"Sure enough."

Burke shot a glance over at her, one eyebrow cocked. "So what are you sayin'?"

"Just groping in the dark."

They rode in silence for a few minutes, and Estelle felt a pang of uneasiness as they turned onto Canyon Road, a fast, macadam two-lane that cut through rumpled farming country, with burgeoning subdivisions here and there. Her son and his fiancée hadn't turned off Tietjen Lane onto Canyon because of the traffic and lack of a bike lane.

Burke slowed a bit as they turned into the wide driveway for Dixon's Tractor and Implement, and then chose the first slot in the flowerbox-lined customer parking area.

She nodded across the driveway at the massive articulated tractor, its double tires easily five feet high or more, the massive machine hitched to an array of plows, and behind that, a rig of discs followed by harrows. "How much do you guess that rig costs?" Burke asked.

"Charlie Stanton would be happy to tell you, and write up the contract for you."

"With my credit, bet not."

She pointed at the Cadillac Escalade that pulled off the highway and headed into the parking lot. "A high roller. Agribusiness pays big bucks."

"A business like this has to *look* prosperous," Estelle said.

"He looks more than prosperous," Susan Burke said. The man who hoisted himself out of the Escalade carried considerable tonnage of his own, but beefy rather than blubbery. His Bermuda shorts revealed the south end of legs like stumps, and when he reached out to pat the hood of the Escalade, the muscles of his shoulders stretched his denim short-sleeved shirt. He slid his aviator-style sunglasses up into his buzz cut, with more gray than the blond it probably used to be.

His smile was salesman warm, and his gaze tracked Estelle as she got out of the car.

"I be Charlie," he announced, and, as if he'd just noticed her for the first time, thrust a hand out to Susan Burke.

"Officer Burke," she said, and nodded at Estelle. "This is Undersheriff Estelle Reyes-Guzman."

His grip was like shaking some piece of substantial farm equipment, his hand heavy and rough. He nodded enthusiastically. "So…you want to take a little walk around to my office, or you want to stand out in the sun?"

"Office would be fine," Burke said.

"Then right this way." He led them forward on the sidewalk that paralleled the showroom, then took a sharp right along the side of the building to three steel doors. While he jiggled a jumble of keys, he looked hard at Estelle. "Undersheriff."

"Yes."

"But not our county. See," and he twisted the key in the substantial deadbolt, "I know Undersheriff Chet Weyland, and you're a long way from bein' him." He grinned and pushed the door open. "Watch your step." They navigated across the polished concrete floor, past a dozen bays all with machinery in various states of repair.

"Home away from home," Charlie said, and held out a hand to a door labeled SHOP MANAGER. The keys were jumbled again, and they entered his office. The walls were papered with brightly colored posters presenting a collection of tractors, motor graders, front-end loaders, skid-steers, and endless varieties of farm equipment—everything polished and clean, no speck of dust to hide the fabulous paint jobs.

"Now then." Charlie gestured toward chairs, and settled himself behind the desk.

"You mentioned on the phone that you had filed a complaint recently," Estelle said. "Was that with the Sheriff's Department or Briones PD?"

Charlie settled back in the office chair. "It was with the very Chet Weyland I mentioned a minute ago. We've been friends for years."

"And the complaint was concerning..."

"Whoa, whoa, whoa." He held up a hand. "First things first. Where are we headed with this? You said that it might have something to do with the business next door?"

"We're trying to look at all possibilities."

"And not to put too fine a point on it, just exactly who are you?" When she told him, he shook his head. "Never heard of your neck of the woods. So what's the deal?"

"We have reason to believe that the corpse found in the dumpster over at the fruit stand might in some way be related to a motor vehicle-bicycle crash last week that injured my son and his fiancée."

Charlie Stanton clasped his hands in front of him and leaned forward a bit.

"That deal over on Canyon Road? Paper said it was a tandem bike got hit by a pickup?"

"Yes."

"And that was your son?"

"Yes."

"Well, hell, I'm sorry."

"Thank you. I need to ask about the complaint you filed with the SO."

"Then let's get right into it." He settled back and folded his hands over his stomach. "Despite a gigantic metroplex practically on all sides of us, we have some kiddos who think they're living out in the sticks. Maybe it's because we're surrounded by hayfields right here. I don't know. They're demo fields, mostly.

A guy wants to see how a machine works, we can just wheel out and demo. But a big field is an attractive nuisance when you're talkin' kids. The reason I called the SO was a recent rash of vandalism. See, we have a three-thousand-gallon diesel fuel tank out back. A very tempting target."

"Someone shot at it?"

"A number of times. Fortunately, with a twenty-two. That tank steel is pretty stout. Little dents, no holes. But..." He raised an index finger. "You can imagine the problems if the kids doing the shooting decided to switch hit to a thirty-ought-six, for instance."

"Did the SO come up with any suspects?"

"Yep. A silver-tongued deputy had some ideas, and he confronted the two most likely candidates. He played with their minds a little bit. Convinced them that he'd found a swatch of twenty-two shell casings, and that he could identify the gun from those. The eleven-year-old spilled the beans."

"Eleven-year-old?"

"Sure enough. His partner in crime was nine."

"What did the parents say?"

"Not happy. Especially when I recommended to CJ that we ought to require a bead-blast and tank repaint out of the deal." He grinned. "That'd cost the little bastards their allowance for a good long time," and then he shook his head in disgust. "CJ wouldn't go that route, though. Soft touch, my boss."

"And that's it?" Susan Burke asked.

"Pretty much. Got a One Twenty that's tied up in an insurance mess." He turned around and touched a color photo of a huge machine, photographed from gopher level to make it appear even larger. "Like this bad boy. Guy bought it, and his barn burned that night, taking the One Twenty with it. Never been used. Had like two hours on the Hobbs. Backed off the trailer during delivery, into the barn, and a little later, *woof*." He mimed a conflagration with his hands.

"Paid for?"

"Sure." He grinned humorlessly.

"Likely arson?"

"What do the news anchors say? 'Investigation continuing.' We'll see."

"Mr. Stanton, I'm most interested in Wednesday late evening into the night. Is it usual for anyone to be here after eight or so?"

Stanton shook his head thoughtfully. "CJ is here late sometimes, catching up on the paperwork. But not this past week. He was off fishing in Canada for a few days. He's got this favorite place in Manitoba that he likes."

"Security patrols?"

"We've never done that. We put most of the smaller units—you know, the easy stuff like lawn tractors and stuff—inside at night. Or daisy-chained together. The bigger ones? Nah. Nobody is going to steal a twenty-ton unit." He grinned. "And they're not as easy to hot-wire as they used to be, either. Cabs are locked, remote starts, all that happy shit."

Estelle fell silent, and Charlie Stanton held up both hands in surrender. "Sure wish there was something I could help you with, but it don't look like there is. You're pretty sure the body went into the dumpster on Wednesday night?"

"It looks that way."

"Well, like I told the cops who stopped in later in the week—Thursday, I think—I mean, I told them just like I told you, we get some vandalism now and then, but nothing serious like that. That's what I told him. We weren't here Wednesday, so..." He shrugged again. "Hard to believe, something like that dumpster thing. Like something out of a gangster movie, you know?"

He spread his hands wide on the desk top. "I don't know what else I can tell you," he said. "Or how to be of help."

"Thanks for taking this time for us," Estelle said. "We're kind of floundering around, chasing any possibility. We appreciate your cooperation."

"No problem." Stanton extended a business card toward her. "Take that, just in case." He laughed suddenly. "Hell, you might even decide you want a good tractor. We'll ship to New Mexico same as anywhere else. Our sales manager will make you a hell of a deal."

Outside, the haze was thick, softening the skyline, limiting visibility to a handful of miles. Half of the late-season alfalfa field next door had been mowed, and the aroma was fresh and strong. Estelle looked out across the field, imagining a nine- and eleven-year-old wading across the field, hoping to scare up something that would make a good target.

"So, what did we accomplish?" Susan Burke asked as they skirted the corner of the building.

"We ruled out a square on the checkerboard," Estelle replied. "That's if you're an optimist. If you're a pessimist, the answer is 'absolutely nothing.'"

"And *that's* interesting." An unmarked police cruiser was parked bumper to bumper with Burke's marked unit. "I didn't call for backup... In fact, I didn't call in our location to dispatch at all. Bad girl, me."

Chapter Thirty-Four

Estelle stepped off the sidewalk onto the dealership's patch of manicured lawn, putting a few feet between herself and Officer Burke. Sergeant Jake Kesserman lounged around the front of his car, a pleasant smile from the nose down. His hawk-like gaze was locked on Estelle.

"Ladies," he said, still ignoring Burke. "Undersheriff, your sheriff wants you to call him."

Estelle kept her tone good-natured. "Sergeant, if the Posadas sheriff wants to talk to me, he has my cell. He has my husband's cell. He even has my son's and Tasha's cell."

"Yeah, well. See, this time I called *him*."

Estelle regarded Kesserman thoughtfully and decided not to ask the question he was begging for. "Okay."

"He's a hard man to reach."

"Sometimes he is."

"Look," Kesserman said, "I'll be frank. I know your friendship with Captain Mitchell goes way back, years and years. But here and right now, you're a complication in this investigation that we don't need. Obvious jurisdictional issues aside, we really can't afford the time and manpower to provide escorts for you twenty-four, seven."

"And you don't need to do that."

"But see, that's the point. We *do.* Number one priority is to keep you safe. But you and whoever we spring free to escort you," and he waved a hand in Burke's direction, "are a team, of sorts. But to my way of thinking, anything you happen to dig up is of dubious value from a judicial point of view. You're not a cop here, you're not even a resident of the state." He thrust his hand out toward the ID around her neck. "Regardless of what that says."

"The chain of evidentiary custody is always intact," Estelle replied. "You've made your opinion on all this clear a time or two before. It's a nonissue. All I'm providing is another set of eyes, another viewpoint. That's all. So far, you're the only one complaining."

"I'm not complaining," Kesserman snapped. "I'm making a simple observation."

"You've made it. And now, apparently, you've made it to my sheriff." She drew her phone out of her pocket, scrolled on, and selected Sheriff Robert Torrez's number. It rang six times before his terse response reached her.

"Torrez."

"Greetings from sunny California, Bobby."

"Yup. How's the kid?"

"Out of ICU, healing a little at a time."

"Okay. So when's home for you?"

"I don't know yet. Look, I'm over in the area where a murder victim was found. No one is sure yet how or if his death is related to my son's crash."

"All right."

"I understand that Sergeant Kesserman of the Briones PD gave you a call."

"Yep."

"A request, I assume?"

"Sure. He says it's time for you to go home."

"That's not his call to make, Bobby."

Torrez scoffed a chuckle. "I woulda told him that if I'd

thought of it. By the way, Schroeder thinks he's got enough to go ahead with a grand jury session. He says he might even hit up the budget to fly you back special for the testimony."

"What a waste."

"Well, maybe. Maybe not. He keeps calling it a 'sensitive' case."

Estelle didn't respond to that. Instead, she said, "The sergeant is standing here at the moment, looking impatient. Do you want to talk to him again?"

"Nah. You follow your instincts. I'll keep you posted on what the DA here decides to do. And, hey? This Kesserman guy? I don't know what his beef is, but it seems to me he should be welcoming any help he can get. He's kinda eager to get you gone."

"Would seem so."

"Be careful."

She rang off, and as she lowered the phone, Kesserman reached out a hand to take it.

"The sheriff didn't want to talk to you, Sergeant." She slid it into her pocket. "I appreciate your cooperation so far, Sergeant Kesserman. And I hope it will continue. If you have any other concerns, I'm sure you'll communicate them to Captain Mitchell."

Kesserman's expression was stony. She watched the ridges of his jaw muscles flex, and then, as if someone had thrown a switch, he blinked half a dozen times and relaxed. "What did you two find here?"

"Some vandalism. Kids using the dealership diesel tank for target practice, thankfully with a twenty-two. The dealer reported the incident to the SO."

"And what was it that you were *hoping* to find out here?"

"A stray three-eighty slug, maybe buried in the seat cushion of one of the tractors parked over there. That would be nice." She nodded across the way at the produce stand. "It would be possible. A couple hundred yards? Not that big a deal. Or maybe striking one of those big showroom windows."

"Talk about a fantasy needle in a haystack," he snorted derisively.

"Yes. A very large haystack. Mostly, I guess I just wanted the perspective. A little outing to clear out the cobwebs."

"You and I are going to have to talk." He turned to Burke. "I'll take the undersheriff back to the hospital, or where ever she needs to go."

"I'm fine with providing escort," Burke replied.

"It wasn't a choice," the sergeant said.

"Thanks for taking the time to bring me out here," Estelle said to Burke, but the officer shook her head and looked squarely at Kesserman when she addressed Estelle. "The captain ordered me to escort you. That's what I think I should do until he rescinds the order."

To Estelle's surprise, Kesserman grinned. "So let's all have a pissing contest about who said what and waste some more daylight. Sheriff, you have my card, you have a cell. Let me know when you have a few minutes free."

"Fair enough." She watched him saunter off to his car, his knuckle rapping a light tattoo on the fender. "Susan, I don't want to see you getting in trouble over me with your sergeant. You'll end up reading parking meters."

Burke started toward her own vehicle. "Not to worry. He'll get over it." She watched Kesserman's unit swing out of the driveway. "To the hospital?"

"Actually," Estelle said, "to the dumpster."

Burke looked askance. "For..." Then she nodded without waiting for an answer.

Chapter Thirty-Five

With her back to the dumpster, Estelle surveyed the field behind the produce stand. The alfalfa, a late fall cut, looked lush. She walked, counting paces, to the wire fence that marked the boundary between the produce stand's parking lot and the field beyond. "Eight," she said.

"Sure enough," Burke agreed. "And guess what. Here's our chaperone." The unmarked Charger pulled in close, and Kesserman took his time getting out.

"This isn't the hospital, Sheriff," he said by way of greeting.

"I had an impulse," Estelle replied, keeping her tone light, almost bantering.

"So tell me." His tone carried nothing of the previous conversation's ire.

Estelle turned to survey the field. "The shop manager at Dixon's tells me that this is more of a demo field than an actual effort at farming." She pointed out across the alfalfa. "We can see that at one point fairly recently, they mowed part of the field, but stopped short of finishing."

"Maybe at the time, it was more important to sell a piece of equipment than to spend the day mowing," Burke said.

"Of course." Kesserman looked at Estelle impatiently. "So what?"

Estelle searched the ground briefly and picked up a fair-sized rock. "About a pound, maybe?"

"So?"

"How's your pitching arm, Sergeant?"

"Just fine."

"Then humor me. If the truck with Wilke's body pulls in here...about here," and she outlined the zone with both arms, "the corpse is dumped." She pointed at the dumpster and held up the rock. "What a grand place to dispose of the weapon, don't you think? If he throws it in the dumpster, almost certainly it would be found if the body is found first. If the body is found, he has to know that the cops will take the place apart. On the other hand, if he takes it with him, who knows. But out there in that field? What an opportunity. The alfalfa is thick and lush. When it's mowed, just a thick stubble remains. And then it gets plowed, disked, and harrowed, as they demonstrate more machinery."

"You must have been an incredible daydreamer as a kid," Kesserman said.

"Sin duda." She tossed the rock to the sergeant, and he caught it deftly. "Throw it as far as you can, out into the field."

"Yeah, I see what you're getting at." He turned, stepped beside the dumpster, and hurled the rock using a grenade toss that would have made a Marine Corps drill instructor proud.

"Outstanding," Estelle said. "An arc of that radius is about what I'd like to explore." She pointed straight out toward where the rock had fallen. "More out that way than down along the sides."

"We could be out here the rest of the day," Kesserman mused.

"Sure enough, we could." Estelle advanced to the four-strand wire fence, tested the tautness of the wires at one of the steel posts, and scrambled over. Burke did the same. Kesserman went to the center of the span, crushed the wire down as far as he could, and scissored over.

"Brush the alfalfa gently with both hands as you walk the

row," Estelle instructed. "You should search so you can see the ground."

"Why not just have Dixon's mow it?" Kesserman suggested.

"For one thing, we don't want the tractor footprints crushing things into the soil. For another…"

"Then they'd have to rake it," Kesserman added, nodding. "I can get a crew out here to assist."

"We can try it first. It's not that large an area," Estelle said. "Remember your rock toss."

"So let's take a turn or two before we end up having to camp out here all night."

It took half a dozen turns before Officer Susan Burke stood up straight, shot both arms into the air and shouted, "SCORE!"

They gathered beside Burke, who was grinning with delight.

"Well, I'll be damned." Kesserman looked down at the pistol where it lay with its muzzle nestled in the dirt. He turned back and surveyed the produce stand parking lot. "So he comes in, tosses the body, and then thinks better of it, and sails the gun way out here. Where either the machinery or the plowing will cover it." He nodded. "Pretty smart." He turned a huge smile on Susan Burke. "But you found it anyway." He poked an index finger at her. "*You* did."

Estelle swept her hands in an arc that encompassed the neighborhood. "Photos need to show all this. The gun's position relative to everything—fruit stand, parking lot, dumpsters, even Dixon's spread." She knelt for a closer look at the pistol. "And be careful with this one. It's not cocked, but we don't know what's in the tube. If it's loaded, which it probably is, it's an accident waiting to happen." She bent down, gently parting the alfalfa for a better look. "A Beretta three-eighty. Nice little gun." She looked up at Burke. "Great thing for a couple of kids to find, no?"

As she examined the gun, Kesserman had moved off, back toward the fence. Now, he made his way back through the vegetation, moving as if he might find something else. He pointed his phone at Estelle. "I got the CSI team coming. A couple of 'em will be here in a few minutes. Mitchell's on his way." He looked up once more at Burke. "Outstanding work, Officer Burke."

"Sarge, this wasn't my idea. I just got lucky."

"I'll take it," Kesserman said. "Now we're even up."

"Even up?"

"Yeah. About the same number of answers as questions. Now we match 'em up."

Chapter Thirty-Six

"Tomorrow starts a new week of fun and games," Carlos Guzman said. His tone was surprisingly cheerful. He looked hard at his mother. "Francisco said that he and Angie are headed back to New York in the morning. By way of Posadas."

"Ah." She moved close to the bed and took her son's right hand in both of hers. "And I have a grand jury waiting on me."

"Then it's time for you to hook a fast ride," Carlos said. "The good doctor says that, for me, it's just a matter of time now. I'll be okay. I feel better today than I did yesterday."

"They're all back at the hotel?"

"Yes. I kicked everybody out. His eyebrows furrowed as if he was thinking himself capable of actually doing such a thing." He brightened. "The good news is that Francisco claims he's found a restaurant that will make a green chile lasagna to order. I'm skeptical about that, but we'll see. That would brighten things up." He frowned. "So tell me what you found out today. We haven't seen much of you."

"Some big news, some insignificant things, *hijo*." She ticked off the points on the back of Carlos's hand. "We found a small amount of blood in the back of the pickup—it turns out to be canine. We'll have to talk with the truck owner about that. We spent some more time looking for the slug that killed Wilke.

Impossible. We have a clear print on the license plate bolt of Wilke's truck that turns out to belong to Barry Whitaker. He touched it when he found the truck over near campus. A touch out of curiosity."

"And that's it?"

"That's almost it. And we may have the gun that killed Wilke. May have."

"That's huge, Ma."

"Maybe so."

"The duo came to see me today. More questions."

"And the 'duo' is..."

"Dinsman and Kesserman. Kesserman gives me the impression that he doesn't believe me. He thinks that I must have at least caught a glance of the truck driver. He asked me the same question about fifty different ways. 'Did he drive by first? When he came in from the side, I didn't see his face? When he was backing up, I didn't see him? Did I see this, did I see that?' I don't know if I convinced him or not." Carlos reached up and rubbed the bandage on his temple. "The question is, if I *knew*, if I'd *seen*, the driver, why wouldn't I have said something before now? Ditto for Tasha."

"*Hijo*, they're as frustrated as I am. So they'll dig for any little thing. Now they have a different avenue. Sometimes it's easy to find the owner of a ditched gun." She held up both hands. "And sometimes it isn't."

"We'll have to hope, then," Carlos said. "I'm not going to like getting out of here and then having to look over my shoulder all the time, Ma. I don't know what I did or said to feed this guy's grudge, but there it is."

She bent down and kissed him between the eyes. "I'll find out who's arranged the lasagna and make sure it gets here bubbly hot. Be sure to invite Mrs. Franklin to stop by for a serving."

"No more lime JELL-O. That stuff doesn't do a thing for my ten scale."

"How's that going?"

He managed a shrug. "If I tell 'em I'm seven or above, they start with the meds...some serious stuff. So I lie a little. If I say 'four,' they leave me alone." He pointed down at his caged leg. "They say next week to start with the leg surgery. Once they're absolutely sure about my guts. Then I'll see if the ten scale goes high enough."

"I wish I could wave a magic wand, *hijo*."

"Yeah, well..." He shut his eyes for a brief moment. "Tasha is all squared away?"

"She is. Her parents will be here shortly."

"Arrrg. Maybe they won't be able to find me. I mean, they're the best, you know. Really great folks. But right now, I'd like to close and lock the door."

"Hey, when you're a celebrity, that goes with the turf."

He shook his head slowly. "I don't know how Francisco stands it."

"He and Angie have their retreat in Posadas. You and Tasha have a wonderful condo here. When the leg is fixed, you can pull the walls in around you and be as much of a hermit as you like."

Carlos chuckled. "You know, before this, I never thought of myself that way, Ma."

"Your gregarious, people-loving self will heal in time, too, *hijo*."

"Save me a piece of lasagna, okay? I promise tiny little bites. No cough, no choke." He grinned. "Green chile heals all things."

"Maybe we can whip some up in the blender for you. Kind of like Gerber's."

Carlos did his best to glower.

Out at the nurses' station, Officer Troy Dinsman was leaning over the counter, trying to read the computer screen that was untended at the moment. He saw Estelle approaching and nodded, pushing himself away from the counter.

"He's making progress, isn't he?"

"Carlos? Yes. Slow but sure."

"I wish we were, at least the sure part. But you guys finding the gun was huge."

"I appreciate you providing a presence here," Estelle said. "I know it's a pain."

"Did Sarge find you?"

"You mean recently? I spoke to him earlier, out where we found the gun."

"No, it's been since that. You might give him a shout. I'm not sure what he wanted."

"Okay." But she didn't reach for her phone. "I'll be back here sometime this evening." She said that last as much to Mrs. Franklin as to Dinsman, as the elderly nurse glided into the nurses' station, settling into a chair with a sigh.

Outside, the haze had settled, thick and fragrant. The surrounding hills were merely vague outlines. She was two steps beyond the portico when a familiar unmarked vehicle pulled into the driveway with considerably more brio than necessary. Sergeant Jake Kesserman leaned over even as he activated the passenger-side window.

"Let's take a ride," he said, his grin overly bright.

"No, thanks." Estelle leaned down, an elbow on the windowsill. "Did you want something in particular? Officer Dinsman said you were looking for me." *The man can't help himself,* Estelle thought as Kesserman's gaze wandered down what he could see of her.

"Just get in the car, Sheriff. You'll want to be in on the fun." His tone was equidistant between friendly request and not-so-friendly command.

"The fun?"

"Christ," he muttered, twisting and looking toward the car's blind spot. "Just hang on a minute."

She straightened as the car lurched just short of squawking its tires on the pavement as Kesserman abruptly turned left and nosed the car into one of the reserved spots. Her own rental was twice that distance away, and she walked out of the traffic lane toward it. Kesserman exited his car and rounded the trunk, stopping by the right rear fender.

He beckoned. A beckon from some people would result in an instant positive response, but Estelle wasn't in the mood to be summoned by this particular cop, despite the show of friendly cooperation, feigned or otherwise, earlier in the day out in the alfalfa field.

"Gimme a break," Kesserman said, and beckoned again. The line to her car would bring her within a dozen feet of him, and Estelle chose that route.

"Look, the gun is a three-eighty Beretta Model thirty-four... It's damn near an antique. You already knew that, though. That's exactly what you said it was. What's interesting is that the registered owner is the deceased. Stanley Wilkes."

Estelle looked at Kesserman for a moment. "So somehow he was shot with his own gun."

"Maybe. We know a couple of things. One, he didn't shoot himself with it. That would be a trick. Somebody else could have been there, watched him do it, and then pitched the gun afterward. That's pretty unlikely. What I can see happening makes more sense. Maybe he threatened somebody with it—somebody bigger and faster that he was. I can see somebody taking the gun away from him and killing him with it. *Then* pitching the gun." He looked at Estelle expectantly. "Some version of that."

"Or...that's not the gun involved in Wilkes's murder."

"There is that, of course, common as three-eighties are." He glanced back toward the hospital. "How's the kid?"

"The kid?"

Kesserman smiled. "Well, compared to us, your son's a kid, wouldn't you say?"

When she didn't respond, he took a step closer, his smile broader. "Look, I don't have scabies or anything like that. How about a light dinner? We've got some things to discuss."

"Here we are."

He shook his head with frustrated impatience. "You're a tough woman, Sheriff."

"Nice to know." She started to step around him, but he moved to block her path. She looked up at him sharply. He immediately took a step to one side.

"What I was going to tell you was that the lab's running every test possible on that little gun. Prints, blow-back residue, you name it. We're going to run up an overtime tab that'll make the chief cringe, but we'll know some more later this evening. Tomorrow morning at the latest. We'll know if this is progress or just another dead end."

"So keep me posted." She held up her cell phone. "I'll be having dinner with my family. We'll be leaving later tomorrow, I'm told."

"You'll miss the fun."

"I don't call it that, Sergeant." Not fun. But compulsion, maybe. And she found the decision facing her daunting. When the Gulfstream—or whatever it was for this ride—roared away from Jackson Field the next morning, would she be on board?

Chapter Thirty-Seven

"I have four surgeries waiting on me back home," Francis Guzman explained, not a complaint, but a simple statement of fact. "Carlos is well on the road, so if I can hook a ride home tomorrow, I need to do that." He knew perfectly well that the same decision was difficult for his wife.

Estelle made a wry face. "You're not the only one who knows how to wield a scalpel, *Oso*." She shook her head in irritation at herself for letting that thought go unbridled. She reached out and rested a hand on his chest. "Do what you think you should, *querido*. If I stay here, rest assured that I'll be pestering you via phone with any little change."

"Not a pester. And the phone lines go both ways. And as far as changes go, it's not our son's medical condition that we're talking about."

She punched him affectionately, just hard enough to say, "Yes." She glanced down the hall, surprised to see Officer Susan Burke approaching.

"You guys are making progress?" Francis asked.

"Maybe we are." She grimaced again. "Maybe *they* are, is what I really want to say."

Francis cocked his head toward Estelle. "So you could go home with me tomorrow. You *could*."

Estelle hesitated. "*Oso*, I wish I could just say yes. But..." As Officer Burke drew close, she reached out a hand and shook the young cop's shoulder. "You're just in time for green chile lasagna," Estelle said, and caught a groan from her husband.

"Lethal," he said. "Be warned."

"I don't do even normal lasagna," Burke said with a crooked smile. She glanced toward the patient's room. "How's he doing?"

Estelle nodded by way of reply.

"Some words from the captain," Burke said. "He thought you would want to know. First of all, the three-eighty shell casing that we found in the cycle shop parking lot? It's a match to the Beretta from the field." She held up a finger. "The firing pin impression on the casing leaves no doubt, the lab tells us. Some scoring of the casing from chamber erosion is more support. So that's one."

Estelle felt her pulse tick upward. "Outstanding."

"Two is even more interesting. The gun belonged to Stan Wilke. Legally purchased seven years ago from Briones Shooting Sports. They assisted him in obtaining a concealed carry permit. Apparently he was in the habit of carrying it while cycling. One of the clerks there told me that he remembers having that discussion with Wilke, who was worried about loose dogs. The clerk says that he told Wilke that shooting someone's pet was a sure way to end up in really deep shit. He recommended a canister of pepper spray instead."

"Wilke's own gun," Estelle said. "And the clerk remembers after seven years?"

"Wilke's been in and out of the gun shop since then, too. Plus, like I said, helping him qualify for the CC permit."

"You folks have been busy."

"Indeed. And the lab is assisting every way they can." She held up three fingers. "A trace blow-back residue on the muzzle of the gun, typed to the victim. Not much, it being just a three-eighty, but some."

"So the gun was held really close."

"Contact, in fact. There's a small cut just above the bridge of the nose that matches the front sight, and a circular bruise around the entry hole that matches the crown of the muzzle."

"Shoved right in his face. A contact shot."

Burke took a deep breath. "A variety of fingerprints, most of them Wilke's. One clear set on the slide, facing backward, as if someone clamped a hand on top of the gun while Wilke was holding it."

"Most but not all Wilke's, then."

"Correct. And for once, all the governmental bureaucracy helps us. Get this: Jim Wayne's prints are on file. He works for a contractor who routinely does work for schools, and he holds a CDL. The prints on Wilke's gun are his. A good, clean thumbprint, some other partials."

Estelle sagged against the wall, and Burke looked at her with what might have been sympathy.

"A little relief, maybe," Burke said. "At least it looks that way." She huffed a sigh. "I'm here to offer you a ride-along, if you wish to go. He'll tell you himself at the scene, but the captain asked me to remind you that if you *do* ride along, you remain in the vehicle unless you're specifically invited. We don't know how this is going to go down."

"Of course. So based on what the lab tells you, Mitchell is convinced beyond a doubt that Wayne is involved."

"What's your line? '*Sin duda.*'" She smirked. "That probably sounds more *Puerto Riqueño* than Mexican, huh?"

"You're going after Wayne now?"

"That's the plan." She smiled. "We understand why you would want to go along, Sheriff. This is important to you. But it has to be on our terms. Our rules of engagement, so to speak."

"I understand that. Who's responding?"

"The mob. Me. Officers Scott and Dinsman. Sergeant Kesserman. Lieutenant Beaumont. The good captain. Some tactical support out on the street."

Her husband hadn't said a word, but he reached out and

rested his left arm across her shoulders, pulling her into a hug. For a moment, they remained silent. Finally, Estelle circled her husband's waist, tightening the hug.

"I'll pass," she said. "You guys don't need me in the way."

Burke looked surprised, and then her eyes narrowed. "You're not thinkin' of driving out there by yourself after I leave, I hope. Some sort of vigilante thing?"

"No, I'm not. For one thing, I don't know where 'there' is, Susan. You guys have a top-notch team, and you don't need me adding dead weight. You rope him in, you prove he did it, and after it's all said and done, I'd like to know why he did what he did. That's all. I'll be a happy camper with that. I don't need to see him go down."

Her husband's deep breath didn't go unnoticed.

Burke regarded her for a moment and then held out her hand. "I'll let you know. Somewhere along the line, we'll get the questions answered."

"Thanks for all you've done, Susan Burke."

She offered a lopsided grin and a fist bump to Francis. "Keep a tight rein, Doctor."

"And you guys be careful."

For a moment, as they watched Officer Susan Burke walking away, Estelle wasn't sure her knees would hold her up if Francis released his grip.

"Let's go make sure Carlos doesn't suffer a relapse," Francis said.

There was no bending of the torso and little at the waist—no sitting up to tackle the lasagna, although a slight elevation brought his head up to reduce swallowing difficulties. Carlos did his best to enjoy the facsimile of green chile lasagna, carefully mashing his piece into an unrecognizable blob and then dipping the plastic fork into the remains, taking barely enough each time to wet the tines. On the first taste, he grimaced, and Estelle wasn't sure if it was the lasagna or the effort of trying to fold his battered torso a degree or two more upright.

"This is really gross," Francisco said, agreeing with his brother's unspoken assessment. Everyone except Nurse Franklin had accepted a piece, further testimony to her good sense. She had thoughtfully provided a clean trash bag for the remains. "And this stuff comes highly recommended?"

"It's the idea of the thing," Carlos whispered. "Thanks for the effort, Bro."

"The chile tastes as if it were grown in a lab somewhere. It sure ain't from Hatch."

"It probably was lab-rat food." Carlos watched his mother take a tiny bite from her portion.

"Ay, caramba," she whispered. "How do they do that?"

She contributed to the growing contents of the trash bag, and Carlos reached out a hand to her. His gaze locked on hers.

"I heard you guys out in the hall." His voice was little more than a whisper. "I'm surprised you didn't take them up on the offer."

"So am I," Estelle replied. She didn't say how little it would take to make her change her mind. Her son's sympathetic smile told her that he could read her mind.

Chapter Thirty-Eight

A hand gently shaking her shoulder jarred her out of an absurd dream in which Johnny Rabke was trying to explain to an unsympathetic jury that the alleged billiard ball he'd flung at Pablo Ramirez was nothing other than a soft, light Wiffle ball. The jury was not buying it.

Estelle looked up, trying to blink away the sleep. Her watch said it was almost ten. She had been back at the hotel, had had a late dinner with the two girls, her son, and Francis, along with Tasha's parents. Unlike the attempt at green chile lasagna, the food at the Thai restaurant was succulent, beautifully prepared, and presented on fine Oriental china.

She and Francis had returned to the hospital afterward and found Carlos sleeping fitfully. Rather than waking him, she and her husband had returned to their hotel room, where she surrendered the fight to keep her eyes open.

Now, she turned to lie flat on her back, one hand over her eyes. "Uh?"

Her husband stroked the cell phone down the inside of her arm, stopping with it touching her right hand. "Your old buddy."

For a few seconds, she didn't move. Finally grasping the phone, she squinted at the small screen and pressed the correct choice.

"Sorry to bother you," Captain Eddie Mitchell said. When

she managed to murmur something unintelligible in reply, he added, "You awake? I debated about calling, but figured you'd be off pursuing vigilante justice if I didn't."

"I think I'm awake."

"Good. Look, the apprehension went down without a problem. You know how it sometimes works. We got the impression that Jim Wayne was relieved that it was all over. Sort of."

"Wayne admits to crashing into the kids?"

"No. Now get this. He says the crash was Wilke all the way. He calls Wayne—Wayne says it was about ten o'clock or so—and feeds him some cock-and-bull story about seeing the white-and-blue jersey, and his first thought is that it's Kesserman. We know there ain't no love affair between those two. So it's just an impulse. A twitch of the wheel. And after the collision, the guy panics. Wayne says Wilke claims to have backed up to see what or who he'd hit, and went too far. It's dark, that truck has shitty backup lights, so he hits 'em again."

"Somebody is a creative thinker, Eddie."

"Well, it could have gone down that way. But Wayne claims Wilke was so shaken that he was just babbling, running on and on, not making much sense. Anyway, he says that he thinks he killed a cop, and what's he going to do. He tells Wayne that the truck is at the bike shop and he's gotta have help or the cops will find it. He pleads with Wayne for help."

"And Wayne falls for that."

"Well, remember, it's his truck. He's smart enough to know he needs some story to protect himself. Reporting it stolen comes to mind."

"So Wilke is at the shop, and that's where Wayne goes?"

"Yup. That's his story. He sees the truck, the blood, the damage, and see, Wayne is smarter than your average bear. '*No way, Jose,*' he thinks. '*I don't want to be involved in this shit.*' But Wilke is beside himself, and next thing you know, he threatens Wayne with that little pop gun he carries. '*You gotta help me. You gotta.*' Bad move."

"Wayne took it away from him?"

"So he says. Thrusts it his face, thinking just to scare the little runt. You know the rest. The gun goes off, Wilke's a dead mackerel. Now it's *Wayne* who's in the bind. He says the whole thing was unintentional."

"They all say that," Estelle said.

"Oh, sure. In this case, it might be true. That little Beretta has a really light trigger. I mean *really* light. Like malfunction light. In the heat of the moment, it could have happened that way. All he had to do was touch the trigger. Or just the hard jar of shoving it in Wilke's face."

"That leaves a bunch of questions."

"Absolutely it does. Like all the whys. He told Wayne over the phone, and again when they argued at the shop, that he thought he'd killed a cop. He mentions Kesserman by name. I can believe that."

"So can I," Estelle agreed. "There was clearly some friction there. Even during the little bit of time I was in the shop. Both Whitaker and Emily will corroborate that."

"We never know what's going to set somebody off," Mitchell said. "And I can believe that after the gun went off and killed his ex-brother-in-law, Wayne concocted the lamebrain plan to ditch the truck, all that shit? Yeah, I can believe that. What he should have done is call the cops, right then and there."

"He got clever."

"That isn't uncommon, my friend."

"He's in lock-up now?"

"Wayne? Yes. No bail set, at least not yet."

Estelle let out a long exhale of relief. "I was just with Carlos. He's sleeping."

"Good for him. Look, I'm confident enough that I'm pulling the troops. Wayne can sit in jail as we sift through all this. But bright and early tomorrow morning, we're going to be spending a *lot* of time with Carlos and Tasha. We'll pick apart that relationship that Wilke had with them, see where the jealousies were. It may be..."

"May be what?" she prompted when he hesitated.

"It may be something as simple as love from afar, you know. Maybe Wilke had a passion for Tasha, let's say. Obviously unreciprocated. Or for Carlos, even. Even more obviously unreciprocated. And we *know* that he crossed swords with Jake Kesserman. So maybe it was something as wild as what you suggest. Wilke sees the bike riders, maybe sees and recognizes the U.S. Postal jerseys, thinks it's Kesserman on the lead seat, taking a girl—maybe Tasha—for a ride. Now who knows?...Whatever happened, Wilke came unglued and did what he did."

"If that's how it all went down."

"Well, Wayne knew enough details about sticking the fake license plate on the truck, about where it was parked and all, that what he says supports his version of the story."

"That's what grand juries are for," Estelle said.

Mitchell grimaced and made a loud noise that turned into a huge yawn. "You're right about that. But look, I gotta get some sleep myself. You're heading home tomorrow?"

"Yes." For the first time, Estelle felt comfortable with her decision. "I don't see anything else I can do here. I don't want to get in the way of you guys, and Carlos doesn't need his mama hovering. We'll keep in close touch."

"Flight time?"

"I think we leave Jackson about ten in the morning."

"You don't want to be in on all this, huh?" He chuckled.

"There are all kinds of reasons why I'd like to be with you, but...I don't want to screw up your case with jurisdictional issues," Estelle said. "Like I said, that's what grand juries are for. Right now, it's enough for me to know that my son and his fiancée are out of danger and healing, and justice is being served. You'll keep me posted, I'm sure."

"I'll do that."

"The kids did well for you? Scott and Burke?"

"'The kids.' I like that. But, yeah, they did real well. There was a brief moment when we thought Wayne was going to go stupid on us. You wouldn't believe how fast Burke drew her Taser. Didn't have to shoot, but man, she had it out so fast. What a gunslinger. I mean, she even beat Kesserman to the draw, and that's an accomplishment."

"Good for her."

"And no...don't go cherry-picking my staff."

Estelle laughed. "Come visit, Eddie. Sometime soon."

"Count on it."

Chapter Thirty-Nine

As was his habit, Posadas County District Attorney Dan Schroeder leafed through his paperwork as if he'd misplaced something, buying himself some moments before facing his witness. The jury waited patiently. So did Estelle Reyes-Guzman, to herself repeating the litany she'd shared with Eddie Mitchell…*that's what grand juries are for.* It was time to trust someone else—twelve someone elses.

"Mrs. Guzman, would you identify yourself for the jury?"

"Estelle Reyes-Guzman, undersheriff for Posadas County."

"And, Undersheriff, how long have you worked for the Sheriff's Department?"

"Thirty-two years."

"That's quite a tenure, Undersheriff." Schroeder, tall, lean, and slightly stooped, flashed a smile of crooked teeth. His glacial blue eyes twinkled with amusement. "A few bar fights in those thirty-two, I would wager." He unbuttoned his suit jacket and swept the right side back as if he were about to draw a gun.

As was *her* habit during a court appearance, Estelle didn't respond to anything without a question mark at the end.

Schroeder waited for a few seconds. "Are bar fights a common occurrence in Posadas County?"

"Yes."

"More so at the Broken Spur Saloon than anywhere else?"

"I don't think so."

"You've never actually broken the numbers down by location?"

"No."

"Okay." He turned to regard a large floor plan that rested on an easel facing the jury. "Do you recognize this location?"

"Yes. The barroom of the Broken Spur."

"On October sixth of this year, were you called to that location in response to an altercation?"

"Yes."

"Approximately what time of day?"

"The call was logged at 9:03 p.m."

"And you arrived there how long after that?"

"I arrived at 9:13 p.m."

"So by our county's standards, you were nearby." He shuffled more papers. "When you entered the saloon, what did you find?" He stopped, holding up a hand. "In fact, it would be helpful if you would approach and point out locations on the graphic while you explain." He held out a dry-erase marker and beckoned her to leave the witness corral.

"A family of four were seated at a booth along the west wall." Estelle circled the booth in blue. "The saloon's owner and his bartender were behind the bar, approximately halfway down." Circled *X*s located Victor Junior and Maggie Archuleta. "A young man we later identified as Pablo Ramirez was on the floor at the base of one of the barstools, apparently unconscious. Another man known to us as John Winston Rabke was attempting to stand approximately in the middle of the floor, about here." She drew two more circled *X*s.

"Was Mr. Rabke injured?"

"Yes. He was bleeding profusely from the forehead."

"What was the nature of the wound?"

"It was consistent with a knife slice. From here," and she touched her own forehead, "to here."

"Were you able to determine who inflicted the wound?"

"I did not witness the assault. So any determination was based solely on statements by witnesses."

"You said that Mr. Rabke was 'attempting to stand.' *Attempting.* Is that because of the injury or because of his state of intoxication?" Schroeder frowned and dug through his documents. "The tests taken at the emergency room state that he blew a point nine."

"He appeared badly hurt. The blood was running profusely down his face. It would have impaired his vision."

"Ah. 'Impaired his vision.' Despite that 'impairing,' did Mr. Rabke recognize you when you entered the Spur?"

"Yes."

"You know each other well, then?"

"We have met on several occasions."

"Not socially, though?"

"No."

"And when you entered the saloon, what did he do?"

"He managed to stand up. He held one hand to his forehead and held out the other toward me." Estelle mimed the movement.

"How cooperative," Schroeder chuckled. "Did he call you by name?"

"No."

"What did you do then?"

"I cuffed him without incident and assisted him to a chair. I pressed a bar towel against his forehead and told him to keep his head back. Then I went to tend to Mr. Ramirez."

"Because Mr. Rabke was handcuffed and no longer a threat?"

"Yes."

"Was Mr. Ramirez known to you?"

"No."

"And what did you ascertain, based on your examination of him?"

"He was unconscious, suffering a broken right wrist and what appeared to be a head injury near the right temple."

"Did he have a weapon in his possession?"

"He was holding what appeared to be a medium-sized hunting knife in his right hand."

"Still? Even with that arm broken?"

"Yes."

Schroeder frowned at his notes, then leaned an elbow on the lectern. "So. Based on witness testimony that you gathered, what's your best explanation of what happened here?"

"Witness testimony is that after some bantering and insults back and forth, Mr. Ramirez took a swipe with the knife, cutting Mr. Rabke across the forehead. At that point, Mr. Rapke swung hard with his pool cue...a 'baseball bat' swing, one witness called it. The blow struck Mr. Ramirez on the distal end of the arm bones, above the wrist, resulting in a dislocation and fracture."

"Upon examination, you could see that the arm was broken?" A defense attorney during a trial would have had a field day objecting, but Estelle understood that a grand jury, with no other counsel present to object to the leading ploy, played by far more relaxed rules.

"Yes."

"Yet he still clung to the knife." When Estelle didn't reply, Schroeder raised an eyebrow to provide the question mark.

"Yes. The fracture was obvious."

"And at that point, Mr. Ramirez did what?"

"He apparently lost his balance and fell near the bar."

"And what happened then?"

"Witness testimony to me confirmed that Mr. Rabke swept one of the billiard balls off the table and hurled it toward Mr. Ramirez."

"A purposeful throw?"

"Meaning what, sir?"

Schroeder stumbled a little and waved a hand. He looked at the jury and shook his head. "As opposed to an accidental toss, I suppose."

"I did not personally observe that instant, but based on witness interviews, it was a hard, sidearm snap."

"And hit its target...despite Mr. Rabke's vision being obstructed by the blood flow from his injury." He paused. "And in fact was a direct shot to the victim's unprotected temple?"

"Yes."

"What sort of distance?"

Estelle pointed at the schematic legend. "Established at sixteen feet, plus or minus."

"And after all this, after a backup deputy and the ambulance arrived and transported the injured for treatment, what did you do?"

"I went to California."

Schroeder grinned up at the ceiling, and Estelle was unsure exactly what was going through the man's mind. He turned and regarded the jurors. Unlike trial jury proceedings, in sessions like this one that were closed to any spectators, no judge or defense attorneys, no media, it was Schroeder's habit to solicit questions directly from jurors, and he did so now.

Baines Swarthout, a recently retired high school math teacher, raised a hand.

"Mr. Swarthout?"

"Yes. Undersheriff Guzman, this puzzles me. You have two men sixteen feet apart, probably both drunk as skunks, both injured, and one of them lets fly with a billiard ball and scores with a perfect hit. Now I sympathize with the injuries here, and the tragic results, but I have to tell you...I find it hard to believe it was intentional, or with any forethought at all, and I find it equally hard to believe that he aimed the shot intending for it to do the damage that we're told it did."

Quick off the mark, Schroeder said, "Is there a question there?"

"Well, yeah, there's a question. How is any of this anything other than self defense? Cut as he was, half-blinded by blood, he strikes out, and flings the ball. How would Mr. Rabke know, given all the circumstances, that Mr. Ramirez was no longer a threat?"

Schroeder turned at the waist and raised the eyebrow at Estelle. Before she could answer, Swarthout added, "And that accurate a throw? He sure as hell wasn't that accomplished when he played baseball for the Jaguars."

Schroeder grimaced and held up a hand. "What Mr. Rabke was or was not is not at issue here, folks. We have to stick with this," and he waved a hand at the schematic. "We have to stick with what we have. Undersheriff?"

Estelle hesitated. "All I can tell you is what I saw, and what witnesses told me. You'll have a chance to hear from those witnesses, Mr. Swarthout."

"What's your opinion, though?" he pressed.

"My opinion doesn't matter, sir."

"Of course it matters."

"You can go ahead and answer that, Undersheriff," Schroeder said.

"My opinion is that Mr. Rabke's actions were the result of injury, temper, and intoxication. He lashed out with the nearest weapon at hand after breaking the cue. Instinctively. He wouldn't have been able to see well enough for a well-aimed shot."

Another hand lifted tentatively. "Undersheriff Guzman," Nancy Tucci said, "do you know what a billiard ball—I mean just a regular such—what one of those weighs?" Estelle was not surprised at the question. As postmistress now in Posadas, Nancy would think in terms of ounces.

"Yes. A standard billiard ball weighs five and a half ounces."

"So even a bit heavier than a regulation baseball? I mean like the major leaguers use?"

"Slightly heavier, yes."

"And a lot harder."

Estelle didn't respond to that. Several jurors were busy

writing notes—or perhaps composing shopping lists. Who knew. Compared to a petit jury that might decide innocence or guilt, the grand jury would decide only if enough evidence existed to take Johnny Rabke's case to trial.

The questioning went on for another ten minutes before Schroeder orchestrated a break for the next witness. He had a string of them, Estelle knew. Anyone able to describe what he or she saw would be on the stand. Even Johnny Rabke would be allowed to testify if he so chose. It had been Estelle's experience that most grand jury targets followed their lawyer's advice and did not testify or even show their faces.

After leaving the courtroom, Estelle skirted through the back halls of the county building until she reached the locked inner door to the Sheriff's Department. She keyed the entry. Ernie Wheeler was busy in dispatch, listening intently to a phone complaint, and Estelle was able to reach her office with no detours.

Settling in her swivel chair, Estelle faced her computer. Upon her return from California, she'd cleaned the thing, deleting more than fifty messages, most of no consequence. Now, two immediately drew her attention, and with a sharp intake of breath she clicked on the first.

Carlos had selected forty-eight-point type for his three-word message:

I SAT UP!

Estelle smiled broadly at the triumph implied by that simple message, knowing how hard Carlos had worked to achieve it. She thought for a moment, remembering her promise to Francisco that she would accept another airlift to California, and then typed her reply:

AND NOW, THERE IS NO LIMIT. SEE YOU NEXT WEEK.

TE AMO, HIJO.

She opened the email from Eddie Mitchell, a far less exuberant message, but welcome nevertheless.

"The lab techs ran that little gun through the ringer, and tell us that when on full cock, less than two ounces is necessary to release the sear. They made it go off by trapping the butt on the bench! So it's not surprising that it went off prematurely when Wayne grabbed it out of Wilke's hand, like he says he did. Your son still will not speak ill of the man, but we believe that Wilke was infatuated with Miss Qarsh. Unless she can shed some light on that, we may never know.

"In the meantime, the DA is looking at a grand jury session. You know lawyers. Who the hell knows what they'll decide. Wayne still contends that he grabbed the gun because Wilke was threatening him with it, trying to force his help in covering up what Wilke had done. He contends that Wilke really believed he'd killed a cop, that Kesserman had stolen the target of his infatuation. We'll see how that flies. Kesserman thinks that's what happened. He claims that he often wears a U.S. Postal jersey very like the one Carlos wore. We put that together with Kesserman's flirting in the shop, and some synapse in Wilke's brain snaps. He takes a swipe at Kesserman—but the swipe is with a three-quarter-ton truck, not an open hand. I've investigated homicides that flew on a lot less evidence than that. Wayne might have walked away with it if he'd just called the cops, instead of tossing the body into a dumpster. That doesn't look too good. For about the fifth time, thanks for your help. I'll do everything I can to avoid hauling you in to testify. But don't be a stranger, Sheriff."

"Fan letters?"

Estelle looked up to see Sheriff Robert Torrez leaning against the doorjamb of her office.

"An update from Carlos. He sat up for the first time. And some details in an update from Mitchell."

He nodded, not exactly brimming with enthusiastic interest. "Okay. How'd grand jury go?"

"It's a good jury, I think." She leaned back away from the

computer. "Thoughtful." She stretched out an arm and touched the wall calendar. "Next Friday morning. Out to Briones, back on Sunday evening."

Torrez almost smiled. "You're getting used to this jet set business."

"It's easy to do. Francisco and Angie have a double performance in San Francisco on Friday and Saturday nights."

"You got free tickets?"

Estelle smiled. "Of course. Do you and Gayle want to go? There's room in the livery."

Torrez snorted out the double positive that actually yielded a negative. "Yeah, right."

ACKNOWLEDGMENTS

Special thanks to first readers Lif Strand and Laura Brush, and to the hard workers at Poisoned Pen Press, who worked so cheerfully with a writer from the Stone Age.

ABOUT THE AUTHOR

Steven Havill and O.T., his 1930 Ford AA farm truck.

Steven F. Havill is the author of more than thirty novels, including twenty-five Posadas County Mysteries. He taught in secondary schools for twenty-five years and earned an AAS degree in gunsmithing in 2006. Havill and his wife of fifty-two years, Kathleen, live in New Mexico.